THE AUSCHWITZ TWINS

ROBERTA KAGAN

ISBN (ePub): 978-1-957207-19-3
ISBN (Paperback): 978-1-957207-20-9
ISBN (Hardback): 978-1-957207-21-6

DISCLAIMER

This is a work of fiction. Names, characters, businesses, places, events, and incidents
are either the products of the author's imagination or used in a fictitious manner. Any
resemblance to actual persons, living or dead, or actual events is purely coincidental.

CHAPTER ONE

The Warsaw Ghetto, in Poland, Winter 1942
An Overcrowded Cattle Train

The entire boxcar trembled as the door slammed shut. The sound penetrated right through Naomi Aizenberg's heart like a butcher knife. The train car was dark. The only light came in tiny slivers that entered through the small cracks in the wooden slats.

The train shuddered and shifted as it sprung to life. Everyone was jittery and nervous. They were stuffed wall to wall, leaning against each other. Naomi had never been so close to strangers before. The frightened people chattered until they were silenced and unnerved by the sound of a loud whistle. An odor of sweat filled the air. It was mixed with a strange smell: acidic, dirty, and nauseating. Naomi decided that it was the stench of fear and desperation, but most of all, loss of hope.

Her body trembled with anxiety. Not only was she worried about where they might be going, but when they boarded the train, Naomi was separated from her three daughters. She had no idea where her children were, and she was terrified. They were her life; without them she knew that she couldn't go on. Herschel, her husband, was standing beside her. She longed to turn to him for reassurance. If only he were the kind of man who would put his arms around her and hold her tightly. But she knew better. Herschel was cold, and when he was frightened or threatened, instead of turning to her so they could comfort each other, he grew even more distant. Still, even though she knew he would not give her much warmth or affection, right now she needed him. And she would take whatever crumbs he might be willing to provide.

Theirs had been an arranged marriage, one that her father had wanted. And although Naomi had succumbed to her father's wishes, things between her and Herschel had never been quite right. They were different in too many ways. He was prideful and hard, refusing to ever show weakness. But Naomi was warm, and she craved human touch. Right now, as they stood surrounded by strangers, she was panicked inside. She desperately needed Herschel to ease her mind. And so, she hungered for anything that might calm her. And although he'd never been one to lessen her anxiety, she still craved any small amount of help that his familiar voice might bring. There was no one else she could talk to. She didn't know anyone else on the train. And she was finding it unbearable to be in the darkness bumping along the rails all alone with her thoughts.

"I am shaking. What will become of our girls? I don't know where they are," Naomi asked Herschel in a small voice. "I am sick with worry about them. Oh, how I wish they were here with us. At least we could face whatever happens in the future together as a family. Right now, all we can do is worry about them."

"Don't worry so much. You're always worrying about something. They'll either get on the next train, or they have already boarded this one and they are traveling in another boxcar. Everything will be all right. You'll see. Shoshana will watch them," he said coldly.

It was just as she had expected. Herschel had withdrawn into himself. *I might as well be all alone here,* she thought. *He can't give me what I need. He has never been willing or able to give me what I need.*

Naomi leaned against her husband, but he moved away. "This is not what the guards promised us when they told us that if we boarded the train, we would be transported to a place where we would have a better life. They said the train would be comfortable. But that's a lie. This is anything but comfortable. Look at us. We're stuffed in here. I can hardly breathe. And people have started using the bucket to relieve themselves. The smell is making me sick. I want to vomit," Naomi said.

"I know. You're right. It's true. The Nazis are good-for-nothing liars. And I should have seen this coming. But I didn't. I let them lie to me. I wanted to believe them. And I am kicking myself for trusting those bastards. I am not a stupid man. How could I fall for such a trick?" Herschel said. There was anger and bitterness in his voice. He wrapped his arms around his chest and tried to push away from the strangers who were smothering him on every side.

"Where do you think they are taking us?" Naomi asked.

"Who knows. They have their own agenda, their own ideas about us and everything else. Nazis look like men, but I tell you they are not even human."

"I wish I knew where we were headed and how long we are going to have to be on this train."

He sighed. "If I were to wager, I would say that I believe they are taking us somewhere where they can work us good and hard. Why not? They figure they'll use us for free labor. They see us as nothing but Jews," he said.

"What kind of work do you think they will have us do?"

"I don't have any idea. But my guess is they're going to work us and work us hard. But if they want us to have the strength to work, they're going to have to feed us. So, we can only hope that in the end we find out that we made a good choice getting on this train."

"I hope so. We were always hungry in the ghetto. They hardly gave us enough in rations," she said.

"The rations in the ghetto were terrible. If it weren't for the young boys who worked on the black market that sold me the extra food, we would have all starved to death."

"Oh Herschel. We wasted so much time hurting each other before the Nazis came to power. If I had known then what I know now, I would have tried harder to make our lives better."

"Yes," he said softly.

"You have regrets too?" she asked.

"What good do regrets do anyone?" he said. "We are here now. Let's make the best of it. Perhaps we are going somewhere where we can get more food and live a better life."

"I just wish I could hold my daughters." She wanted to lay her head on his shoulder and weep, but she knew that he would not welcome her affection. He would gently pry himself away from her the way he always did when she got too close.

"All right, listen to me," he said with his usual voice of authority. "If we can't find our girls when we arrive at our destination, we'll tell the Nazis we want to go back to the ghetto to get them," Herschel said.

"And you think they'll let us, just like that?"

"We'll see. I have some money. I'll pay them off if I have to." Then he sighed. "I'll do whatever I have to do to take care of this. Now, if you don't mind, I don't feel much like talking. I need some peace and quiet. I can't hear myself think, and I need some time to sort out my thoughts. Why don't you lean up against the wall and try to get some rest? I know it's not easy to sleep standing up. But you won't fall down if you fall asleep. You couldn't; there are too many people in here. We're all stuck holding each other up."

She nodded. "All right," she said in a small voice. Tears ran down her cheeks. *I'm glad it's dark and he can't my face. He would be angry that I am crying. But I can't help myself. I know it's a sin, but I can't help myself, I wish Eli were beside me instead of Herschel. He would understand my feelings. And even though he, like the rest of us, would be powerless against these guards, he would at least hold me and comfort me,* she thought. Then she reminded herself, *These are selfish thoughts; I should be glad he is in Britain with his wife. He is safe there. Our love for each other was a sin. I knew it was wrong. I was a married woman, and he was a young scholar. But we couldn't help it; we fell totally and desperately in love. It was wrong, but those were the best days of my life. Our love affair has been over for years. And I am sure he has gotten over it. But I never did, not even when he got married. I don't think I ever will.*

CHAPTER TWO

Ⅱ

Even with all the degradation and mistreatment that he and his family had been forced to endure, Herschel Aizenberg had never felt so humiliated or angry as he was stuffed into this train. And although he was too prideful to ever admit it to anyone, he was terrified. Before he arrived at the ghetto, he'd been a high-powered lawyer in Warsaw. He'd always been in control. But the Nazis had stripped him of everything. He looked around him. In each tiny ray of light, he could see expressions of fright and terror on the faces of his fellow passengers. Others had fallen asleep and were leaning against the strangers beside them.

He was remembering how he and Naomi had been separated from their children. It was Shoshana's fault. Shoshana, his headstrong eldest daughter. They hadn't spoken in months because she had defied him and refused to marry the boy he'd arranged for her. During those months, he had forbidden his two younger twin daughters from having any contact with Shoshana. But when they saw Shoshana at the train station, they went running to her. He'd asked the guards to allow him to wait for his daughters to return, but they had laughed at him and forced him and Naomi at gunpoint to board the train without the twins. And now he had no idea where they were.

Naomi had stopped talking, and for that he was grateful. He had no answers for any of her questions, and he hated to admit that he just didn't know. She was standing beside him. He could hear her weeping softly. He wanted to put his arm around her, to hold her close to him and to comfort her, but he knew that if he showed even the slightest bit of weakness, this whole hard exterior of his would crack, and he would be nothing but a useless, blubbering, and pathetic excuse for a man. The train ride was rough, no water and no food. As the hours passed, some of the passengers became motion sick; others just needed to relieve themselves. And the smell of vomit, urine, and feces grew strong in the already stifling air.

A woman was standing just a few feet from Naomi, embracing an infant who had been crying when the train ride began. Now the baby was silent. Herschel thought that the child must be dead. As the train took a sharp turn, a ray of dust-filled light illuminated the woman's face. Herschel caught the dull look in her eyes as she sang the same song in Yiddish to the dead infant, rocking the child over and over again. From the silhouette of her shadow, Herschel could see she was tall, slender girl who wore a head covering of some kind. Her voice cracked like tiny broken bells as she sang the familiar lullaby to her child. This sight of her made Herschel feel sick to his stomach, because she reminded him of his eldest daughter. *She is probably about Shoshana's age,* he thought. *And if Shoshana had listened to me and married Albert, she might even have had a child by now.*

As time passed, Herschel felt worse and worse. His lack of ability to control the outcome of this situation made him want to panic. But he knew better. If he went into a rage it wouldn't help anything. All it would do was weaken him. So he stood quietly chewing on his lip, but his hands trembled. He watched the dancing, tiny rays of light as they disappeared when night fell, and then return hours later at dawn. And by this system of dark and light, he figured that they had been riding on this train for three days.

Then one morning as the rays of light began to enter the boxcar again, the train came to an abrupt stop. The train jerked everyone forward. Those who'd drifted off to sleep were awakened. Several people began banging their fists on the sides of the train car. They shouted "Let us out. It's hot in here. We need food. We need water. Help us, please. People are dying."

And it was true. It was hard to tell who was alive and who was dead because of how tightly packed they all were. But there were those who no longer spoke or moved. Herschel wondered how many other people were dead in the other overfilled boxcars. The passengers kept pounding on the walls and doors, but no one answered. They were so relentless that Herschel wondered if their fists were bleeding. But finally, after a long while, they stopped beating on the wood. There was snoring, and Herschel knew that at least some of them had fallen asleep from the heat, hunger, and pure exhaustion.

The train began to move again. Naomi lay her head against the wall and slept. Herschel watched her. *God bless her; she can sleep anywhere. That is such a gift,* he thought, and a sad smile came over his face. *I know that she is worried sick about our daughters, Bluma and Perle. I know she's worried about Shoshana as well. I must admit that I am worried too. But worry doesn't do anyone any good. And I know she likes to talk things out, but I've found that discussing things that are upsetting only makes them worse. I am relieved that, at least for the moment, she is quiet, not asking me any questions. And she is resting.* He longed to reach out and touch her shoulder, to caress her and let her know that no matter what the future held for their family, they would face it together. But he couldn't bring himself to do it. His fingers trembled with the longing to caress her. Herschel turned his head away so as not to look at her.

He had learned as a child to close himself off from feelings. His father had laughed at him whenever he was emotional. He'd laughed and called him weak, like a woman. This hurt young Herschel deeply because he admired his father, and so he fashioned himself to be like him. At first it was difficult, but as the years went on, the wall

Herschel built became thicker and unable to penetrate. By the time he was married, he was strong. To his father's delight, he never wept like a woman, but he was cold. And now, because he was used to pushing his feelings aside, he could not open his heart and tell Naomi what he wanted her to hear. He knew that they might be close to the end of their lives, and he wished that for once he could tell her just how much she had really meant to him during all the years of their marriage. Herschel opened his mouth to speak, to say the things his heart longed to express, but the words would not come. Instead, he just sighed and watched her sleep.

A slight wind blew through one of the openings in the slats. He sucked the fresh air in and swallowed it deeply. Then he leaned his head back against the wood and closed his eyes. Herschel thought about his oldest daughter, Shoshana; they had not spoken for almost a year. He was regretting that decision at the moment. He knew that the twins had missed her terribly, as did Naomi, who was devastated when Herschel had thrown Shoshana out of the apartment where they lived in the ghetto. At the time Herschel was angry, and when he was angry, he was stubborn. Naomi begged him to reconsider, but he refused. He had gone through the motions of sitting shiva, mourning as if Shoshana were dead. In fact, even now, as he stood in this crowded train car, he still wore the torn cloth of mourning on his lapel. He reached up and touched the piece of cloth.

I don't want to scare Naomi, but I don't trust the Nazis. I don't know where they are taking us. The truth is we may never see Shoshana again, and I may never have the chance to tell her that I forgive her and that I love her. So many regrets. I have so many regrets, he thought. *And my little ones, my sweet little twins, Bluma and Perle. I should have spent more time with them, but I was too busy trying to impress the world. I wanted to be an important man, the kind of man my father would have admired. What I failed to realize was that my father was dead, and my children needed me much more than they needed all the material things I provided. Ahh, the mistakes I made. So many. And now, it might be too late to redeem myself.*

When they were boarding the train, he remembered how angry he was at Bluma and Perle for running to their sister. The whole scene was chaotic. He stood there glaring at them. But they must have been afraid of the future, too, because they had defied him when they saw Shoshana; they ran to hug their older sister. And before the twins had a chance to return to their parents, the Nazi guards began to load the train. Naomi and Herschel were at the front of the line, and there was no way to step out of line. The Nazis forced them onto the boxcar without the twins.

Herschel shook his head as he remembered the morning at the train station. Until he was separated from Bluma and Perle, leaving them in Shoshana's care, Herschel had not seen how any good could come from Shoshana's independent streak. He'd despised her strength. Women were not supposed to be tough; they were supposed to depend on men. But now he was relying on Shoshana's vigor. It was the only hope he had for the survival of his daughters. His head ached with worry. If he had been alone on this train with no one who relied on him to be strong, he would have shown how angry he was. He would have roared and pulled out his hair. However, he knew if he did, it would scare Naomi, and he wanted to keep her calm. Besides that, he wouldn't give the Nazis the satisfaction of seeing him weak and vulnerable. No matter what they did to him and his family, he would laugh in their faces, because he knew that he was not a man to beg. And besides, begging would do him no damn good.

Once again, the train came to an abrupt stop. Everyone was thrown forward. A woman screamed. But the guards paid no attention. Naomi woke up and grabbed Herschel's arm. "Where are we? What's happening?"

"It's nothing," he said reassuringly, although he didn't believe his own words. "Everything is fine. We've just stopped for a few minutes. We'll be on our way soon enough. Go back to sleep."

She did as he asked.

Herschel could not say how long he stood there, sweat beading on his brow, worrisome thoughts filling his mind. Hours passed. Herschel knew day had turned to night and the sun had gone down.

Most of the people in the boxcar fell asleep, but Herschel was alert. He felt something was happening. He was tired, but it was not safe to let his guard down and go to sleep. *These filthy Nazis will not sneak up on me. I will stay awake and keep watch.* He was still furious with himself for believing the lie the Nazis told them, that this train was on its way to a better place and that the ride would be safe and comfortable. He quickly glanced over at Naomi. She slept quietly. *I am glad that, at least for the moment, she is at peace.* The silence in the boxcar was eerie. The baby had died, so its incessant crying was silenced forever. That thought made him sad. Not even one of the passengers snored, passed gas, or coughed. It was as if all of them were dead, all of them ghosts. Then the wind howled, and somewhere outside an owl hooted. Herschel closed his eyes for a moment. But then he overheard the voices of two guards. They were speaking right outside the boxcar. Although they spoke in German, he understood them completely, because not only had he studied German in law school, but he was fluent in Yiddish, and the language was very similar.

"I know they're nothing but rats. But I still feel a bit sorry for them," one of the guards said to another.

"Do you really? It's not as if they are really human. We know they are not. In fact, they are nothing but a stain on the fatherland. And they are Christ killers."

"But I can't imagine just murdering all of them. Did you see how many of them we loaded onto this train?"

"Yes, I did. And by the end of the week, they'll all be dead. No longer will they be a plague on society. You know, one day the world will thank us for ridding them of the Jews."

"But there are women and children here. We will be murdering little children. That makes me ill."

"Rolf, you sound like a weak fool. Please don't speak this way to anyone else. I am your friend. We have known each other since childhood. So, I will keep my mouth shut about all these treasonous things you've said today. But make sure you don't talk like this in front of the other guards. The things you are saying make you sound like you are unfit for your position. And believe me, they will tell on you. Everyone wants to get recognition. By turning you in, they could get a promotion. They don't care what happens to you."

"You're probably right, Bert."

"I know that I am right. You must keep your mouth shut about feeling sorry for Jews. No matter whether they are women and children or not. They are still Jews. An Aryan man must be strong. You should know that from the days we were in the Hitler Youth together."

"I'll try to be strong."

"Try hard, because the future of your career and maybe even your life depends on it," Bert said.

Herschel pushed through the crowd of sleeping bodies and looked out through the slats of the train car. He saw one of the guards walking away, and the other remained standing there staring up at the stars.

When the guard was alone, Herschel began to try to signal him without waking anyone. "Shhhh. I have something to tell you that you will want to hear," Herschel said.

The guard turned to look at Herschel, and their eyes met through the slats.

"Come closer so I can talk to you," Herschel said.

Rolf walked over suspiciously.

"It's all right. You're safe. Look, you can see that I can't get to you. I couldn't break out of here if I wanted to; I am securely locked in this train car. Come closer, I just want to tell you something," Herschel said in a conspiratorial whisper.

Rolf edged closer. "What do you want to tell me?" he asked suspiciously.

"I have a proposition for you."

"You hardly look like you're in any position to proposition anyone."

"That may be true. But perhaps not," Herschel whispered. He was nervous. *This could all go wrong and backfire on me. But I have to try.* "In my former life, before the Warsaw Ghetto, I was a successful lawyer, and I was a very rich man."

"So how does this benefit me?"

"I am about to tell you. You see, I have a four-carat diamond that I hid when we were being arrested. No one knows about it. But, it's a blue and white, a perfect stone. Worth a lot of money. If you had it, you could quit work. You could buy a home somewhere and live in peace."

"So, how do I get it?" Rolf asked. "What? Do you want to tell me where it is?"

"I want you to let my wife and I go. Free us, so we can go into the forest and try to survive on our own. We will need two days' worth of food and water."

"No chance. If I let you two go, what guarantee do I have that there is a diamond? By the time I go to look for it, you and your wife will be far away from here."

"All right. How about this, then," Herschel said, clearing his throat. *I will sacrifice my life for hers. She deserves that much for putting up with me all these years,* he thought sadly. "If you will just let my wife out of here. Give her two days' worth of food and water, I will tell you where to find the diamond. You can keep me for collateral. If it turns out that I am lying, you can kill me."

"You will tell me where it is anyway, or I will kill you right now."

"I overheard you and your coworker talking. You have plans to kill us when we arrive at our destination. And if you murder my wife and I, then what will you have? Only our dead bodies. If you don't agree to my terms, you will have no diamond."

"Interesting idea."

"Yes, a flawless blue-and-white diamond is worth a lot of money. A lot of money."

"How do I know you aren't lying to me?"

"Because, you will still have me in your grasp. You can torture me if you find that I am lying. Now, do you think I would want to suffer at your hands? Not at all. Once you have the diamond, I would expect you to show some integrity and free me. But for now, all I ask is that you free my wife."

"Why didn't you pack the diamond when you were told you were being sent to the ghetto in Warsaw?"

"I didn't because I planned to someday escape and go back and get it. I'll give you a clue. I hid it in my office. Once you know where to look, it will be easy for you to find. And it will be all yours. All yours."

Herschel had been a lawyer long enough to know when he was winning an argument. He saw Rolf's eyes twinkle with greed, and he breathed a sigh of relief. *I am probably going to die. But at least I will be able to help Naomi.* Herschel knew that there was power in silence. He did not say another word. Naomi's life hung in the balance as he trembled waiting for the guard to speak. He remembered the words of his favorite law school professor: "Silence is your most powerful negotiation tool."

Several moments passed, and finally Rolf said, "I could probably arrange this. However, if I find out that you are lying, Jew, I will make you wish you had never made this deal with me. Do you understand me?"

"Of course."

"And . . . to sweeten things, I will make you a promise."

"Oh?"

"I will let your wife go now. And, if you are telling the truth, and I do find the diamond, I promise you that I will let you go, too, as soon as I have the stone in my hand."

He's lying. But he's smart, Herschel thought. *He is aware that I know that we are all on our way to our death, and he thinks that once he's let Naomi go free, there will be no diamond and nothing he can do to punish me. So, he is offering me my life and my freedom. But I know that he won't keep his promise. Once he has the diamond, I'll be murdered just like every other Jew on this train.*

"And, you needn't worry. You will have the jewel. It will be yours. Of course, I want to live, so I wouldn't lie to you. I believe you will set me free once I have proven to you that I am trustworthy. Now, just let my wife go, as I asked."

"Very well. you have ten minutes to say goodbye. I will have some food and water ready for her to take with her. But she must leave the train in ten minutes because it is almost dawn, and then the other guards will be awake. This is your only chance, Jew. We will not be making another stop before we reach Treblinka."

"She'll be ready to go in ten minutes," Herschel said.

"Ehhh, wait a minute, you tricky little vermin. Where is the diamond?"

"Not until my wife is gone. Then I'll tell you."

"You are a real Jew." Rolf laughed, "But I'll indulge you because your life depends on it. All right, go now and say goodbye. You have ten minutes. No more."

Herschel sat back down beside Naomi who was still asleep. Gently, he nudged her shoulder. "Naomi," he whispered her name into the darkness, and the vocalizing of it brought back the memory of the first time his father told him that Naomi would be his wife.

"Herschel, what is it? Are you all right?" she asked.

"I have to talk to you, and there isn't much time," he said.

She wiped the sleep from her eyes. "Yes, what is it?"

"You are leaving this train."

"Me? You mean us?"

"No, you are going alone."

"What? Herschel, I can't. I must get our destination to be reunited with our daughters."

"I am hoping they never boarded the train," he said, and there was such a tone of doom in his voice that she shivered.

"What do you mean?"

15

"I overheard the guards talking. You must get out of here. I've arranged it."

"What did they say, Herschel?"

And he told her.

Her throat felt like sandpaper, and her body was trembling. "My children, my little ones," she said. "If it's true, what will become of them?" Naomi began to cry. Just then, an old woman who was standing beside her said, "It's dark in here, and I know you can't see me, but it's me, Mrs. Weinstein. I overheard your husband. You needn't worry about your children. I saw them get onto a truck. They never boarded this train."

"Are you sure?" Naomi said, a flicker of hope in her voice.

"I am quite certain of it," Mrs. Weinstein said. Then she coughed a little and added in a whisper so as not to alarm everyone else around them, "Your husband has arranged for you to get off the train. You should listen to him. You are a young woman. If what he says is true, and we are all headed to our deaths, if you get off, you'll have an opportunity to find your daughters again. Do as he says."

"What about you?" Naomi asked Mrs. Weinstein.

"Me? I am old. My only son is married. He lives in Belgium. He hardly ever comes to see me anymore. My husband, his soul should be a blessing, died last year. I have no one. I am not afraid to die."

Herschel interrupted the old woman. He was growing impatient. He only had a few minutes left to convince Naomi to go. "Naomi, I haven't always been a good husband. I know I am not an easy man to love, or to live with, for that matter. But . . ." He hesitated, and knowing that this would be his last chance to speak to her, he forced himself to say all that was in his heart. "I love you. I have always loved you. I could not always show you, because that's my weakness. I have a hard time with expressing myself. But, I have chosen to save your life rather than my own, and that is because I love you. Now, you must go. Stay in the forest. Make sure you stay far away from the main roads where you could be spotted by soldiers. Try to remain hidden as much as you can. The guard is going to give you two days' worth of food. After that, you must steal from the farms at night. Be careful. Please, be careful."

She couldn't help herself. She knew he hated to be touched like this, but she needed to feel human contact. So, she put her arms around him and laid her head on his chest as she openly wept. "I can't go. I can't let you go to your death alone. And what about our daughters?"

"I will be all right. I'll find a way to survive; you know me. I am a clever one, yes?"

She tried to smile and nod, but she couldn't. She was weeping even harder.

"And, listen to me. You must survive so that when this is all over, you can find our girls again."

"I'm scared, Herschel. I'm scared for the girls, but I am scared for you and me too. I want to stay with you." For a mere second she considered telling him the truth about Shoshana, that she was not his daughter. That Shoshana was the child of her lover, Eli. It would feel good to finally unburden herself of that terrible secret that she had carried deep in her heart since the day Shoshana was born. But she looked into Herschel's eyes and decided against it. It would not help him to know the truth. It could only hurt him. And if by some miracle he was to survive and be reunited with his daughters, he would never feel the same way about Shoshana. They already had problems getting along with each other, and she didn't want to say or do anything that might further separate them. She took a long, ragged breath. "I am not going without you."

"I forbid you to stay here. You will do as I say."

She sighed. In her way, Naomi loved him. She knew that he was making a great sacrifice for her right now. He was trading his life for hers. She'd never known that he cared that much about her, and she wished they had more time together to try and make things better between them. But there was no time. In the next few minutes, she would be escaping into a forest, dark and frightening. All alone.

CHAPTER THREE

A few minutes later, Rolf appeared at the opening in the wood slat. "Let's go," he said.

"She's right here," Herschel said.

"I'm going to open the door. I'll be pointing a rifle at the opening. That's because I don't want anyone else to try and get out. So, don't be afraid, just come to the door and do as I say."

"All right," Naomi moaned. Then she turned to Herschel. "I don't want to go without you."

"I demand it," he said coldly. "Now go."

Rolf opened the door. The sound awoke several of the other passengers. They tried to rush the door, but when they saw the gun, they backed up.

"Come on, get out of the train."

Naomi did as Rolf commanded. Then he slammed the door. He handed her the small bag of food and water. "Now, get out of here. Go, run, into the forest."

It was as if her feet caught flight. She began to run. For a fleeting second, a frightening thought crossed her mind. *He could shoot me in the back.* Naomi ran faster, faster than she ever knew she could run. It seemed like the safety blanket of the trees was a thousand miles away, but in reality it was only a few more feet. Finally, she was welcomed by the darkness of the forest and the open arms of the trees.

Rolf turned to Herschel. "Tell me now, or I swear I'll shoot you dead."

"Of course, I'll tell you. I am a man of my word," Herschel said, and he began to explain where he'd hidden the ring. "There is a tile behind my desk. That tile is removable. Pry it off the wall and you will find an empty space. Reach inside and pull out the cloth. The diamond ring is wrapped in that very cloth," Herschel said.

Rolf was satisfied. "Good, I'll go looking for it as soon as we arrive at Treblinka," he said.

Herschel didn't answer. He just sighed. He was glad he'd freed Naomi. But when he looked over at the space where his wife had stood only a few minutes ago, he felt lost and alone. Hot tears stung his eyes, but he wiped them away quickly as he saw his father's face in his mind's eye.

So, this is the end, he thought. *Who knew that this was how my life would end? I always thought I would die surrounded by my grandchildren who would adore me and be grateful to me for the fortune I left them. Ehhh, I'll never see grandchildren; all I can do is hope that my wife and children survive.* The dismal, dark train car, the knowledge that soon he would be dead, and the memories of his life with his wife and children, made him realize just how much he had, how much he was losing, and how much he had loved Naomi.

CHAPTER FOUR

Ⅱ

Shoshana Aizenberg, who was only a teenager herself, held her eight-year-old twin sisters, Perle and Bluma, to her breast as they sat in a room filled with twins that was located in the hospital at Auschwitz. None of them had been sick, so she couldn't understand why the doctor with the straight black hair had sent them here. He seemed fascinated by the fact that Perle and Bluma were twins. As she looked around the small room, she realized that all of the others there were a part of a set of twins. *I am the only person in here who is not a twin. This is like that nightmare that Perle had. I wonder if it was a premonition after all.*

Since she was a small child, Perle had been having strange dreams as their mother had. Shoshana was trying to sort out her thoughts. She had seen her parents board that train. And she and Ruth would have boarded it, too, if Ruth's Nazi boyfriend had not come with a truck and told them to get in. He'd said he had come to save their lives. He said that anyone who was on board the train was headed to Treblinka, where they would be murdered as soon as they arrived. Beads of sweat had formed on Shoshana's forehead because she knew her parents had boarded the train. But there was no way to save them. And there was no time to think. She was responsible for her sisters now, and she had to act fast. So she'd followed Ruth, and she and her sisters had climbed onto the truck. That was how they ended up here at Auschwitz.

If what that Nazi friend of Ruth's said is true, and I pray it's not, then our parents are probably dead already. A chill ran through her as she considered this. *Or perhaps he tricked us, because from what I can see, he brought us to some kind of a terrible prison. The doctor with the dark hair who sent us to this room that he calls his twins' room looks exactly like Perle described him when she had that dream. He seemed to be kind when we met him, yet I don't trust him. He, like Ruth's Nazi friend, is one of them. And every day we are reminded that Nazis are not human; they are monsters. Only monsters could do the things they do.*

Shoshana closed her eyes and remembered her parents as they'd been the last time she saw them. They were standing together at the front of the line to board the train. Her mother turned to look at her first. When her mother's eyes caught hers, she wanted to run into her mother's arms. But it was impossible. There were too many people in line between them, and there was so much chaos.

Then her sisters, Perle and Bluma, had seen her, and somehow, unexpectedly, they pushed their way through the crowds to get to where Shoshana stood. Perhaps they'd been able to get through the masses because they were so small. When she could hold them, she was so filled with love that she grabbed them and hugged them. It had been a long time since she'd last seen her sisters, and she hugged them tightly, her arms filling with all the love she'd held so deep in her heart during those lonely months. But who could have guessed that this tiny act, this one moment when her sisters came to say hello to her, would have changed all of their lives forever? Because just at that moment, the Nazi guards had begun to load the train, and although she saw her mother trying to wait for the twins to return, the Nazis had forced her and Shoshana's father onto the train.

Papa is such a hard, stubborn man, she thought, and she remembered how he had turned and looked at her for a single moment before he climbed on board the train. But there was no affection in his eyes. They were blank as if she were nothing to him, as if she were a stranger. How she had longed for his forgiveness, but he didn't offer any. And now it was too late; she had no idea if she would ever see him or her mother again. Shoshana knew she was helpless as far as her parents were concerned. All she could do now was try her best to save her sisters.

"Where did that Nazi guard send Ruth?" Bluma asked Shoshana. She was still staring at the angry red skin that surrounded the tattoo that had been cut into her forearm when they arrived. Shoshana looked down at it and hoped it was not going to get infected.

"I don't know. I wish she had been allowed to come with us."

When Shoshana and her sisters arrived at Auschwitz, they had been given a shower and then the three girls had each been tattooed with numbers on their forearms. It had been very painful, but none of them cried. Bluma looked at the guards defiantly. Perle surrendered as she always did. And Shoshana kept her head down, hoping to find a way out of this place. They saw other prisoners whose heads were being shaved. But Shoshana, Bluma, and Perle weren't sent to have their hair shaved. These were regular prisoners, not twins like Perle and Bluma. From what everyone said, twins were Dr. Mengele's favorites. And right now, this seemed like a good thing, because Mengele's favorites were permitted to keep their hair.

"I think Ruth is dead," Perle whispered softly.

"Do you think that her Nazi boyfriend tricked us?" Bluma asked. Then Bluma continued, shaking her head. "I can't believe that Ruth would have a Nazi boyfriend in the first place."

Shoshana thought about it. She was certain that the Nazi Ruth had been sleeping with had betrayed her. But she didn't think her sisters were old enough to discuss such things.

"No, I don't think he tricked us. I don't think he knew that this place would be like this," Perle said.

Perle, she is always looking for the good in people, Shoshana thought.

It was a known fact in the Aizenberg family that Perle had a gift, the gift of sight. It had first shown itself when she was very young. It had started through her dreams. But now she sometimes just had a knowing. This had not come as a surprise to Perle's mother, Naomi, because she had grown up with the gift as well. Not always, but sometimes, Perle was able to predict the future or know the thoughts of other people that no one else knew.

"You really don't think he knew where he was taking us?" Bluma asked again referring to Ruth's boyfriend.

"I don't think so. I believe he was trying to help us," Perle said. "But, I am scared. I am scared of that doctor with the black hair."

"Do you remember the dream you had a few years ago about a doctor who looked like him?" Shoshana asked.

"I remember. And I believe that's him," Perle said.

"But he seems so nice." Shoshana tried to make things seem less frightening. "At least to twins."

"He's not nice," Perle said. "I promise you, he's not."

"I saw so many dead people, Shoshana. There were piles of dead bodies. Did you see them? If that Nazi boyfriend of Ruth's was really her friend, he would never have brought us to this place. He's nothing but a Nazi. And, I think he tricked her and us. Now, she's dead. Ruth is the youngest person who I have ever known that died. I mean, I remember when Bubbie died, but she was old and very sick. Ruth was young. In fact, I still remember that she had just spoken to us before she was taken away. And now, she's probably dead." Bluma shivered. Then she wrapped her arms around her chest and in a small voice said, "My stomach hurts. I'm hungry, and I don't feel well."

"I don't feel well either," Perle admitted. "But I am afraid that if we let anyone know we are feeling sick, these Nazis will make things even worse for us. Didn't you see when we first got here? They were shooting people for no reason. I saw it happen to two different people as we were coming in. Nazi guards just shot them dead. They fell on the ground like rag dolls. They didn't even look like people.

One was a young woman; the other was a small child. I think she was a little girl, but I couldn't tell because she was covered in blood. They both were. It seemed almost as if it was a dream. A nightmare. Like one of my nightmare dreams. Bluma, I am sure that the best thing we can do is to keep quiet and keep to ourselves. It's the safest thing to do. Let's play our game of pretending to be invisible like we always have. It's best if they overlook us. After all, why would the Nazis care if a couple of Jewish children are sick? My guess is that if they thought we were ill, rather than risk catching whatever we might have, they would just shoot us too."

"I don't want to die," Bluma said. "And I don't want to lose either of you. I'm scared here."

"It will be all right. Just don't make a fuss. Stay quiet," Perle told Bluma.

It's frightening how grown up Perle is, and she is only eight years old. It makes me angry that she has to be so grown up. My poor little sisters have never had a real childhood, because our family has been stuck in that ghetto in Warsaw. They are so thin because the rations were never enough. It's just not fair. And now, we're here in a place that's even worse than the ghetto. It shouldn't be this way. We've committed no crime. The only thing we ever did wrong was to be born Jewish. My sisters are innocent. They should be outside playing with their friends, not here in this filthy, smelly prison, surrounded by death. No child should ever see so much death. No person should either, Shoshana thought.

Bluma took Shoshana's hand. "At least that doctor allowed you to come with us and take care of us."

Perle's eyes glazed over. "Just remember what I am telling you. We must be very careful of him. We can't trust him. We will never be able to trust him. He let Shoshana come with us, but he is not good. He is not nice."

"Stop it, Perle. It's bad enough here. Don't start predicting things," Bluma said. She was edgy and nervous.

The twins never fought like this. At least they had never fought in the past. But now, Bluma was frightened, and hearing Perle voice her terrible, intuitive feelings only made things worse.

"I'm sorry," Perle said, hugging Bluma. "I would never want to scare you."

"How long do you think we'll be in here?" Bluma asked Shoshana. Shoshana shook her head.

Just then a boy of about twelve, who was also a twin, walked over to them. "Hello, I'm Asa," he said. "That's my brother, Ari. I overheard you ask how long you will be here. No one knows the answer to that. We keep praying that something will happen to get us out of here. But as long as Hitler is in power, we will be in here. All we can do is hope for a miracle."

"What will happen to us?" Bluma asked.

"That doctor you met . . . was he tall with dark hair and a pretty big space between his front teeth?"

"Yes," Perle said.

"His name is Mengele. He demands that we call him Uncle Mengele. But he's no uncle of mine. In fact, you're going to find out that he's a devil," Asa said. "He's a sadist and a beast."

Bluma was shaking.

"This isn't helping," Shoshana said to the boy. "You're terrifying my sisters."

"Well, it's true. You'll see. You just don't know him yet. But you can believe me when I tell you, he is the devil. In fact, people around here call him the angel of death."

CHAPTER FIVE

♊

T he night before Ernst was to return to work at Auschwitz
with his new bride, he was overcome with a deep feeling of
dread. He never wanted to return. That place brought back
bad memories. As he thought about what Dr. Mengele expected of
him and all the horrors he'd witnessed at Auschwitz, he found he
could not fall asleep. His beautiful new wife, Gisele, the woman of
his dreams, lay softly breathing beside him. Her golden curls spread
out like a gilded fan on the pillow. *I love her so much. I don't ever want
to lose her. So, I can't tell her how I feel about returning to work with Dr.
Mengele. She thinks I am someone important because I am an assistant to
the most important doctor in the Third Reich. A beauty like Gisele would
never have looked twice at a man like me if I did not earn such a good
salary and have such a prestigious job. She has no idea what goes on in
that place. The horrors I have witnessed watching Mengele torture innocent people, innocent children.* He shivered. Gisele must have felt him
move because she turned over in her sleep. Ernst watched her, and
his heart ached with love for her. I have to find a way to tolerate this
job. I must overlook Mengele's horrific behavior in that poor excuse

for a hospital. I just can't lose this job, because if I do, I will risk losing my wife.

The following morning, they left early and boarded the train for Poland. As they passed the farms and golden fields, Gisele turned to Ernst and said, "You have plenty of money. I think you should purchase an automobile. It would be much more comfortable to be in our own car rather than on this train. Don't you think so?"

He didn't want a car. But if it made her happy he would buy one. "Have you ever ridden in a car?" he asked.

"No, but I want to," she said, smiling at him.

She is so damn pretty, he thought. Then he laughed. "All right, Mrs. Neider. If you want a car, I'll buy one."

She clapped her hands, then she leaned over and kissed him. His heart was filled with joy.

The gentle rhythm of the rails rocked her to sleep. As Gisele lay with her head on Erns's shoulder, he thought about the future, about what would happen once they were in Poland and once she could see where he worked. He was worried about what she would think of the barbed wire and the guards in the tower when she saw them in the morning light. She would definitely know that Auschwitz was some sort of a prison. But she wouldn't know that it was not criminals who were contained there. He had to admit that there were some prisoners who could be considered criminals, people who were enemies of the Reich. But for the most part, that horrible prison was filled with innocents who suffered at the hands of the Nazis.

Dawn came, and the sun lit the sky with a soft rose-colored light. Ernst looked over at Gisele. She slept soundly, missing the light show of the sunrise. He would have liked to wake her to share this beautiful moment, but he knew that traveling had made her tired. And in a few hours they would be at their destination. He was hungry, and his arm where she lay on him had fallen asleep. The tiny feeling of pins and needles was uncomfortable, but he loved her so much that he dared not move and disturb her.

As the sun grew brighter in the sky, Ernst remembered that soon he would have to return to Auschwitz, and the beauty of the morning sky lost its allure. By this time tomorrow he would be back at work, back under the direction of the cruel and unnerving Dr. Mengele. He was exhausted because he had not slept, not even for a few moments.

When the train pulled into the station, Ernst gently kissed Gisele on the forehead. "We're here," he whispered softly.

She awakened. They left the train and then headed for his apartment.

"Your apartment is rather small for such an important man," she said.

"I'm sure once Dr. Mengele knows I am married, he will ask the party to give us a house," Ernst said, hoping it was true. He knew Mengele didn't like him very much. But he would be impressed with Gisele's Aryan looks even if she was French.

That afternoon Ernst took Gisele for an early dinner at a small local restaurant. Then he surprised her and bought an automobile. It hadn't been as difficult as he thought it would be. He telephoned Mengele who made a call, and he was able to buy a car within a few hours. She was delighted, and the fact that he'd made her happy filled him with pleasure. The man who sold him the automobile showed him how to drive it. Ernst drove slowly, but she enjoyed it just the same. They drove around for a short while and then returned to his apartment.

Gisele went into the bathroom and came out naked. He thought she looked like a statue of a goddess. They made love until she said she was tired. Then she turned over and fell asleep.

Ernst knew that in the morning he must return to Auschwitz, and even though he was beyond tired, he couldn't sleep. When the sun peeked through the dark clouds, he rose from the bed.

Quietly, he went into the bathroom and washed his face with cold water. Then he got dressed in his uniform and put his doctor's coat over it. He leaned down and kissed Gisele who stirred awake.

"I'm off to work," he said, not expecting her to get up and prepare his breakfast. If anything, he would have prepared hers.

"Don't forget, you said you are going to try to get us a larger place to live. Like a house of our own," she said. "This room where you lived as a bachelor is hardly big enough for a married couple."

"Of course. You're right, darling. And don't worry, I won't forget. I'll speak with Dr. Mengele today and see what he can do for us." He leaned down and kissed her. "I'll be home this evening."

She smiled and turned over, closing her eyes and drifting back to sleep.

CHAPTER SIX

♊

The horrible smell of death greeted Ernst when he drove
through the iron gate at the front of Auschwitz. *I should be
used to it,* he thought, *but I don't think I will ever be.* He trembled as he parked his car. *What horrors does this day have in store
for me?*

Oh, how he longed to be far from Dr. Mengele and his terrible
experiments. But he dared not quit this job lest he ruin his career and
disappoint his wife. So with his head down, he walked into the
hospital.

"Heil Hitler," he said to the nurse at the desk.

"Heil Hitler, and welcome back," she answered, smiling. "How
was your holiday?"

"Very nice," he managed to say. "Is Dr. Mengele in his office?"

"Yes, I believe he is."

"Thank you," Ernst said. He walked slowly, dreading the moment
he would see that wicked smile with the space between his two front
shiny white teeth. Ernst stood at the door to Mengele's office for a
moment. He took a deep breath and steeled himself. Then he
knocked.

"Who is it?"

"Ernst Neider."

"Do come in," Mengele said in a jolly voice.

Ernst walked inside the office where Mengele sat behind his desk sipping from a cup.

"Heil Hitler." Mengele saluted.

"Heil Hitler."

"Welcome back to work," Mengele said, and then there it was— that smile. There was a cruel glint in Mengele's eyes. He'd seen this look on Mengele's face before just when Mengele was about to do something terrible to someone. As soon as Ernst saw that expression on Mengele's face, he wanted to run away. But there was nowhere to run. He had to please Gisele, had to keep her happy. If he ran out of here now, he would lose this job and be lucky to ever be permitted to use his medical license again.

"Thank you, Doctor," Ernst said respectfully. Then looking away from Dr. Mengele, he added, "There is something I must discuss with you?"

"Oh?" Mengele raised his eyebrows, looking amused. "Why don't you sit down?" I'll have my secretary bring you a cup of coffee, or would you prefer tea?"

"Nothing. I'm fine. But thank you."

"Nonsense. I insist."

"Coffee, then."

Mengele nodded. Then he called out to the young girl who sat at a small desk right outside his office. "Bring Dr. Neider a cup of coffee, Alice."

Mengele took some candies out of his pocket. Ernst felt a chill run down his spine. He knew that whenever Mengele gave candy to his patients, the next thing he would do was send them to the gas. *What does this man have in store for me? I know him, and I know it is something cruel.*

"Candy?" Mengele offered graciously.

"No, thank you."

"I'm surprised you can resist candy. You're such a chubby one," Mengele said. Then he laughed and popped a piece into his mouth. "All right, Neider. What is it you wanted to speak to me about?"

Ernst took a deep breath and gathered his courage. "While I was on holiday, I went to Berlin where I met a girl. I got married."

"Well, well, isn't that good news? You should be bringing us plenty of Aryan children."

"Yes." Then Ernst shuddered. *I must tell him the truth.* "She's not German, I'm afraid. She's French."

"OH?"

"Yes, but she does have Aryan coloring. She has blonde hair and blue eyes."

Mengele let out a laugh. "Hmm, well, French isn't so bad, I suppose. After all, it could be worse. She could be a Jew."

"She's not Jewish," Ernst said firmly.

"Yes, well. All right." Mengele smiled again. "And, I have some news for you too. While you were off on holiday, I needed extra help. So, I hired another assistant." He took a piece of candy, unwrapped it, and popped it into his mouth.

Ernst felt his throat go dry. "You mean I am out of a job?"

Mengele stared at Ernst for a long moment. Then he let out a laugh. Ernst felt his stomach turn over. "No, you're in luck. I am still keeping you. I've decided that you and my new assistant will work together. We could use the extra pair of hands."

The secretary arrived and put the cup of steaming coffee in front of Ernst. Mengele turned to his secretary. "Alice, tell Dr. Schatz to come into my office."

"Yes, Doctor," she answered.

Ernst wished he could believe Mengele that everything was going to be fine, that he and this new person were going to work together. But he didn't believe that for a minute. Ernst didn't trust Mengele. He was afraid that Mengele was training this new doctor to take his place. He thought that just when he let his guard down and became friends with the new doctor, Mengele would drop the bomb.

That is the way Mengele operates. He likes to make his victim feel secure as if everything is fine, then he destroys him.

There was a knock on the door.

"Otto, is that you?" Mengele called out.

"Yes, Doctor."

"Well, what are you standing out there for? Come in," Mengele said in a joyful tone.

"Heil Hitler."

"Heil Hitler."

"I'd like to introduce you to someone. This is Ernst Neider. Dr. Neider," Mengele said.

"Arschgeige," Otto said, laughing. "It's been years."

"You called him an Ass violin?" Mengele asked Otto, amused.

"Actually, that was his nickname when we were children, in school."

"So, you two are old friends." Mengele smiled.

"We are. Aren't we, Ernst?" Otto said in that same mocking tone of voice.

Ernst was appalled. He felt his throat tighten. It had been a year since he'd suffered humiliation at Otto Schatz's hand, but seeing Otto again brought back every terrible day he'd spent trying to avoid Otto and his constant bullying.

To make matters worse, Otto had grown up to be handsome. He was an athletic young man with a cap of curly blond hair and bright blue eyes that twinkled as he walked into the room. He carried himself with an air of charm. His uniform was immaculate and pressed, and he seemed to have everything in his world under control. Otto nodded at both Ernst and Dr. Mengele, then he smiled a winning smile.

Mengele winked at Ernst and then returned Otto's smile. He looked evil.

Then Ernst caught a look of camaraderie that passed between Otto Schatz and Dr. Mengele, and he felt like they both saw him as an inferior. It seemed to him that the two of them had formed a special bond when Ernst was gone. The look in their eyes spoke of an understanding that did not include Ernst. A half smile came over Mengele's face, and Otto matched that smile.

"I think we are all going to work very well together," Mengele said. "What do you think, Neider?"

"O-o-of course. Y-yes. We'll work very well together." Ernst watched the unspoken communication between Otto and Mengele, and he felt as if they had left him to freeze, standing outside on an ice-cold winter day looking in the window of a room he was not privy to enter. *Mengele is enjoying this. He loves watching me squirm. Damn this stutter. I've been rid of it for years, and now it's back. All because of that bastard, Otto.*

"Otto has been wonderful while you were off running around. He has been a gem helping me out here at the hospital. You know how much work there is to do, with keeping an eye on those doctors who are prisoners. They are doctors, so they tend to be smart, and that means they require my constant surveillance. And to further complicate things, now it seems we are having problems with a breakout of noma in the Gypsy camp. I would like to find a cure for that, but let's face it, noma is a disgusting disease, and if we happen to have a surprise visit from Himmler or Goring, I know they would be repulsed. So, I've decided that if I don't find a cure soon, I am going to gas the entire Gypsy camp just so I don't have to worry about it anymore."

"I quite agree with Dr. Mengele. I think that if we don't find a cure soon, we might as well get rid of them. They're just worthless, lazy Gypsies anyway. So why risk having that miserable illness spread through the camp. After all, who's to say that one of us won't catch it."

"That would be terrible," Mengele agreed, then he continued, "Anyway, while I've been busy doing selections, Otto has been doing an excellent job of carrying out your duties. He has been taking care of the morning blood draws on the twins and the misfits," Mengele said. "However, now that you have returned, Otto can get on to more important things, and you can get back to your own work."

Ernst said nothing but he swallowed hard. *So, Mengele thinks that silly fop is worthy of more important work than I am. I doubt he did as well as I did in medical school. I've seen his type before. He's handsome and relies more on his looks than his brains or his abilities.*

"That's all. You can both go now."

Otto nodded and then smiled at Ernst. "It was a pleasure seeing you," he said, but Ernst didn't believe him for a moment.

He feels superior to me. His tasks are important. Mine are mundane. That's what Mengele implied anyway. "Y-y-yes." Ernst was miserable; his stutter was back. Mengele had not heard him stutter before, and he looked directly at him as if he were seeing him for the first time. And not liking what he saw.

"You two will be working very closely together. I can promise you that," Mengele said.

"I look forward to it," Otto said cockily.

Ernst said nothing. He just stood up, straightened his uniform jacket, and started to walk toward the door.

Otto stood up and headed out the same way.

As Ernst followed Otto to the door, Mengele stopped him. "Neider," Mengele said in a soft but maniacal voice.

"Y-y-yes?"

"I have decided that I would like to meet that new wife of yours. How about tomorrow night? I think we should go out for a beer."

"Y-y-yes, Doctor. I-I-I'm sure s-s-she would like that." Ernst wished he could cut out his own tongue. He was so angry with himself because he was unable to control the damn stutter.

"Good. Then it's settled." Mengele smiled. "Off with you both. I have work to do. And . . . Neider, start by making your rounds this morning. You won't need to do that anymore, Schatz."

"Yes, Doctor," both answered.

Ernst left the room. *I hate myself for this stuttering. And to make matters worse, the last thing I want is to stutter like this in front of Gisele, and I know I will if we are with Mengele. He will love it. He will enjoy seeing me at my worst in front of my beautiful young wife. I wish he didn't want to meet her."* He sighed. *"Besides, I am so angry with myself. I didn't even have the courage to ask him about a house. And the truth is, how can I expect him to award us larger accommodations when he hasn't even met her yet? So, I am going to have to arrange this meeting. Damn him. He is the most horrible person I've ever known. What if he tells her about his so-called work at this camp? How could I ever explain that I have been a party to such dreadful things. My stomach is killing me, and I have to be here working in this hell for the rest of the day.*

CHAPTER SEVEN

♊

Ernst tried to calm himself as he walked into the room where Dr. Mengele kept his twins. It was getting late, and he had still not done his morning blood draws. *Morning blood draws,* he thought, shaking his head. *They are unnecessary blood draws on healthy patients. He is torturing people for no reason, and it makes me sick, especially when I see what he does to the children. I must control myself. I cannot allow my conscience to get in the way of my keeping this job. My wife is beautiful. She is far more beautiful than any woman I've ever met. And I am afraid she is going to discover the truth, that she is too good for me.* Ernst had always been a shy, introverted boy, a little overweight, not good looking, not athletic, and never popular. In his experience, girls like Gisele never seemed to be interested in men like him.

He did not look at the patients; instead, he stared out the window. "Good morning," he said.

The patients in the twins' room answered, "Good morning, Dr. Neider."

Ernst placed his black leather doctor bag down on the table and began to lay out his equipment when he noticed that there was a new pair of twins. They were two small, dark-haired little girls accompanied by a pretty teenage girl with bright, intelligent eyes. It was rare to see someone who was not a twin in the twins' room, and this sparked Ernst's curiosity. *I wonder who she is, and why is she here? I don't see her twin, so I don't think she has one.*

"I'm Dr. Neider, one of Dr. Mengele's assistants," he said to Bluma. "And who are you?"

"Bluma Aizenberg," Bluma answered defiantly, crossing her arms over her chest.

"I see. And you, what is your name?"

"I'm her sister. My name is Perle Aizenberg. And this is our older sister, Shoshana."

"And are you a twin, Shoshana?" Ernst asked. He didn't stutter when he was away from Mengele.

"No, I am not a twin," Shoshana said. Her voice was soft, almost like a caress. "But the other doctor, the one called Uncle Mengele, said it was all right with him if I stay here to take care of my sisters. Please, may I?"

Ernst looked at Shoshana. She was looking down at the floor. He noticed her hands were trembling. She was a soft-spoken girl. Very respectful. "Of course," Ernst said.

Bluma, who was standing behind her sister Shoshana, put her hand on Shoshana's arm as if to comfort her, and then, very slowly, she walked around and stood in front of Shoshana as if to shield her. Ernst realized that this was a message, a clear message. *I can see the message in Bluma's eyes: "Don't touch my sister, Doctor. Don't hurt her." But even more, Bluma's eyes say, "I know I am just a child, and I am not capable of much. But believe me when I tell you I would kill you if I could. I would kill every Nazi here if I had the chance."*

Ernst looked at Bluma, who was looking right back at him with those insolent eyes.

Bluma is just a child. She is so bold, I wonder how she will fare here with Mengele. Poor thing. He won't put up with this, and I don't know how I can help her, Ernst thought. He liked Bluma; he liked her gumption. He would try to buffer the situation between her and the other doctors as much as he could. "I understand you," he said in a soft voice.

"Good. Then we understand each other," she said.

He decided that he would give her a special treat.

Ernst took three of the candies that Mengele had given him out of his pocket and gave one to each of the girls.

"Thank you," Shoshana said. "This was very kind of you."

Perle took the candy but didn't eat it. She held it in her hand and glanced up quickly into Ernst's eyes.

But Bluma was still rebellious. She didn't want his friendship. There was anger in her voice when she said, "I don't want your candy. I want to leave here so I can go and find my parents. Let us out of here," Bluma said, and she threw the candy at Ernst.

Perle's face turned white. "Please, forgive my sister. Don't hurt her. She didn't mean it . . ."

Ernst knew he should be angry. But all he could feel was pity for these three helpless girls. Especially for Bluma. He knew that if she had behaved this way in front of Dr. Mengele, he would have been very angry. Ernst shivered; he could have quite possibly sent this child to the gas. At the very least, if he was feeling generous, he would have beaten her severely. Ernst couldn't treat a frightened child that way. The truth was he couldn't treat anyone that way. *I have always been the fellow who couldn't kill an insect,* he thought. However, he knew that he was not doing Bluma or her sisters any favor by coddling her. If he was kind, it would only lead Bluma to believe that she could behave this way with Mengele, or with Otto, and then what would happen to her?

Ernst sucked in a deep breath. Then he turned to Shoshana. "You'd better take control of your sister. This place is not a playground. You are going to discover that it's very dangerous for a child to be so outspoken and bold. And the last thing you need is for Dr. Mengele to take a disliking to your sister. He has absolute power here in this hospital. So, if he so decides that he doesn't like you, he can make your lives a living hell. And that's if he decides to let you live. I am not like him, but I know the ropes here. And I am warning you to be careful."

"I'm sorry. Please forgive my sister. I promise you that it won't happen again," Shoshana said.

Ernst looked at the young girl; she had to be about seventeen or so, and she was quite pretty. Like the others in Mengele's special rooms, she was permitted to keep her hair, which was thick and black and hung down in soft waves all the way to her shoulders. *I still wonder why Mengele decided to allow her to stay here with her twin sisters. This is unusual for him because she's not a twin or deformed in any way. In fact, she's perfect. I wonder if he is planning on raping her. I truly hope he is not. She is so sweet, and she doesn't deserve that. But it might not be that. It could be something else or nothing at all. The truth is that nothing Mengele does ever makes sense to anyone but him. His allowing these twins to have the comfort of their older sister seems to be a kindness. However, I have seen his kindness turn to cruelty many times. And I wouldn't be surprised if he had some sinister plan in mind for these poor girls. I just don't know what it is. Or if I can find a way to stop it.*

Ernst turned to the girls and said, "I am going to have to take blood from each of you twins. I'll be very gentle." Ernst picked up the syringe.

"No, I'm not getting stuck with a needle by you," Bluma said. "I won't let you stick me. I won't."

"I'm afraid we both have no choice, Bluma. Your name is Bluma, isn't that right?" Ernst said. "I don't want to stick you. And, I promise you I will be very gentle. I won't hurt you."

"You remembered her name," Shoshana blurted out. She hadn't meant to say anything, but she was shocked that a Nazi had taken the time to learn her sister's name. Then she looked away, and in a small voice she asked him, "Is it really necessary to take blood? Both of my sisters are healthy."

"I'm sorry, but Dr. Mengele demands that I take blood from every one of the twins each morning. I wish it were my decision but it's not. It's part of my job."

"I'll go first," Perle said bravely, and she put her arm out.

Ernst's eyes caught Shoshana's, and he felt such a wave of pity come over him that he had to look away. For a moment he felt unable to move. He just sat there breathing heavily. Then, as gently as he could, he took the blood from Perle.

"It wasn't that bad," Perle said to Bluma. "I hardly felt anything at all."

Bluma shook her head. "No! I don't want to do it. I won't do it."

"Shhh, please, don't yell," Ernst said. "If Dr. Mengele comes in here, he will be far worse to you than I am. Please, just be quiet."

Shoshana was shaking. She put out her arm and said, "Let me give you my blood. Just tell the doctor it's hers. Please, I am begging you. We just got here, and she is so afraid. By tomorrow she will be more relaxed. I promise you."

"I'm not afraid," Bluma said as she angrily wiped the tears that were falling down her cheeks. "I want to leave here and go to wherever my parents are. I don't want to be in this place. I would rather die."

"Don't say that," Shoshana said. "Don't give yourself a kinehora."

"What?" Ernst said.

"The evil eye," Shoshana said. "A kinehora is the evil eye." She was trembling. "Please forgive my sister. She is too outspoken for her own good. She misses our parents."

"I completely understand, Bluma," Ernst said. "And I wish I could help you, but I have no way of sending you anywhere. I am not the superior officer here. I am only his apprentice. Now, since I don't want to make this worse for you than it has to be, I will break the rules for you today. I'll take Shoshana's blood, and I'll say that it's yours." Then he turned to Shoshana. "But by tomorrow you must make Bluma understand that she is a prisoner here and that Dr. Mengele won't be as kind or tolerant of her outbursts as I have been."

"Thank you," Shoshana said. She gave him her arm. And he took her blood.

Then, without saying another word, Ernst made his rounds taking blood from each of the twins in the room. After he'd finished, he took the test tubes filled with blood and left.

CHAPTER EIGHT

Ⅱ

S hoshana sat down on the bed and held her sisters, one wrapped in each of her arms. None of the girls spoke. Shoshana thought of her parents and of Ruth. *Is it really true? Is it really possible that they are all dead? My dear, sweet mother? My best friend, Ruth? And my stubborn but always constant father? Is it just me and my sisters who are left now? What will become of us here in this place? Bluma is so outspoken and so defiant. I am afraid for her. I am so afraid that if Mengele finds out, he will hurt her. But I don't know how to convince her that she must obey the rules. I might be a fool, but I am not afraid of Dr. Neider. He seems to be a good man, although I don't really know him, and I can't be certain that he won't turn on us. But I am truly terrified of Dr. Mengele. I think he can turn into a raging animal if he is angered. And Bluma is just the type of child to enrage him. Somehow, I must make Bluma do what they tell her to do and stop fighting.*

Shoshana tried to speak to Bluma about struggling against the doctors.

"Bluma, you must not forget that we are prisoners here. We must do as they say," Shoshana said.

"And how did we end up here anyway? I'll tell you how it happened; your friend Ruth was tricked because she trusted a Nazi and because she was so stupid, we all ended up here."

"I know. I shouldn't have trusted him, but everything happened so fast. I am sorry. I will do what I can to get us out of here. But for now, you have to listen to the doctors, so they don't get angry with you. Can you please try?"

"But why? I have done nothing wrong. Why am I in prison, and why should the doctor stick me and take my blood? I'm not sick."

"I know, and you're right. But at least this Dr. Neider is gentle, and he won't hurt you. You must try to cooperate with him. It could be your only chance of survival."

"I don't care," Bluma said, crossing her arms over her chest. "I won't let them do it to me."

"I know you don't care what happens to you. But what about Perle? What if they punish Perle because you refused to cooperate with them?"

"But why would they do that? Perle has nothing to do with it."

"They might do it to punish you. I suggest you go along with whatever they tell you to do," Shoshana said. "If not for your own sake, then for Perle's."

Bluma glanced at Perle. Then she nodded. "All right. I'll do it. But only because of Perle . . . and you."

"Thank you, Bluma. You are very brave," Shoshana said. Perle stood up and walked over to Bluma, then she wrapped her sister in her arms and hugged Bluma tightly.

Later that night when Bluma was asleep, Perle gently nudged Shoshana awake. "Do you remember that dream I had about the doctor?"

"I remember some of it," Shoshana said, still groggy. "Why do you ask?"

"Because I recognize the doctor from my dream: it was Dr. Mengele."

Shoshana gasped. "You must try to sleep," she said. "You need to get some rest." Perle nodded and lay her head on Shoshana's shoulder. She fell asleep almost immediately. But Shoshana lay awake for the rest of the night trying to remember everything she could about the dream.

CHAPTER NINE

♊

Finding herself alone in the forest, Naomi looked around. There was very little light. Wild animals hooted and howled in the distance as the sun set and night began to fall. Through the trees, the forest was steeped in shadow. It was growing darker by the minute, almost claustrophobic. Naomi's eyes strained; she could feel the forest closing in around her, her skin crawling as she imagined spiders falling from the trees into her hair and onto her face. Naomi shivered. She had never been alone at night in such a place before, and she was unsure of where to go or what to do. Most of the trees were bare, but not all, and those leaves swayed in the wind. As she stepped through the ice and snow, she heard the sound of twigs snapping and crunching beneath her feet.

What am I going to do? How am I ever going to find my children? I felt safer on the train with all of those other people. And although he isn't much company, at least Herschel was with me. Now I am totally alone. I am still shocked that he sacrificed himself for me. I never knew he cared so much. In fact, I never really believed that he loved me. But he must have, or he would have saved himself instead of me. Poor Herschel. We were mismatched from the day my father arranged our marriage. But in the end, he came through for me. When I think he might die in the next day or two, it breaks my heart. However, I am powerless to help him. In fact, I don't even know where the train went. Once I entered the forest I left the train forever.

Dark and tall trees with thick branches, twisted and tangled and snaked together in a way that made her feel like she would fall, seemed to be reaching out to grab her. Their bark was a patchwork in shades of dark brown, but as the evening grew darker, everything looked black. She wanted to cry. But she knew it was pointless. No one could help her. There was no one to hear her cries. Herschel had done all he could for her. He'd saved her life. He'd traded his own life for hers. She wanted to tell him how much she appreciated this final gesture. *If what Herschel overhead those Nazi guards saying turns out to be true, then I must accept that I will never see him again. It's hard to imagine that. He has been a part of my life for so long. We had three children together. I know we had a tumultuous marriage. Neither of us were faithful. But right now, my thoughts of Herschel are like a warm, old blanket. They are filled with familiar memories. And the very idea that I will never see him again makes me sad and frightened.*

Her heart was filled with worry for her children. *What will become of them? All I can do is pray that God will watch over them because I cannot. I am here alone in this unfamiliar place without a soul in sight. And I will probably die of hunger or thirst, because once this food is gone, I can't imagine how I will find more. The Nazis were the soldiers in my nightmares that began so many years ago. I told Herschel about those nightmares and how I thought they were premonitions, but he refused to believe me. I don't think it would have mattered anyway. What could we have done? Leave our homes, leave Poland, all because of a dream? But, I have known since the Nazis sent us to the ghetto that they were the soldiers in my dreams. I recognized that flag with the black spider right away. And the cruelty. Oh, and their terrible, inhumane cruelty. Dear God, please help me.*

Then she heard a sound. She whirled around and looked up. *Could my eyes be playing tricks on me, or is that the shadow of a man over there in the darkness?* The hair on the back of her neck stood up; she grew tense like a prey animal. *Who could be here in this forest in the middle of the night?*

CHAPTER TEN

♊

hen the transport arrived, and the passengers were
ushered out and forced to line up, Rolf walked over to
Herschel.

"You owe me, Jew. I sent someone to that office where you told
me to look. There is no diamond there. Now, tell me. Where is the
diamond?"

Herschel let out a laugh, a bark that was so foreign, it was frightening. He sounded more like a hyena than a human.

"What in the hell is the matter with you that you laugh like that?
Tell me what you promised."

"You Nazi fool," Herschel said. "I can see that what you said is
true. Everyone here is being lined up to be murdered. You were
honest, at least." He laughed again. "But I lied. I will not tell you
where the diamond is. My wife is free. And either way, I am headed
for the end."

"Is there a diamond?"

"You'll never know. But it will eat you up inside for the rest of
your miserable life. You stupid Nazi bastard," Herschel said. He was
laughing again.

Rolf took the butt of his gun and hit Herschel across the face. "I can make this very bad for you."

Herschel laughed as his blood splattered onto the ground. "You're going to make this worse than it already is? That's funny. And how do you plan to do that? I am already about to be murdered. What else can you do to me? I've already lost my wife and children and spent the last several days in a boxcar, a filthy one at that, with no food or water. People were dying every hour from thirst and disease. There were corpses all around me. I had to watch young mothers going mad as they sang lullabies to their dead babies. And now, you are going to kill us all. Perhaps you plan to kill every Jew in Poland. But as far as I am concerned you've already taken everything away from me, so I have nothing left to lose." He laughed again "So, my Nazi friend, how exactly, may I ask, are you going to make this situation even worse?"

"I could beat you to death. I could torture you. Make you suffer. Give you pain, even more pain than you have now."

"You could," Herschel said, "but I have a surprise for you."

The Nazi stared at Herschel in disbelief. How could he be so bold and seem so fearless. "I could hurt you. I could torture you."

"Not anymore," Herschel said, laughing again. "You see, I guess I will tell you the truth about the diamond. You want to know, don't you?"

"Yes, I want to know. Where is it?"

"Be patient," Herschel said, enjoying his moment of control. "There was a diamond. But, I traded it for something better. I met someone and made a trade while I was on this heinous transport. Do you know what I got in return?"

Rolf was intrigued. This was the strangest Jew he had ever met. So bold. So uncooperative. He wanted to kill him, yet he also wanted to know what Herschel had traded for the diamond. And he wanted to know who had it now. "What did you get, and who did you get it from?"

"Well," Herschel said in a condescending voice, "I traded it for this little pill." He pulled a small white pill out of his pocket and popped it in his mouth.

"What? What the hell is that? And who the hell has the diamond?"

"It's just a little pill. Hardly looks like it's worth anything. Right?"

"Shut up, Jew. Stop talking in circles. Tell me where the diamond is. Tell me who has it. Anyone who was on this train is doomed to die. So, whoever gave you that pill will never enjoy that diamond."

"But I will have my prize. Do you know what that prize is?"

Rolf stared at Herschel, but he didn't answer

Then Herschel said in a threatening whisper, "I am going to thwart you of your chance to torture and kill me. This pill is cyanide. I am going to bite into it, and I'll be dead before you can do anything about it." Herschel smiled, then he bit into the pill. It was almost instant. There was a sharp pain in his chest, then he felt his soul leave his body. He felt like he was drifting high above the trees, but he was able to look down at his lifeless body. He saw Rolf, the Nazi standing over him in disbelief. He saw the lines of people who had been on the transport. He looked inside the gas chamber where he witnessed the murder of innocents. Shuddering, he thought, *I did the right thing. I gave Naomi another chance.*

CHAPTER ELEVEN

All the way home, Ernst worried that Dr. Mengele was going to fire him, that he had hired Schatz to take his place. Ernst would have been happy to give up his job if it hadn't been for Gisele. More than anything he wanted her to be happy and to respect and admire him. And he wondered how she would take it if he was fired and had to find a position as an ordinary doctor at a local hospital.

He walked into his apartment, and when he saw her sitting on the sofa looking at pictures of his parents that she must have found in his drawer, he was overcome with tenderness.

"I hope you aren't angry that I found these," she said sweetly. "I was putting away your clothes from the trip, and they were right there in the drawer. I didn't think you would be opposed to me looking at them."

"I'm not," he said as he walked over and kissed the top of her head. Then he sat down beside her. "Those are my parents." He pointed to a man in a white shirt and black slacks and a woman in a light-colored casual housedress. In the woman's arms was an infant "And that's me," he said.

She smiled. "You look the same," she joked.

His heart was filled with love for her. "Oh, you think so?" he chided.

"Yep, you were quite an adorable baby."

He leaned over and kissed her. "I spoke with Dr. Mengele today."

She put the picture down, no longer joking, and glanced up at him. "Yes, what did he say about a house for us?"

"I didn't ask him about the house yet. I thought I should let him meet you first. When he meets you, he will be charmed, that I promise. And I am sure we will get a house."

"What did you tell him about me?"

"I said that I got married when I was on holiday. And that you are the kindest, sweetest, most beautiful woman in the entire world. And you know what? He wants to meet you tomorrow night. Would it be all right if we meet him for a beer?"

She giggled. "Yes, of course, it would be wonderful. But I hope he isn't disappointed. You gave me quite a résumé to uphold."

"Just be yourself, and he won't be able to resist you."

"Do you think so?"

"Of course I do. I can't resist you," Ernst said.

"Do you really think he'll allow us to live in a house? Will we have to pay for it, or will it be given to us to use as part of your job benefits?"

"I believe he will give us the use of a house. Many of the officers live in houses given to them as job benefits by the Nazi Party," he said. What he failed to say was that the homes were confiscated from Jewish families who were murdered every day, in the camp where he worked. That was the shameful part, and he hoped she would never find out what he did for Dr. Mengele, how he helped his boss who was a poor excuse for a doctor, to do horrific experiments. *If she knew the truth of what happens at Auschwitz, she might think differently of me. But, I wish I could tell her. I wish I could tell her that I want to quit, that I hate this job. If only I knew that she would stand behind me and not leave me if I were no longer Mengele's apprentice.*

"What shall I wear to meet your boss?" she said, putting her hands on her hips and standing up to go and look in her closet. "I don't know what to wear. I must go and look through my clothes."

"No need to worry. I have an idea. Why don't you go out and buy a pretty new dress? There's a ladies' dress shop right in town. It's not far from here. Walking distance. I could give you directions."

"But I don't have any money," she said, looking down at the floor and waiting for him to say something.

He knew what she wanted to hear, and he smiled. "I'll give you plenty of money, of course. Don't you worry about that. I'll give you enough for a dress, shoes, and a hat to match. How does that sound."

"It sounds like I married the most generous, kind, and successful doctor in the world," she said, throwing her arms around his neck and kissing him. Then she reached down and gently squeezed his manhood. "Why don't we go to the bedroom before dinner."

His heart skipped a beat. He nodded, and she stood up, taking his hand and leading him like a child.

When Ernst made love to Gisele, he forgot everything, including the guilt about his work that usually followed him everywhere. She was so beautiful and so much more than he'd ever expected to have. Before they met, he had always wondered if he would ever marry. He knew he was an unattractive man and that women weren't drawn to him. But he had hoped that one day he would find someone who was willing to give him a chance. He'd thought that she would probably be plain, but he hoped she would be kind and intelligent. However, never in his wildest dreams had he imagined that a woman like Gisele would marry him and then lie naked beside him each night.

After they finished, she whispered in his ear, "Are you hungry?"

"Yes, I am."

"Please don't be mad at me, but I didn't make anything for dinner. I was hoping it would be all right with you if we went out."

"Of course, darling. Anything you want." Ernst was very tired, but he didn't want to disappoint Gisele. But he wondered if she was ever going to cook or if they would have to go out every night after he worked all day.

They got dressed and walked to a nearby restaurant. She looked stunning as always, even though she only wore a casual dress. However, when she walked into the restaurant, all of the men turned to look at her, and Ernst's heart swelled with pride.

After dinner they went back to the apartment. He was too tired to shower, so he lay down on the bed and closed his eyes. In minutes he had drifted off to sleep.

He was awakened by a flash of lightning and a huge clap of thunder which heralded the arrival of a storm. Rain poured down in sheets outside, battering the windows, and the roar of thunder began rolling over, one after another. Gisele lay beside him asleep. He glanced over at her. There was another flash of lightning, and he didn't know what came over him. But all of a sudden, Ernst began to cry. The tears fell down his cheeks and splashed across the pillow. He couldn't stop, so he turned away from Gisele hoping she would not awaken and see him like this. His shoulders heaved and he covered his eyes.

The storm that raged outside was mirrored inside his mind. He was a man caught in a cycle of sin and punishment. He was not a cruel man, but he had done cruel things. And as he cried, he prayed, asking God to forgive him. Yet he didn't feel like he deserved forgiveness. In his mind, he replayed a night about a year ago. It was early evening a few weeks after he'd first arrived at Auschwitz. Ernst had just finished eating dinner and was in his apartment when he had received a telephone call. It was Dr. Mengele who instructed him to go back to Auschwitz. "Collect these Jewish prisoners and bring them to the ravine. Do you know where I mean?"

"Yes," Ernst said.

"There will be some guards there waiting for you. Here is a list of the prisoners' numbers. Make sure that the numbers tattooed on their arms match the numbers I am giving you. Do you have a pencil to write this down?"

"Yes." Ernst grabbed a pencil and paper.

Mengele spouted off ten numbers, then he demanded that Ernst read them back to him. Ernst did as he was told.

There were no further instructions, and he had been too afraid to ask. So he hung up the phone. It was growing dark, and he was tired, but he walked back to the camp. Even now as he was remembering the incident, he could still recall how he'd been accosted by the smell of death and decay that had emanated from the crematorium when he entered the camp.

He went to the guards' office where he asked a couple of guards to help him locate the prisoners whose numbers he'd been given. Once he had them all lined up, he loaded them onto an open truck. One of the guards who accompanied him was standing in the back of the truck with a gun trained on the prisoners, and another drove the truck as they headed out to the ravine. Ernst had no idea what to expect when he arrived at the ravine, but he followed the orders he'd been given. And to this day, he felt sick whenever he remembered how he had delivered the prisoners to the guards, who were waiting at the ravine. *What did I think was going to happen?* he asked himself. *Did I really believe that they were just going to be questioned?*

His entire body trembled as he remembered the guards lining the prisoners up and then shooting them in the back. They fell quietly into the ravine as if they were not human beings, as if their lives had not mattered. But he knew that they were human and that each of them had a past, a life that had ended abruptly that night. *If only I had the power to go back in time. If only there was a way I could reach out and stop it. But even if I could go back, I would have no way of changing the fate of those poor people.* It was growing dark that night as he stood there helpless by the side of the ravine. He remembered that there was a full moon. In the light of that moon, his eyes became fixed on one of the men who had been shot. The man was moving. He was still alive. Ernst didn't say anything. He knew if he did, the guard would shoot the man in the head. So he stayed silent and watched as the man died slowly. It made him sick. Even now, the memory of it made him ill.

"You can go now," the head guard turned to him and said.

Ernst had nodded. Then he got back into the truck, and the driver drove away. They dropped him off back at his room. But once he was alone, he found that he began shivering. *Did they bury that poor soul alive? I don't know if I did the wrong thing by keeping my mouth shut. Would he have been better off if I had said something? He would have been shot immediately . . . would that have saved him further misery? I don't know. I will never know, but what I do know is that day will haunt me for the rest of my life.* The following day when Ernst reported for work, Dr. Mengele sent for him.

Mengele was sitting behind his desk toying with a strangely-shaped ashtray. Ernst stared at the ashtray. He'd seen the bones of a woman's pelvis before when he was in medical school but never as an ashtray. It was hard to believe that he was actually seeing such a horrific thing. "You passed the test," Mengele said.

"What test?" Ernst had asked, still staring at the ashtray.

"I wanted to see if you had the guts to follow orders regardless of how distasteful those orders might be. And, it seems that you do."

"I am a doctor," Ernst had said as strongly as he could manage. "I am a healer, not a killer. What happened last night was appalling to me."

"Yes, yes," Dr. Mengele said in a condescending voice. "You are a healer. We are all healers. But even more so, we are scientists. And fortunate scientists, at that. We have the opportunity to test all of our theories here at Auschwitz without any rules. We have the power to use human subjects. Now you must admit, that is quite a gift that the Nazi Party has given us." Mengele smiled.

Ernst nodded, but he couldn't manage a smile. "May I ask you something?"

"Of course." Mengele smiled.

"What is that?" Ernst pointed to the ashtray.

"Oh, I don't smoke. But it's an ashtray. A special one. Would you like to see it closer?" Mengele handed the ashtray to Ernst.

"It looks like the bones of a female pelvis," Ernst said.

"Of course it does, because that's exactly what it is," Dr. Mengele said, smiling.

Ernst put the ashtray down on Mengele's desk. He looked away. He could hardly breathe.

"That's all. You can go. Get back to work," Mengele said.

Ernst stood up. As he was going to leave the room, he tripped over the leg of a chair but caught himself before he fell. Then he walked out of Mengele's office and practically ran outside where he gulped the fresh air until he was able to breathe normally again.

And after that night, Mengele made Ernst his surgical assistant. His duties were to assist in all of Mengele's atrocious procedures. That had been the beginning of Ernst's nightmare. *I should have left then and there,* Ernst thought. *But I was so afraid of ruining my career, my future, and I was seduced by the money and benefits that the party awarded me for working with Mengele. And, it all paid off; just look at me now. I have the wife of my dreams. I have an automobile. I have plenty of money, and more than enough to eat, but I am still living that nightmare.*

CHAPTER TWELVE

♊

Otto Schatz was full of ambition as he walked to the apartment where he lived. His mind was on Ernst Neider. Before Ernst had returned to Auschwitz, Mengele had told Otto a little about him. He'd said that Neider was a brilliant man, but he lacked courage, confidence, and inner strength. And because of this, Mengele said he was losing respect for Neider. "I need a man who isn't afraid to do what I tell him to do. I need an assistant who doesn't question my every command."

"I can be that man," Otto had promised Mengele. And so, Mengele hired him. Once he was hired, he found that the job was not easy. Mengele was demanding. And he was vicious with the prisoners. Otto didn't care about the Jews, or the deformed, and he didn't give a damn about the twins either. But the oath he'd taken in medical school sometimes bothered him, yet he brushed it off. *First, do no harm.* The words, as his professor had read them, echoed through his mind. But he knew if he was going to succeed and make a name for himself in the Nazi Party, he was going to have to break that oath.

Otto was told that the SS wanted detailed medical reports of all of Mengele's patients and their condition. And that he was required to keep meticulous records. Mengele made it clear that it was very important to him that the twins be authentically twins. "You must make sure to check this fact out very carefully," Mengele had warned Otto. "You see, these Jews are masters at manipulation and lies. Once, I discovered that two brothers who had been taken to the twins' room were not really twins at all. They were members of a family of seven siblings. I suspected that they were lying. So, I gave one of the young ones some candy and he told me the truth. The brothers were not twins. Although they looked alike, they were a year apart in age. I gassed all seven of them together. Then I hung them up right where the prisoners go for roll call. I made an example of them. After all, we can't have Jews thinking they can go around tricking us, now, can we?" Mengele said.

"No, we must retain power at all times," Otto said.

"Absolutely. And it serves those dirty little Jews right for lying. Don't you agree?" Mengele asked Otto.

"But, of course," Otto said.

"Good, I am glad you agree. So, to prove to me that you are as capable as you claim, I want you to go my twins' room where you are going to find the two young girls whose eye color I have been working on this past week. I was attempting to change their eye color from brown to blue. But the injections into the eyes were ineffective, and now they are blind. Both of them. So, take them out into the field and shoot them. When you have finished, return to my office. Go now."

Otto nodded. "Yes, Doctor," he said, but he was trembling. Until that day, Otto had never killed anyone. And the thought of shooting two blind children was disgusting to him. But because he didn't want to appear weak, like Neider, he did as he was told. When he returned to Mengele's office, Otto was flustered, but Mengele was waiting for him with a glass of whiskey.

"Good job," Mengele said. "I had a couple of the guards watch you, and you did a good job."

Schatz nodded.

Mengele patted him on the back. "It's only hard the first time. You'll get the hang of it. In fact, you'll start to enjoy the power you feel when you take a life. You'll see."

Otto nodded. *Well, I can do this, even if this job is going to take some getting used to.*

As he ate his dinner, Otto remembered that day, and he thought about Ernst. Otto understood him. And he pitied him. Ernst had too much compassion to ever rise to a high position in the Nazi Party. He would never make it. Otto knew how Ernst thought because he, too, had been filled with ideas of saving the world when he first started medical school. He'd wanted to be like a god, healing the sick and gaining admiration from everyone he met. However, he quickly learned that this was not the way to success with the Nazi Party, and unlike his competitor, Ernst Neider, Otto Schatz had a ruthless side. He was a chameleon, and if using his medical degree to carry out Mengele's atrocities was the way to achieve his dreams of becoming an important man, he was prepared to do just that.

CHAPTER THIRTEEN

The forest was filled with shadows and strange noises. All of Naomi's senses were on high alert. She wished she could see in the dark. Her eyes darted around frantically; she couldn't be sure she had really seen a man. Had she really seen a person there in the forest, or was it just shadows? A cold chill came over her. Who, but another refugee, would be alone in the forest at night? And if he found her, what would he do to her?

More than likely, it was just a trick of my mind, she tried to reassure herself.

Her teeth were chattering. The damp cold from the forest floor had penetrated her clothing. *I am never going to get out of this forest alive.* She had no idea which way to go to find shelter. Or even if there was shelter to be found. But if someone was there, it was best to get away. Naomi walked forward and as she did, she tripped over a large root and fell, scraping her knee. Pain shot through her, and she began to cry again. It would be easy to just lie there and freeze to death. But when she thought about the sacrifice that Herschel had made to keep her alive, she decided that she owed it to him to try to survive. And to survive, Naomi had to keep moving, although she didn't know where she was going or even why. Wearily, she pushed herself up onto her knees. She reached above her and grabbed a branch to pull herself back up to her feet. Then slowly, and even more cautiously, she began to walk again.

It was hard to say how far she'd gone or how much time had passed when she broke through the thick line of trees and found herself standing in a small, brushy clearing. Her body was stiff from the cold. She arched her back and then straightened, and she stretched out her arms as she yawned. Her eyes and mind were blurry, but she tried to take in her surroundings.

Blinking a few times and then shaking her head, she realized that she was standing in front of a rusted fence. The fence was old and crumbling. There was a farmhouse in the distance and a barn beside it. The place looked abandoned. *It is so cold. And there are wild animals and strange shadows. I could never sleep outside. But I am so tired. I wonder if I could sleep in the barn. It looks like there is no one here.*

There was no lock on the gate. The rusty iron moaned and creaked as she pulled the door open.

This had once been a nice home. It was large and sprawling. *Someone wealthy lived here at some point in time. I wonder what happened to them,* she thought as she walked into the empty barn. It was large and seemed as if it had once been well maintained, with enough stalls for six horses. Cobwebs hung from the ceiling and in the corners of the empty stalls. She thought she could still detect a faint smell of manure. *At least it's warm. And I am afraid to go into the house. What if I am wrong and someone is still living there? I can't take that chance,* Naomi thought. *And I can't stay outside in this frigid weather. I'll die for sure. Besides that, I am so terrified of being alone out there in the forest. I'll spend the night here in this barn and leave as soon as the sun comes up. That way if there happens to be anyone living in the house, I'll be gone before they can find me.*

Cradling the small bag of food she had been given by the Nazis before she left, Naomi lay her head down on a pile of straw and tried to sleep. At first she was acutely aware of every sound from the forest. It was warmer inside the barn, but it was still cold. *What I would give for a blanket, or a warmer coat.* Shivering, she lay on her side on the ground looking out through the open windows of one of the stalls. A full moon hung like a giant silver coin reflecting light through the tall trees across the glade.

The hay had grown soft from the past rains and snows that had come through the open stall windows. It was dry now, but if felt like a warm feather pillow beneath her head. Exhaustion overcame her. Closing her heavy eyelids, Naomi slept. She dreamed of her daughters. The three of them were together again. In her dream, she reached out with longing to hold them tightly. She felt Perle's hair against her arm, just as something jarred her awake. Her eyes flew open. In the darkness, she saw his shadow. It was a man. *Am I dreaming? Is this real? Dear God, please help me. Please.* The shadow was standing over her. Her heart raced as she kept her eyes glued to him. Then she gasped as he reached down to where she lay. She was frightened that he was trying to touch her. *I must not scream,* she thought. *Because if someone is in that house and I scream, they will come. But if this is real and that man forces himself on me, I will die. I can't let him do that to me. I just can't, but I am not strong enough to stop him. Still, I must find some way to try.* She turned over and kicked upward hitting him in the shin. He let out a small scream.

"What the hell did you do that for?" he said.

"Get away from me, or swear I'll kill you," Naomi growled.

He laughed. "Oh? With your bare hands?"

"Don't you dare try to touch me. I am armed. I have a gun."

"I know it's dark in here, and I can't see a thing, but I'd bet my right arm that you aren't armed, and if you were, you wouldn't know how to use a gun."

He sat down, and then he added, "I didn't mean to be so rude. I'm sorry. I'm just starving, and I saw that bag you have there. I thought it might be food. And I hoped you might be willing to share some of that food."

"It's not food," she lied.

"Oh, and what is it, then? Wildflowers?" he asked sarcastically. "Everyone who is hiding in the forest in the middle of the night carries bags of wildflowers with them, now, don't they?"

The mention of the word wildflowers brought her mind back to Eli. She shuddered, both from the cold and from fear. "Leave me alone. Please, just let me be. I am begging you."

"I'd like to. I promise you; I'd walk away from here if I could. But I am in a bad way. However, if you'll share the food you have tonight, tomorrow I will go out and hunt or fish. I'm a good fisherman, not a bad hunter either. My father taught me when I was just a boy. I'll bring back food for both of us."

She had no choice. If she didn't agree to share the food, she was afraid he might take all of it. So she said, "All right. But can I ask you a question?"

"Sure, why not?"

"Who are you? You are speaking German, not Polish. Are you a Nazi?"

"You're right. I am speaking German. And you are speaking Yiddish, right?"

"Yes," she said.

"The languages are so similar that we understand each other. That's a good thing, yes?"

"Yes," she said. "But please, tell me, who are you?"

He let out a painful laugh. "I am what you might call a deserter, a traitor to the fatherland. But it's not Germany I want to destroy. I love my country. It's that bastard, Hitler, and his henchmen that I want to rid the world of. I believe he is going to be the downfall of the German people. So, I have to say, I am a German, but certainly not a Nazi."

"And how do you plan to rid the world of Hitler? You are one man alone. Aren't you?"

"No, I am not alone. At least not at the moment. Right now, I am here with you," he said, and she heard the lightheartedness in his voice.

"I meant you are alone in your quest to destroy Hitler."

"Oh, I don't know about that. You'd be surprised how many people hate him but won't dare to say how they really feel."

Naomi sat up. She shook the hay out of her hair. *How can he be so flippant when he has deserted his platoon and is now hiding in the forest with a Jew. What a strange man he is*, she thought.

"So, what is your name? Or if you don't want to give me your real name, what can I call you?" he said as he took her bag of food and opened it.

"I'm Naomi."

"Nice to meet you. I am Friedrich." He looked inside the bag.

"You were a Nazi at some point, weren't you—before you deserted? I know it's dark in here, but that looks like a German uniform you're wearing?" she asked.

"Yes, I suppose you could say that, technically, I was a Nazi. But to be more specific, I was a German soldier, like my father and his father before him. I was willing to give my life for the fatherland. But when I found out the truth about Hitler, I couldn't stand behind him and his party."

"What did you find out?"

"Plenty," he said. "Plenty."

She didn't ask him anything else. In the darkness she saw him take half of a hunk of bread and then hand the other half to her.

"When was the last time you ate?" he asked.

"It's been a couple of days. I was on a transport. I suppose you know I am a Jew."

"Of course I know. I know because you speak Yiddish."

"You don't hate Jews?" She looked at him, puzzled. "I thought all of you hated us."

"It's statements like that, that puts rifts between people. What if there was no you and no us?"

"I don't know what you mean."

"Don't you? You are the Jews, in my case anyway. I am one of the Christians. That makes us different. Or does it?"

"I don't understand."

"What I am trying to say is that under our skin, we are all just people."

"So, you don't hate the Jews."

"Why would I? Only the ones who do things to me to make me hate them. I don't hate anyone for their race or religion," he said. "Eat the bread. I promise you; I'll get us more food tomorrow."

She nodded. "I was a little bit afraid to eat it. Because once it is gone, there is no more."

"I know, but I'll go out in the morning, and I'll get us more. Besides, you would have had to eat it eventually. So, you might as well eat it now."

"I suppose you're right," she said and began to gobble the hunk of bread. It was hard and a little moldy, but it was food. And she'd been hungry since they left the ghetto.

"So, tell me a little bit about you. You said you were on a transport?"

"Yes," she said. "I'll explain. When Hitler took over Poland, he rounded up the Jews in the small village where I lived and sent us all to this place that we came to know as the Warsaw Ghetto. While we were there, we were sent to live in a very crowded apartment with another family. The ghetto was dirty because it was so crowded, and the Nazis rationed our food. We never had enough to eat. Then one day, the guards had promised us that if we were to get on this train, we would be sent somewhere where we would have work. And because we were working and valuable to the Nazi Party, we would have more food. So, we went."

"Where were you going?"

"I'm not sure. All I know is that the transport was terrible. We were stuffed onto the train so tightly that we could not sit down. We were not given food or water. The smell was so bad that I can't even describe it. And people were dying all around us. Then we made a stop. I don't know why. You see, I was asleep. But my husband over-heard some of the guards talking, and he became convinced that we were being sent somewhere to be murdered. I find it hard to believe that the Nazis were going to murder so many people. I was certain that they were taking us somewhere to work. But my husband was so sure that we were in danger that he made a deal with one of the guards to let me go. That's how I ended up here in the forest. He is still on the train."

"Hmm," Friedrich said. "Yes, that sounds like something the Nazis would do, and that's one of the reasons I can't fight for Germany."

"I don't understand," she said.

"Well . . ." He sighed. "It's true. The Nazis are a killing machine. And I mean that they are not just soldiers fighting a war. But crazy men murdering innocent women and children. Your husband was right to get you off that transport. He must have loved you a lot."

"Yes, I suppose so. But . . ." She coughed and cleared her throat. "Are they really killing people? Children too?"

"I'm afraid so."

Naomi let out a sound like a wounded animal. "Before we got on the train, I was separated from my daughters. I don't know where they are. I don't know how to find them," she said, her voice cracking with desperation.

"There is nothing we can do tonight. I wish I could help you find them." Then he added, "Do you have any idea where your husband was being transported to?"

"I'm not sure. I only know that he overheard the guards saying that all of the Jews on the train were going to be killed."

"Probably a death camp."

Naomi winced. "A death camp. Is there really such a thing?"

"Yes, I am afraid so. I am ashamed of Germany right now. This is a terrible thing they are doing."

"Do you think my husband is dead?"

"I'm sorry to have to tell you this, but yes, probably. He's either dead or on his way to being murdered."

She gulped. "Oh, dear Hashem, how could you let this happen to me?"

"I'm sorry? I don't understand. What the hell did you just say?" he asked.

"Never mind," she answered, afraid to ask him anything more, especially anything about her children.

"Listen, we have all suffered loss. I know that I have. But, you're stronger than you realize. I promise you that," he said as he chewed loudly on the bread.

Even though she was famished, it was hard to eat. The bread stuck in her throat. She put the rest of her piece down on the ground. *I can't bear to live anymore. I want to die if my girls are gone.*

Then, as if he were reading her mind, he said, "Your daughters could very well be all right if they didn't get on that train. That was probably the best thing that could have happened to them. They could be anywhere, but you can't give up hope. They might just be alive."

"You would help me try to find them?" she said in a small voice.

"I might. I don't know yet. It's risky. But then, so is everything right now. The Nazis are hunting me because I am a traitor. The Russians see me as the enemy. Ehhh, I haven't got a chance, huh?" He let out a short, bitter laugh. "So, maybe I will help you. We're both sort of doomed. Maybe we can do something good together."

"Where would we start?"

"Where you left them, of course."

"In the Warsaw Ghetto?"

"I think so, don't you?"

"Yes, actually, I do," she said, and at that moment, she felt as if she had a glimmer of hope. "How will we get back there?"

"By limousine, of course, my lady." He laughed.

She laughed too. "Stupid question, I suppose."

"It's all right. I understand. The truth is we are going to have to make our way there on foot. But I think we should wait until the weather warms up a little. It's too cold right now. I think for the time being we should take shelter right here in this barn."

"How long, do you think?"

"I don't know. As soon as it warms up, we can try to walk to Warsaw."

"Is it a long way from here?"

"It's not close."

CHAPTER FOURTEEN

$$\text{♊}$$

Gisele looked stunning in her hunter-green silk dress. It hugged her perfect shape in all the right places. She studied her reflection in the mirror. Her hair had been cut and curled at the local beauty shop, and she wore real silk stockings which Ernst had given her. She loved those stockings because they were almost impossible to get, and they made her long, shapely legs look perfect and alluring. *He's not a bad husband. I just wish he were more attractive. It's difficult to make love to him, especially with the light on. He's so fat, and pale. But, at least he is good to me. And . . . tonight is so special. Tonight, I am going to meet my father for the first time. I don't know if I should tell Dr. Mengele that he is my father right away or not. I think I should get to know him better first.*

Ernst walked into the bedroom and looked at Gisele admiringly. "You look beautiful," he said, smiling.

"Thank you. I love the silk stockings." She smiled.

He returned her smile. But inside he was cringing. He'd stolen the stockings from Kanada, the place where all of the possessions from the Jews who arrived on the transports were sorted, and anything of value was sent to Germany. He had heard about Kanada before, but he'd never gone there. The very idea of seeing the possessions of those who had just perished in the gas chamber made him feel sick. But when he couldn't find anywhere to purchase real silk stockings, he decided to muster up the courage and check Kanada. And sure enough, he found two pair. He took them. But then as he was leaving, he saw Otto Schatz standing outside and watching him. Dr. Schatz smiled at him and winked. It was a threatening half smile that never traveled as high as his eyes.

Ernst felt a cold chill run through him. It would not be good if Schatz knew he'd stolen the stockings. *I am going to have to watch my every move from now on. He is after me, for sure. I know he wants to get rid of me. If he can, he will get my job, and he'll become Mengele's right hand. Or at least that's how he sees it. I am certain. I know he wants to become someone important in the party and he sees this as the way. I've seen his kind before. I'm sure Mengele has made it clear to him that he doesn't like me. But, because of my wife, I can't lose this job.*

Otto didn't speak. But he smiled as he knew what Ernst had done. And he kept his eyes glued on Ernst as Ernst walked away, the silk stockings tucked under his uniform jacket.

"I know you said that we are meeting for a beer. Do you think we will have dinner, too, or should I eat something now?" Gisele asked Ernst.

"I don't know. I never know what Dr. Mengele is thinking." *Isn't that the truth*, he thought. "If you're hungry, eat something light before we go."

"Do you want anything?"

"Sure," he said.

CHAPTER FIFTEEN

♊

When they arrived at the beer hall, Mengele was already seated. As they approached, he stood up to show respect for Gisele. He pulled out her chair and she smiled.

"Good evening, Ernst. And who is the beautiful woman? No, don't tell me." Mengele smiled, revealing the gap between his front teeth. He was doing his best to appear charming, but Ernst could see beyond his façade. "This must be your lovely wife." A hint of cologne, the kind that costs a month's salary, wafted out from him, heady and strong.

"Yes, this is Gisele," Ernst said. Then he turned to Gisele and said, "Gisele, this is Dr. Mengele. My boss."

Gisele was beaming. Her lovely face lit up like a candle. "It's a pleasure to meet you," she said.

Mengele is very charismatic right now, that's for sure. But, if she knew the things I do, I wonder if she would still be so awestruck by him, Ernst thought.

Mengele was a delightful conversationalist that night. Ernst was surprised to see how well he handled himself around women. He was funny and clever, and Ernst decided that no one would know by looking at him that he was a sadist. *I wonder why he didn't bring his wife with him,* Ernst thought. *He knew Gisele would be here tonight. It seems only right that he would have brought Irene with him. I don't trust him. He's up to something. He's always up to something.*

It was getting late. Mengele was still telling amusing stories of his days in medical school.

Ernst watched Mengele, repulsed, as he worked the table like a famous entertainer. *I am exhausted,* Ernst thought. *I'd rather be home asleep than listening to this man whom I have no respect for. Yet, I dare not say a word about wanting to go home. Mengele would be offended if I tried to end the evening. He must be the one to end it. I don't want him to get angry for any reason. I can only hope that this tavern will close soon,* Ernst thought. He glanced around him. There were lots of Germans eating, laughing, and guzzling dark beer after dark beer at the tavern. Many of them he recognized as guards from the camp. *How can they enjoy themselves so wholeheartedly, when they spend their days committing murders? It baffles me. The tavern reeked of sweat and smoke, of beer and sauerkraut.* In his mind's eye he saw the faces of the children in the twins' room and the Gypsy children who ran around the Gypsy camp. Then he thought of the piles of dead bodies waiting for their turn in the ovens. Gisele was laughing at something Mengele said. Mengele looked smug as he smiled at her. Ernst began to feel a headache coming on. He was nauseated.

Bile was rising in Ernst's throat. He swallowed hard. "Excuse me. I am going to the bathroom," he managed to say. He hid in the stall and gagged. He vomited up a sea of beer. Then he leaned against the wall breathing heavily. *I wish I could separate myself from my work. These guards who are here enjoying themselves are able to do it. Why can't I?*

After splashing his face with cold water, Ernst ran a comb through his thinning hair. Then he walked back to the table where Mengele was animatedly telling another story. None of the little anecdotes Mengele told that night were about his work. They were all cute and clever, but most of all they hid the true monster that lived within Dr. Mengele. Gisele was smiling, her golden hair illuminated by the light of the chandelier. She reached for Ernst's hand. He gave her his hand as he sat down. Then Ernst swallowed hard. He managed to smile at Gisele. *I just have to get through the rest of this night.*

Finally, a half hour later, Mengele declared that he was tired, and it was time for him to get home. "It's very late, and as Ernst knows, I must be at work early in the morning." Mengele sighed.

"Yes, we both are required to be at work early tomorrow morning," Ernst said.

Mengele insisted on paying the tab.

Ernst and Gisele were about to leave when Mengele stopped them. "Before you go, I'd like to invite you both to a dinner that is going to be given for the high-ranking doctors in the SS. It's to take place next week. Would you like to attend?" he asked Gisele.

"Oh yes!" she said enthusiastically.

"Good," Mengele said, "then I'll give all the details to your husband. Time, place, that sort of thing." He smiled.

"Thank you for inviting us." Gisele beamed.

"It's my pleasure."

"And is it all right with you?" Mengele said to Ernst; there was a slight mocking tone to his voice.

Ernst half smiled. "Yes, of course we would love to come," he said.

"It's settled, then. I'll see you next week," Mengele said, then he left.

"He's wonderful," Gisele said. "You must really enjoy working with him."

Ernst nodded. He couldn't speak. But he wondered why he had not known about this party before tonight. He was certain that Mengele would have had the invitation for some time, and he was sure that if it had not been for Gisele, he would not have been invited. *Perhaps Otto is going to be attending. I have this nagging feeling that I am being pushed aside.*

CHAPTER SIXTEEN

♊

G isele was removing her makeup with cold cream. She
stared at herself in the mirror admiringly. She replayed
the evening's events in her mind.

*If Dr. Mengele wasn't my father, I could fall for him. He is the most
fascinating and exciting man I have ever met. I wonder what he was like
as a young boy when my mother fell in love with him? If he was anything
like he is now, I can completely understand her attraction to him.*

Ernst walked into the bedroom and began to get undressed for
bed. He glanced at his wife. "You are so beautiful, have I told you that
today?"

"Yes, you have." She giggled. "You tell me all the time, but I never
get tired of hearing it."

He smiled. "It's true, you know." Then he added, "Did you have a
nice time tonight?"

"Yes, I had a very nice time. And I am so excited to be going to
that dinner for important doctors." Then she looked at him with
admiration in her eyes. "I am so proud to be married to you," she said
as she carefully removed the silk stockings.

His heart swelled. He tried not to think about the stockings and the woman who they had belonged to. A woman who was most likely dead.

Gisele walked over to Ernst and planted a kiss on his lips. He put his arms around her. Her hair fell soft against his hands. He buried his face in it and inhaled the smell of her skin. Then once again, he kissed her sweet mouth. She took his hand and led him to the bed. As he lay down beside her, he thought, *I can't lose this job. She admires me. She thinks I am someone important. I have to find a way to get rid of Otto. I can't let him replace me.*

CHAPTER SEVENTEEN

♊

G isele had shopped all week for the perfect dress to wear to the doctors' dinner. She finally decided upon a silky black cocktail dress that hugged her curves and was cut low enough to expose her ample cleavage. As she dressed for the dinner, she looked in the mirror, and she knew she looked stunning. Carefully, she put on her silk stockings and black high heels. Ernst walked into the room and gasped. "You will certainly be the most beautiful woman at this dinner," he said.

"You are so sweet to say that," she said humbly, but she knew it was true. *I am quite beautiful,* she thought. *I look so much like my mother that I am surprised that Dr. Mengele can't see it. Perhaps he will tonight.*

When they arrived at the banquet hall, they were shown to the table where Dr. Mengele sat with his wife, Irene. Otto was there and so was a woman doctor who Mengele introduced as Herta Oberheuser. Herta was a stern-faced woman. Her light auburn hair was pulled into a severe bun, and she wore no lipstick or rouge. It seemed to Gisele that Dr. Oberheuser and Otto were seated beside each other because they were both single. But as Mengele was introducing them both to Gisele, she thought that neither of them seemed interested in the other. Dr. Oberheuser was quiet and withdrawn, but Otto Schatz was delightful. He smiled admiringly at Gisele as he looked her up and down. "Your wife is quite the looker," he said to Ernst, who nodded.

"Yes, s-s-she is," he said, but he glared at Otto.

"Thank you," Gisele said, and she dropped her eyes. But then she glanced back up at Otto to see if he was watching her. He was. And she saw the desire in his eyes. Ernst sat between them. So, Gisele found herself seated between Mengele and Ernst.

"You have a French accent," Otto said to Gisele. "It's lovely. If I am correct, it sounds to me like you are from Paris."

She nodded, not wanting to say anything more about France because she knew that the Germans thought the French were inferior to them. And she didn't want to bring it to light.

"French girls are so beautiful. They are always so up on the latest fashions," Otto said, smiling.

"Have any of you been to France?" Gisele asked everyone at the table. But she wasn't paying attention to their answers. Instead, she was watching Dr. Mengele. She wanted to see if he had any reaction. He had none.

Then Herta interrupted, "I have never been to France and have no desire to go. I am an Aryan woman. We are the superior women, and to be quite frank with you, good German women don't have time for such nonsense, like fashion and beauty. Himmler has made it clear that pure Aryan women should put their focus on more important things. Children, Kitchen, Church. I'm sure you are familiar with this, Dr. Schatz?" Herta said in a gruff tone of voice.

"Yes, of course, we are all familiar with this," Otto said, trying to be as charming as possible, but Gisele could see that he found Herta to be annoying.

"Well then, you should be touting the attributes of German women and not be swayed by the externals of women from lesser countries." Herta sneered.

"Now, now, let's all be civil. This is a dinner party after all." Mengele smiled. But he was watching Ernst. Ernst was fidgeting. His eyes were fixed on Otto, who was openly admiring his wife.

This continued through dinner. Then after dinner the band began to play a waltz. Before Ernst even had an opportunity to ask Gisele to dance, Otto was on his feet with his hand extended. "You won't mind if I dance with your lovely wife, will you?" he asked Ernst.

"N-no, of course n-not," Ernst said. His face showed that he was clearly feeling unnerved by Otto's request. Mengele was smiling that wicked smile that he reserved for moments when he was making other people uncomfortable.

"Why don't you ask Dr. Oberheuser to dance?" Mengele said to Ernst. "I'm sure she would love to dance with you. And, meanwhile" —he turned to Irene and smiled—"I am going to dance with my own lovely wife."

What can I do? Ernst thought. *I have no choice; I have to dance with her. If I don't ask her to dance, it will be awkward. Leave it to that bastard Mengele to make things uncomfortable. He likes to do that. It gives him pleasure.* Mengele was watching Ernst intently. He turned to the female doctor. "W-w-would you like to d-d-dance?" he asked Herta. "I'm not much of a d-d-dancer, I'm afraid." *Damn stutter*, he thought.

Herta nodded. "I'd love to dance," she said as she stood up. Once she was standing, Ernst could see her better. Herta was a skinny, unattractive woman. She wore an unflattering dress, and he decided that she was not very feminine. But Ernst had agreed to dance with her, so he took her hand, and they began to waltz. Neither of them proved to be very agile on the dance floor. "So, I assume you work with Dr. Mengele at Auschwitz?" Herta asked.

"Yes, I do. So does Otto. We are both his assistants."

"Oh, Otto. I can see by looking at him that he's some kind of a fool," she said. "However, you are not. In fact, I must admit, I've heard impressive things about you. It's been said among your colleagues that you are a brilliant doctor."

"Thank you for saying that. I haven't heard it. But I am flattered."

"I don't flatter. I speak only from facts," she said coldly.

He nodded. "Well, thank you."

"Have you heard anything about me?"

"Actually, I haven't. I am sorry. I'm so busy working that I don't have an opportunity to socialize much."

She nodded. "I work at Ravensbrück. That's the only all-women's camp. And I am the only female doctor who is so highly respected within the party. I am surprised you haven't heard of me before tonight," she said.

"Like I said, I don't have much opportunity to speak to any of the officers."

"I am doing some important work. You see, I have been running some experiments at Ravensbrück."

"Oh," he said. He didn't want to know anything more.

But she went on talking anyway. "You may find it hard to believe, but the women prisoners are as rough as men. I can tell you that is for sure. Right now, I have a group of Jew women that I have been working on. And let me tell you, those Jews are liars and thieves by nature. If you don't keep your eyes on them at all times, they will steal a hunk of moldy bread that no one would have any use for, just to be stealing something. That's how corrupt they are. But, of course, I can handle them, and that's because I am an Aryan, and that makes me naturally smarter than they are. I have found the best thing to do is keep them terrified of me. They require strict punishment for the least little thing they do wrong, or they'll get out of line. And I make sure that when I punish them, I punish them severely. If they know they will suffer terrible consequences, they are less likely to break the rules. I'm sure you have similar problems at Auschwitz."

"I don't know. I don't pay any attention." Ernst wanted to get away from her. He wished the music would stop.

"I would love to speak to you about our work. Perhaps we can meet and have a beer sometime. I know it's a distance from here to

Germany, but I would be willing to travel. After all, I could use a couple of days off," she said.

"I am very busy. Dr. Mengele keeps me busy during the day, and after work I like to go home to my wife. So, I don't have much time for meeting with colleagues. I'm sorry," he said.

"That's a shame. I would love to tell you all about my work."

The music ended, and Ernst was relieved to return to his seat.

When he sat down at the table, he watched Gisele. She and Otto were standing close together on the dance floor.

Gisele was giggling, and her face was lit up by a slight blush as Otto whirled her back to the table and pulled out her chair. She gazed up at Otto as she sat down. Her eyes were bright and glistening with appreciation. Gisele gave Otto a smile, and her smile was as luminous as the first time she'd smiled at Ernst. Ernst saw it, and his heart was breaking. Then Gisele spoke in her broken German with that sweet French accent that was like a melody. "Thank you for the dance," she said. Her golden hair curled about her face like the sun setting over the green hills.

The world around Ernst turned black as he watched his beautiful young wife laughing and gazing into the eyes of his handsome rival. Ernst's vision was blurred; he felt dizzy and nauseated. *I have to get out of here. I need some air.* "E-excuse me," he said, then he stood up and walked quickly out the door. Once outside, he sucked in the fresh air, but he felt as if he were being squeezed between the earth and the sky. It was difficult to catch his breath, and his heart felt as if it were being crushed in his chest.

CHAPTER EIGHTEEN

♊

Otto and Gisele danced several more times that night until finally it was over. Ernst and Gisele returned home. Gisele sat down at her dressing table and got ready for bed. She could see that Ernst was tired. He didn't even wash up. He just undressed and climbed into bed. She walked over and planted a soft kiss on his lips. "You look very tired," she said.

"I am. It's been a long day and night."

Gisele climbed into bed beside him and gently touched his forehead. "Get some rest," she said.

"Good night, my darling." After Ernst fell asleep, Gisele climbed out of bed. She wasn't tired. In fact, she was too excited to sleep. She was enthralled with her new life. Mengele and Otto were both handsome and charming, and they had fawned over her all night. *It is going to be even more difficult to make love to Ernst after spending time with such attractive men. I'm glad he was too tired tonight. One is my father, and the other could be my lover,* she thought whimsically. *I belong here in this world. It is my rightful place. After all, I am the daughter of the famous Dr. Mengele.*

She thought of Otto, and her mind drifted back to the evening.

How he'd taken her hand to lead her to the dance floor. He was not clumsy like Ernst. He was a skillful dancer and a wonderful conversationalist. His compliments had made her eyes sparkle. She closed her eyes and imagined that his cologne wafted across her nostrils, a mix of spice, flowers, and bay leaf. It made her think of a time long ago, when she had searched for the perfect perfume in a Parisian boutique. Of course, at that time she had been window shopping. Perfume was not a necessity, and she'd grown up poor, unable to afford such things.

But this evening, she'd spent dancing in the arms of a handsome man, and she'd enjoyed every minute of it. She was also the wife of a very wealthy one. *Too bad they are not one and the same.* She sighed. *I wish I could be in love with Ernst. I wish I had the feelings of excitement around Ernst that I feel when I am dancing with Otto. After all, Ernst has so much to offer. He is kind, generous, and loving. He would be perfect, except he is hard to look at. And I am so young. I want to feel that same wonderful excitement in his arms that I felt when I danced with Otto. But it's just not like that with Ernst and I. Making love to him is never unpleasant. He is gentle and considerate. But he is also boring and predictable.*

Ernst walked out of the bedroom. His hair was a mess. It stood up around his head like the mane of an old, worn-out stuffed lion, and even in the shadow of darkness she could see the outline of his large, protruding belly. "Darling, are you ill?" he asked with true concern in his voice.

"No, I just couldn't sleep. I am probably just restless from all the excitement," she said.

"Can I make you a cup of tea? Do you think that might settle your nerves?" he said as he walked over to her and placed his hand on her forehead. "You're not warm. That's good."

"No, thank you. No tea," she said.

"Then please, darling, why don't you come back to bed and let me rub your back. That should help you calm down."

"All right," she agreed.

He took her hand and led her back to bed. Then he poured some lotion into his hands and warmed it before laying his hands on her back. Gently, he massaged her shoulders until she fell asleep. As he watched her sleep, he thought, *I hope my love and kindness toward her will keep her away from Otto's arms. To him she would be nothing but another conquest. I've seen his kind before. But to me, she is everything. She is all I have in the world. I can't lose her.*

CHAPTER NINETEEN

♊

Shoshana could see that Ernst was in a sour mood when he arrived the following morning. But when their eyes met, he managed to smile half-heartedly. "Good morning," he said as he prepared Perle's arm for her morning blood draw. Ernst's hair was messy as if he had not taken the time to comb it properly. His blue eyes were slightly bloodshot, his nose red and slightly puffy. The uniform he wore had not been ironed. His breath was foul, and Shoshana could smell the stale perspiration on him. She noticed all of this because this was unusual for Ernst. He was normally well groomed and smelled clean, with just a faint twinge of a fine after-shave. But today, the strong odor of sweat hung on him like a garment of shame, mingled with the odor of dirt, fear, death, and smoke from the crematorium.

"Good morning," Shoshana said. Her eyes narrowed as she watched him closely. Even when she worked as a singer in the café, she was shy and kept to herself, so she didn't have much experience with men. But Shoshana was sensitive to the feelings of others, and it was easy to see that he needed someone to talk to. The sadness and despair in his eyes told her that something deep and important to

86

him was on his mind. She reminded herself that even though he seemed to be kind, he was still one of them, and therefore she must be cautious. It would be dangerous to entirely trust him. Still, she must test him, slowly and carefully. He might be the only person willing to help her save her sisters.

She steeled herself. This could be dangerous. If she overstepped her boundaries, he might get angry, and then she was afraid she would see another side of him. *This is my only chance to make friends with him. I have to do what I can and hope he doesn't turn on me. I need him to protect my sisters. I wish Ruth were here. She was so experienced with men. She always seemed to know what to say and do around them.* Shoshana cleared her throat. This was a risk. Speaking to him could either make him want to befriend her, or it might have the opposite effect and make him angry. And he had the power to make her, and her sisters, suffer if he chose to. *Still, I have to try. He just might be able to help us get out of here.* "I know it's bold of me to ask, but, well, Dr. Neider, are you feeling well?"

He whirled his head around to look at her. "I'm all right," he said, and she saw that she'd shocked him by asking.

She swallowed hard. Her throat felt like sandpaper. "I don't mean to offend you. It's just that, well . . . you just look a little pale. I hope you don't mind me saying so," she said, then she continued in a small voice. "It's just that . . . well, I am concerned. I mean, I hope you are feeling all right." Shoshana was nervous; her heart was racing. "I mean, you are the only person here who is kind to us and . . ."

Ernst sighed. He turned to glance at her. "I had a bad evening last night." The words exploded out of him. "I went to a dinner party with my wife and some other doctors. And, things . . ." He hesitated and drew a long breath, then he said, "Things just didn't go the way they should have."

She was surprised he was speaking so candidly to her. But she hoped that this was an opening to begin a friendship that might save them. "I will listen if you want to talk," she said.

He shook his head quickly. "No, I'm fine," he said as he finished taking Perle's blood and then began to take Bluma's.

"I'm sorry. I didn't mean to pry into your personal life. I hope you aren't angry at me," she said, looking down.

"I'm not angry. I appreciate your concern. It's just that I can't share personal things with a prisoner," he said.

"Of course. I understand," Shoshana said.

CHAPTER TWENTY

♊

After Ernst left the room and was making his way to his next stop, the room where Mengele kept the dwarfs, he thought about Shoshana. *She is a nice girl and so observant. It's a shame that she is in such a terrible position. I am grateful every day that I am not a Jew, but I feel so much sympathy for them. She cares more than anyone else I know. She cares enough to see that I need someone to talk to. I have no one I can turn to. I can't trust Mengele, that's for sure. And my wife, well, my wife, is the reason I am distressed. Perhaps I can talk to that girl even though she is a prisoner. She is young and tender, and she seems understanding. More importantly, I don't think she would dare tell anyone what I say to her. Of course, she is afraid. I don't blame her. Her sisters are in mortal danger. She is, too, for that matter. Any day, Mengele might tire of the twins, or if one of them gets sick and dies, he would think nothing of sending her sisters to the gas.* The very idea of Shoshana and her sisters facing the gas chamber made him angry and terrified at the same time because he knew that he didn't have the power to stop an order that Mengele gave.

He pulled open the heavy door and entered the room where Mengele kept the dwarfs. Heaving a sigh, he looked around. Otto was drawing blood from one of the females. "I am back from my holiday. Why are y-y-you here m-m-making my rounds?" Ernst asked Otto. He was annoyed to see Otto doing *his* job. In fact, he was annoyed to see Otto at all. *Damn stutter.*

"Sorry, dear boy," Otto said mockingly. "I didn't mean to overstep. However, I am here because Dr. Mengele asked me to take over your rounds in this room and to tell you when you arrived that he would like to see you in his office."

Ernst felt a chill run through him. *Mengele's going to let me go. And then what am I going to do about Gisele?* he thought. Without another word to Otto, Ernst turned and left the room. He forced himself to have courage as he began walking toward Mengele's office. *I am having terrible heartburn,* he thought as he felt the bitter acid bubble up in his throat. *I hope it's not my heart. But I doubt it is. I'm sure it's just all this aggravation. Everything important to me is at stake here. And this despicable man is in control of my life right now. If he fires me, what will I tell Gisele? She was so excited to be at that party last night. She desperately wants to be a part of that group. She can't see them for what they are. But I can. I have a feeling that they are second-rate doctors, and most of them are sadists like Mengele.* He belched as quietly as he could, but one of the nurses at the desk overheard him and gave him a look of disgust.

Ernst turned away from her. He knocked on the door to Dr. Mengele's office.

"Come in, Neider. Close the door behind you," Mengele said. Once Ernst was inside, he said, "Heil Hitler."

"Heil Hitler," Ernst answered.

"Nice party last night, don't you agree?"

"Y-y-yes, very nice."

"Such good food. The Reich provides us with everything we need. We are the fortunate ones, huh? We are members of the greatest party on earth. It's only right; we are the superior race after all."

Ernst nodded.

"Sit down, you make me nervous," Mengele said in an irritated tone of voice.

Ernst sat down, but he was leaning forward, waiting anxiously for Mengele to speak. He was ready to hear the worst.

"What did you think of Dr. Oberheuser?"

Ernst looked at him blankly.

Mengele let out a laugh. "She was so unmemorable that you don't even know who I am talking about, do you?"

He shook his head. "I'm sorry, no I don't."

"The woman at our table at the dinner last night. I know you must remember her. After all, you danced with her, and it was only yesterday."

"Yes, of course I remember," Ernst said, but he thought, *I hope Mengele isn't going to try to have me transferred to Ravensbrück to work under her.*

"Dr. Oberheuser works at Ravensbrück. I don't know if she had an opportunity to tell you about it, but she is working on the causes and effects of infection. She was telling me a little about her work. Would you like to know more?"

"Of course," Ernst said, wishing he could leave and go back to work.

"Infection is very interesting. Don't you agree?"

"It is."

"Well, anyway. First, she must cause an infection so that she can study the infected area. So, the prisoner must first be wounded. Then in order to create an infection, the wound is filled with rusty nails or glass. After that, they must record how long it will take for the wound to become infected. Once the infection sets in, time must pass in order to see if the patient will heal on their own. If they don't, which is quite often the case, the patient must be disposed of. So, they are injected with gasoline, or some other lethal substance. Once they are deceased, their limbs and organs are removed for further experiments in order to determine how far the infection has spread. Brilliant, don't you agree?"

When Ernst didn't answer, Mengele went on. "I visited Ravensbrück once, and I had the opportunity to see some of her work.

"She's not a pretty woman, but I must admit, her work is rather fascinating," he said. "Perhaps you would like to go and visit her camp sometime in the future, yes? I can arrange it. By the way, there are some very pretty women there. In fact, I had a little fun with a girl named Ilsa a while ago. If I remember correctly, she had a friend named Hilde who would be just perfect for you."

"Perhaps. But not right n-n-now, if t-t-that's all right w-w-with you. I am just getting back to work, and I want to immerse myself in your work. I hope that's all right. Besides, I am a married man now," Ernst said proudly. *So, that's why he's telling me all of this. He wants to get rid of me so he can take more time working with Otto. But, the last thing in the world I would ever want to do is go and visit another sadistic doctor.*

Mengele let out a laugh. "You're an Aryan man. It's not only your right, but it's your duty to spread that pure Aryan seed."

Ernst blushed.

Mengele smiled that half smile that Ernst had come to know as his wicked smile. Then he said, "Very well. Perhaps next year, then." Mengele added, "Would you like a piece of candy?" He pulled some candy out of his pocket. Ernst shivered. Mengele smiled. He popped a hard candy into his mouth and said, "I have been planning to do some work concerning typhus using a set of my twins. I am looking for a cure for the disease. As you know, that damn disease has been plaguing Germans for quite a while. It's even gone rampant at this camp."

Ernst nodded. *At least he isn't going to let me go. I was sure this was the end of this job.*

"I plan to inject one twin in a set of twins with the disease and use the other one as a control. Then I'll give them various cures I am working on. I am going to need your help with this project."

Ernst nodded. *Typhus. Dear God, he's going to inject someone with typhus. This man is mad. Why can't he use someone who already has the disease? Why infect a healthy person? There are more than enough people who are infected right here at the camp. But he won't use them. That's because he's a sadist, that's why.*

"I was thinking about using those two little Jews who came in the other day. I'm sure you know the ones. The pretty little girls who are in the twins' room with their older sister."

Ernst was shocked and stunned. But he knew he had to hide his emotions. If Mengele even suspected that he cared about the two twins and their older sister, Mengele would find a way to torture them all. He must find his voice and find a viable excuse quickly. "I t-t-think those two girls are t-t-too young. Personally, I would b-b-b-be more apt t-t-to work with an o-o-older set of twins. You will be able to use higher doses of m-m-medication. And thereby y-y-you s-should get a more accurate reading."

"Hmm, interesting idea. I suppose we could give that a try," Mengele said. "I know just the twins that would be perfect for this. Do you know the two boys who are about fifteen? They have red hair. Redheaded Jews. What will we see next in this place, huh, Neider?"

Ernst nodded, but he felt sick to his stomach.

"Yes, I think they will be perfect. We'll use them for this. I am sure we'll probably need to waste more of my precious twins. After all, this is one difficult disease. However, let's go ahead and start with the red-haired boys."

Ernst felt even sicker than he had a few minutes ago. "All right," he said. *It's my fault that he's chosen to torture one of those young men. But I had no choice; he forced me to choose between them and the girls. And I couldn't let him do that to those girls, especially not with the way I feel about their older sister. However, now one or both of those boys will probably die. And their blood is on my hands.*

"That's all, then. We'll start this thing with the redheaded boys tomorrow."

Ernst nodded. The less words he had to say, the less opportunity he had to stutter. He stood up and headed for the door.

"And by the way," Mengele said just before Ernst opened the door, "that Otto is quite the ladies' man, don't you agree? Your wife seems quite taken with his charm. If I were in your position, I'd watch that woman very closely. She's a beauty, I tell you. And beautiful women are always trouble for their husbands."

"Is t-t-that all?" Ernst needed to get outside; he needed a breath of fresh air, or he felt as if he might pass out.

"That's all, Neider," Mengele said and he gave Ernst a smug smile. "Go now, and finish your work."

CHAPTER TWENTY-ONE

♊

Otto waited until late afternoon when Mengele had left the camp, to go into Mengele's office and make the call he'd been planning to make all morning. He leaned back in Mengele's chair for a moment and considered what it might be like to be the famous doctor. *I am smarter than he is and far more handsome,* he thought. *Mengele is old, and although he still has the charm of a person who was raised with money and education, his looks are fading fast. I wonder if... once I rid myself of Neider, I can work on taking over Mengele's place in the party. My looks are certainly more Aryan than his. He has that dark, Jew-like hair, while mine is golden like an Aryan god. My eyes are as blue as the sky on a spring day in the fatherland, and my build is athletic. I embody all the traits the party admires.* Otto leaned back and sighed.

Then he thought about Gisele. She's not a German girl, so she's not someone to consider for marriage because I would more likely be promoted if my wife were German. And besides, she would know all the rules. When I do marry, I'll marry a girl who will have so many babies for the fatherland, that she'll win the medals. The truth is, Neider is a fool. I can't believe he has such an important position, and he actually married an inferior. It's

95

no wonder we nicknamed him ass violin when we were children in school. But of course, he would marry a French girl, an inferior. He was lucky she would have him.

He's hideous, and I must admit Gisele is a beauty. Still, I would have slept with her but never married her. The girl I marry will be of pure Aryan blood. She will be so blonde that her hair will be almost white, and she'll be so stunning that she will strike the interest of the führer himself. A girl like this can further a man's career. Still, why should I let a gorgeous French girl like Gisele slip by me. I must conquer and bed her. And why not? If I want to get rid of Neider, the best way is to break him down completely. First, I will take his wife away. That will break him. Once he is shattered, it will be easy to steal his position. I've already convinced Mengele that I am the superior man for the job.

Otto picked up the receiver

"This is the operator. How can I help you?" a sweet, young female voice said.

"Get me the home of Dr. Ernst Neider."

"One moment, please. I'll connect you."

CHAPTER TWENTY-TWO

♊

T he phone rang. Gisele was in the process of setting her hair in pin curls, and the sound startled her for a moment.

No one ever called except Ernst. And he didn't telephone unless he had something very pressing to tell her. She got up and lifted the receiver: "Bonjour. I mean, Allo?"

"Allo, sweet lady," Otto said. "It's Otto, Dr. Schatz. Do you remember me from the doctors' dinner the other night?"

"Yes, of course I remember you," she said, a little taken aback because she hadn't expected to hear his voice. A pump of excitement shot through her. She felt her face grow hot. There were butterflies in her stomach. *This is so unusual for me. I have never felt this way about a man. There is just something so charming about him.*

"I realize it's rather bold of me to telephone you. I do hope it's all right that I did. But well, you see, I just had to tell you that I thought you were the most beautiful girl at the party the other night, and I thought you should know that I can't get you off my mind."

"Well . . . that is rather bold," she said, not knowing what else to say. *He makes me uncomfortable, and yet I don't want to say goodbye. I want to hear more, but it isn't right. I am married to Ernst. I should get off this call.*

"Please forgive my daring behavior. I hope I haven't offended you."

"No, you haven't. But if that's all you have to say, I really should go."

"Please." His voice was heavy with emotion, and it made her tingle all over. "Please, Gisele, don't hang up. I don't mean to be forward. It's just that I can't help myself. Thoughts of you have infiltrated my every waking moment. And when I sleep, your lovely face haunts my dreams."

"I don't know what to say," Gisele said. "As you know, I am Ernst's wife."

"It's such a pity. A rare beauty like yours should not be wasted on a man like him."

"I must stop you. Please, Otto, don't speak that way about my husband. He is a good man. He's intelligent and kind," she said. It felt as if her heart would pound right out of her chest. *I know that I should hang up the phone. My life with Ernst is good. It's not perfect, but what is? And I've been through so much since my mother's death. When I am with Ernst, I feel safe, and that's the best my life has ever been. I should tell Otto to leave me alone. But I can't. I am drawn to Otto like a magnet. He is so handsome and captivating.* In her mind she envisioned kissing Otto, his warm lips on hers, his blue eyes filled with affection as he looked at her. *What am I thinking? This is trouble. My feelings for him could destroy my marriage. They could destroy my life.* She tried to push these thoughts of Otto out of her head. "I really must go now," she managed to say.

"Forgive me. I meant no harm. It's just that you are so superior to him that I find it hard to believe that the two of you are married."

She cleared her throat. "Well, thank you for your compliments. You are very kind. But, I really must go now."

"Please, I am begging you, don't hang up. Not yet. Please tell me that you will have lunch with me."

"Oh no, I must not," she said, but she thought, *I would love to. I would love to spend more time getting to know him. I would love to be alone with him so I could look into his eyes without Ernst looking on.*

"What is it that I can do to convince you? I promise nothing inappropriate will happen. We will have lunch, nothing more. I will do anything you ask in return. Anything at all. Shall I buy you a pretty dress? Or a necklace?"

"I don't know," she said. Then she was silent for a moment. Thinking.

There was something she wanted, something she needed. And she had been avoiding asking Ernst because she felt uncomfortable. If he knew that she thought Mengele was her father, he might think that was why she married him, to get closer to Mengele. She hadn't wanted to ask Ernst to arrange a private meeting between herself and Mengele. *I don't want to lose Ernst. I enjoy being the wife of a successful doctor. Since I met Ernst, I haven't worried about money at all, and for a girl from my background, that means a lot. I was so proud to be Ernst's wife at that dinner the other night. I can tell he's respected by his colleagues. And I know why. He has a wonderful mind. He's very bright and intelligent. The truth is, I wish he looked more like Otto.*

I can't help being attracted to Otto. He's so handsome, and his body is so strong and healthy. But if this was all there was to it, I would walk away. I would force myself to hang up the phone and never speak to Otto again. I swear I would. However, this is an opportunity to have that meeting with Mengele arranged without telling Ernst a thing. I am a strong woman; I can control my desires for this man. I know how men are. They only want one thing from a woman. At least most of them. Not Ernst, of course, but I can tell that Otto is the type who would bed a girl and then leave her. He's probably had a long line of girlfriends during his lifetime, and he's still unmarried. I'm sure he loved them and left them. As long as I remind myself of this fact, I won't fall for him.

"Well . . . there is something you can do for me," she purred.

"Anything, beautiful. Anything at all."

"I need for you to arrange a private meeting with Dr. Mengele and myself. My husband must not find out about it. Can you arrange such a meeting?"

"For you? I could arrange for the stars to drop out of the sky and do a ballet in front of your apartment building. So when you glanced out the window and saw the dancing stars, you would think of me."

"And in exchange for this meeting, you and I would have lunch one afternoon? And that's all? Just lunch?" she said timidly.

"Yes, that's all I ask."

"But, how can you get off from work to meet with me?"

"Don't you even concern yourself about that. You just leave that to me. I'll call you next week with all the details. Times and places. Until then, thoughts of you will dominate my every moment. Goodbye."

"Goodbye." She hung up the receiver. *What have I done?* she thought. But even though she was afraid of ruining her marriage, she was excited too. The thought of spending time with Otto made her giddy. She tried not to think about him as she went about her day. But as much as she tried to keep her mind off him, it was impossible. When she ate her bowl of soup for lunch, she thought of his blue eyes and how his arms had felt when they danced.

For the past week, Gisele had been working on embroidering beautiful cotton napkins with her and Ernst's initials. The mindless work kept her busy. She sat down at her sewing table, her hands still trembling, and took out the napkins. As she carefully moved the needle in and out of the fabric, she wondered what Otto's lips would feel like on hers. Would he be warm and tender, or wild and passionate? *Wild and passionate*, she decided. Then she thought of making love to him.

His body is perfect, like a statue, she thought. *Not fat and soft, like Ernst.* As soon as she thought these things, she was angry with herself. *Ernst is a good husband. He is a good person. I shouldn't feel this way about him.* But she did, and she secretly wished she didn't have to spend the rest of her life sleeping beside him and feeling his soft, plump hands on her body. Then she remembered that she would soon have her meeting with Mengele, who she believed wholeheart-edly was her father. *How will he react when I tell him who I am. Will he be happy to hear the news, or will he be upset by it? And if he is upset, will he fire Ernst? I don't know if it's a good idea to tell him, and yet I feel I must. For my mother's sake. For the sake of my future. I refuse to believe that he will reject me. He is so charming and kind, I believe he will be glad to know that I survived.*

He might have tried to find my mother all those years ago but couldn't because her parents had thrown her out of the house. She was a beautiful woman. So I'll bet he was miserable with love for her. She daydreamed. *And once he finds out I am his daughter, I'll bet he will claim me, and everything in my world will change. I won't need Ernst anymore. And even though Ernst is kind, it will be good to know that I don't have to stay married to him if I don't want to. I'll be able to leave him and find a man more like Otto without worrying about falling into poverty. I'm sure a man as well respected and successful as Dr. Mengele would want to take care of his daughter, once he discovers who I am . . .*

CHAPTER TWENTY-THREE

♊

Ernst was a sensitive man, and therefore he was readily able to see the changes that were occurring within his marriage. His wife didn't seem to want to make love to him anymore. She was always making excuses. When he spoke to her, she did not look into his eyes. He knew she was trying to hide things from him. And he could see that she wasn't as happy with her marriage to him as she had been before that night when she'd danced with Otto. *I am not surprised. Otto grew up to be another Nazi monster; he was a louse when we were children. He is a lot like Mengele. I must admit I am surprised that he became a doctor. He was cruel and sadistic as child. Doctors should be healers, not killers. They should care about the human race. At least ideally. But neither Otto nor Mengele have a conscience,* Ernst thought.

A gray-haired nurse knocked on the door of Ernst's office.

"Come in," he said.

She told Ernst that Mengele wanted to see him in his office. Ernst nodded.

"Thank you."

When he arrived at Mengele's office, Otto was already there

sitting across from Mengele. Mengele leaned back in his chair as he told Ernst to sit down. Then he smiled and said that Ernst and Otto were to begin the typhus experiments with the redheaded twin boys the following afternoon. Upon hearing Mengele mention the typhus experiments, Ernst felt his gut tighten. He hated what he was being forced to do. But Mengele and Otto seemed to be excited about the possibilities of this experiment.

"Can you imagine the acclaim we will receive when we find a cure?" Mengele said. Then he added, "After you both finish your rounds tomorrow morning, I want you to report to the operating theater. I'll see to it that the twin boys are strapped down and waiting for you."

Once you both arrive, Otto, you will infect one of the boys with typhus. Do you know the twins I am referring to? The two redheaded boys? Have you observed them during your rounds?" Mengele asked Otto.

"Yes, Dr. Mengele. I've observed them."

"As you both know, in each set of twins, one is always stronger, healthier. Do you know which one is the stronger one in this set Dr. Schatz?"

"Yes, I do." Otto sat up straight and answered quickly and clearly.

I doubt he knows. He hardly pays any attention to the poor prisoners. But I know which one it is. Still, I won't say anything. I can't. It would be like choosing which child to kill, and I am having a difficult time with this as it is.

"Give the typhus to the stronger one. Let's see if the cure I have in mind works on him. And if not, how long the typhus will take to kill him."

Ernst shivered.

"And you"—Mengele pointed at Ernst—"you watch and learn. Because you are going to do the next set of twins."

Ernst nodded. But he felt cold inside. His stomach ached and he was miserable.

CHAPTER TWENTY-FOUR

♊

Ernst was making his rounds slowly the following morning. He dreaded what was to come.

As he was finishing his blood draws, Otto approached him. "I'm going to the operating theater to begin the typhus work. You are taking a longer time than usual today. That doesn't surprise me, ass violin, you've always been slow at doing things. However, I am forced to wait for you before I begin. So, hurry up and finish, so you can join Mengele and me."

Ernst glared at him, but he nodded.

"And move your fat ass, Neider. I would like to go to lunch at a reasonable hour today."

Ernst didn't answer, but he hated Otto. He hated everything about him. He'd seen Otto draw blood. The man was careless, and because he was, the patient suffered. Only just a few days ago, Otto was drawing blood. He was fast and didn't place the needle carefully. The child he'd been working on jumped from the pain. And because of this, the needle had broken in the boy's neck. It was a very young boy, a dwarf. Blood spurted out and the child began screaming. Ernst had been working with another child but when he heard the cries, he ran over to help. However, before Ernst had an opportunity to remove the needle, Otto had already given the child a shot which immediately euthanized him. The child stopped moving and was quiet. Otto put his fingers on the boy's neck. "He's dead," Otto said. Then he shrugged.

The little boy's mother who was also a dwarf was screaming. "No, oh, please no, not my son. Not my boy." Tears spilled down her face. "Help me, someone. Please, help me."

"Shut up or I'll stop your incessant wailing," Otto said. But the mother didn't hear him. She was in shock at the death of her child, and she continued to scream. With shaking hands, the woman lifted the child into her arms and held him close to her. Then she put him back down and lay her head on his chest. Loud animal-like cries of grief and horror sprung from her lips.

"This is unacceptable. She is going to alert Dr. Mengele, and he won't be happy that I wasted the use of that little dwarf. I'm sure he'll say that child could have been better used for an important experiment," Otto said aloud to no one. But Ernst overhead.

Otto's face turned red with anger. He shook his head and then pulled a pistol out of his pocket and aimed it at the mother. "I've had enough of you. I hate loud noises," he said angrily. "I can't stand your screaming."

"Wait. Please, w-w-wait. Give m-m-me a moment with her," Ernst said pleading with Otto. Gently he pushed Otto's arm so the pistol was not aimed at the mother. "Listen to me Otto, it would be worse if you lost two of them. What would Mengele say? One is bad enough, right? Please, just give me a minute. Please just let me talk to her."

"Go on. Do something. Anything. Stop the noise. Stop her screaming or I am going to put an end to it. Now do it quickly. I can't stand it," Otto said, and he put his gun away.

Ernst was trembling as he knelt beside the woman. Kneeling hurt his knees and bothered his hip, but he knew that this grieving mother needed him to be face-to-face with her. Eye to eye, on the same height level, so she could look into his eyes. It was important that she be able to see that she could trust him.

"I'm sorry for your loss," he whispered. "But listen to me, you must be quiet. Please, I am begging you. I know that you have another child here. Don't you? Isn't that little girl in the corner over there your daughter?" Ernst indicated a cute little dark-haired girl.

The mother nodded. She was shaking. Her hair was streaked with gray, even though she was young. Her face was sunken and gaunt but it was her eyes that haunted him, dark eyes that reflected pain and misery as they sank deep in their sockets.

"Now, if you keep screaming, Dr. Otto is going to shoot you. Chances are he will probably kill you," Ernst said as softly and kindly as he could. With his head, Ernst was indicating Otto. "I won't be able to stop him. And if you are dead, who will be here to protect your little girl? Your daughter needs you. You must be quiet for her sake."

The woman looked at her daughter. Her eyes grew wide, and it was as if she had been awakened from a dream. Terror came over her face and she stopped screaming. She stared at Ernst, but she was silent.

"Good job, Neider. You finally did something right," Otto said as he walked out of the room and over to the nurse's station. Ernst followed him. He heard Otto tell the nurse, "Have that child's body in there removed and sent to the crematorium, and mach schnell."

CHAPTER TWENTY-FIVE

Ⅱ

The two young red-haired boys were strapped to the table in the operating theater when Ernst arrived.

A pair of terror-filled blue eyes followed Ernst. He could feel the weight of them, but he could not look directly at the boys.

"How nice of you to finally make it here, Neider," Mengele said. "You took long enough. It seems to me that you are quite inconsiderate. After all, this is not only your time you are wasting, but you are wasting my time and Otto's too."

"I'm s-s-sorry," Ernst said.

"Very well, get on with it. Examine the boy," Mengele said.

Ernst pulled the dirty sheet that had been placed over the naked boy halfway down in order to examine the child. He left the sheet covering the boy's private parts. It was difficult to look at a healthy child and know that soon he would be very ill, and for no reason at all.

Ernst observed and noted on the paper that the redheaded boy's skin was pale, but his eyes were surrounded by brown freckles and deep set into a youthful face.

Ernst felt sick. *Something terrible is about to happen. I wish I could believe that Mengele was doing this to this innocent boy for a good cause. But I know better. I've seen Mengele do horrific things for no reason. There are plenty of poor souls who are dying of typhus right here in the camp. He doesn't need to inject a healthy person with the disease to test his cure. He just wants to watch this young boy die a painful death. And why? Because he's a bastard, that's why. I've seen him at his worst. I watched him perform several unnecessary amputations on these sets of twins and on the poor people he keeps in his room filled with what he calls his misfits. He calls them misfits, but the truth is he is a misfit. And so is Otto. I've witnessed them both test the potency of poison by injecting it into a subject and then standing by and watching the pitiful person die a painful death. And I'll never forget that horrible day when I arrived at work and saw that Mengele had sewn a set of twin girls together for no reason at all. They were in horrible pain and unable to move. Men like Mengele and Otto should be in prison, not working in a hospital. So, it is hard to believe that this experiment with typhus is anything more than another sadistic attempt by that monster Mengele to exercise his power over the weak and helpless.*

"You're taking a long time to do a simple exam Neider," Mengele said, clicking his tongue. "Otto here tells me that everything you do seems to take you forever. Slow and slovenly. That's a good nickname for Dr. Neider. Isn't it, my boys? Or do you prefer ass violin? That's what everyone called Dr. Neider when he was a boy," Mengele said to the twins who lay strapped to the table. Then his eyes twinkled, and he put his face next to the closest red-haired boy's face and he added, "You look so frightened. I don't know why you boys would be so afraid. Answer this for me: would Uncle Mengele hurt you?"

The twins glanced at each other. Then their eyes, wide with fear, traveled from Ernst to Mengele.

Again, Mengele clicked his tongue. Then in a mocking voice, he said, "Ah-h-h, Otto. I am so good to these twins, and yet they are afraid of me anyway. How sad, isn't it? I am like an uncle to them. I give them candy. I play with them. And then when I need their help in an experiment, they look at me as if I am some kind of a monster."

You are, Ernst thought. *How can a man play with children, give them candy and tell them to call him Uncle Mengele and then turn around and hurt them? And often kill them. The children know. They see what happens to the others who Mengele takes to his operating theater. They know what kind of man Mengele is.*

Mengele didn't explain what he was doing. He just handed the syringe to Otto who injected it into the boy's arm. The boy struggled to free himself, but he was tied down too tightly.

"See, it was just a quick injection. Nothing to be so frightened about." Mengele smiled. "Ernst, first take this boy to the hospital," he said, "and after you drop him off, take the other one back to the twins' room."

As they walked to the hospital, the stronger twin, the one who'd been injected with typhus asked Ernst, "What was that he gave me?"

"I don't know," Ernst lied. He couldn't bear to tell this teenager the truth, that within twenty-four hours he would be suffering terribly. He would be very sick and even possibly on death's door. *I wish I could have stopped this,* Ernst thought.

An old nurse with an angry face and hair in a wiry gray bun greeted them at the hospital door. "I've been waiting for him. Dr. Mengele told me to expect his arrival. But I thought it would be an hour ago," she said, then she turned to the red-haired boy. "Get in that bed." She indicated a bed in the corner. The boy did as he was told. His twin brother ran to him and put his arms around his brother. He held him tightly for several moments. "All right, that's enough," the nurse said. "Get up and go with Dr. Neider."

"I'm sorry," Ernst added. "Come with me. I'll take you back to the twins' room."

They walked in silence for a few minutes, then the boy said in a soft voice, "Is Uncle Mengele going to kill my brother?"

Ernst looked into the boy's eyes. He shrugged. "I don't know," he said. "I hope not." They had arrived at the twins' room and Ernst was glad to be getting away from the boy as he opened the door to let him into the room. But when he opened the door, he saw all of the children sitting on the floor gathered around Shoshana. In a soft haunting soprano voice, Shoshana sang to them. The song was in Yiddish. But he could understand the words. It was a lullaby. Her eyes were closed as if she were lost in a dream.

Ernst was drawn to the sound. *Her voice is gentle like a rushing river, deep like a cathedral, musical like a harp, and melodious like a piano. I can't take my eyes off her. As she sings she moves her head and her loose black hair sways gently, like a tiny bird swept up in a mild whirlwind. I'm so glad that Mengele allows his special inmates to keep their hair. It would be a terrible loss for her to have been forced to shave those lovely raven-colored locks.*

He recognized the children's lullaby. His mother had sung it to him in German. And because Yiddish was so much like German, he understood and remembered every word. The sweetness of the song brought a tear to his eyes as he drifted back to memories of his own mother who had passed away. Ernst was mesmerized. He was unable to move. Standing there in the doorway, watching, listening, enthralled he was transported back to his childhood home. Then one of Shoshana's twin sisters looked up. She saw him and nudged Shoshana who stopped singing. "No, please, don't stop. Go on," Ernst said. He walked into the room and sat down on one of the cots.

Shoshana swallowed hard. She'd lost the connection to the dreamlike state. And now she sang but her voice trembled.

Sheyn vi di levone,
Likhtik vi di shtern,
Fun himl a matone,
Bistu mir tzugeshikt!

When she finished the song, Ernst smiled at her. "You have a lovely voice."

"Thank you," she said.

"My mother used to sing that to me. But I can't recall the name of it. Do you know the name of that song?" he asked.

"It's called 'As Pretty as the Moon.'"

He smiled. "Did you ever sing professionally?"

"Actually, yes, I did. I sang in a café in the ghetto. I know it was a silly dream, but I was hoping I would have a career as a singer before I came here to this place."

"It's good to dream. And there are no silly dreams," Ernst said.

"That's true for you. But not for me," Shoshana said boldly. "I am a Jew. We don't dare to dream because we don't know if we have a future."

He felt a smothering kind of sadness come over him, because he knew it was true. At any time, Mengele could decide to destroy all of these children, and within a few hours they would be dead. He remembered a time only a few months ago, when he'd seen that very thing happen with a group of Gypsy children. Mengele had taken Ernst into the Gypsy room. He said he wanted to show Ernst how he played with the children. At the time, Ernst knew that there had been a flare-up of noma in the Gypsy camp. It was a hideous disease that caused terrible disfigurement to the victims' face. He knew that Mengele wanted to discover a cure for it, but at the same time he was deathly afraid of catching it. He'd done some experimentation on several victims only to euthanize them quickly.

Mengele talked openly with Ernst about eliminating the entire Gypsy camp in order to eradicate the disease. However, so far, none of the children had come down with it, so, Ernst thought they might be safe. When they arrived at the children's room, Mengele raised his arms in the air and said, "Who wants candy?" All of the children came running to him, crying out, "I do, Uncle Mengele. I do." Mengele hugged them and smiled. Then he gave them each a piece of candy from the pocket of his jacket. While they gobbled the much-coveted treats, Mengele smiled at them, and turned to Ernst. "Let's go," he said and winked. Ernst nodded. He had no idea what was in store. But as soon as they left the room and closed the door behind them, Mengele walked over to the guard who stood right outside and said in a calm voice "Gas them all."

"The children?" The guard asked.

"Yes, the Gypsy children in that room." Mengele pointed to the door where they had just been. The sound of giggling echoed into the hall. Ernst was shocked. He had been convinced that Mengele had some affection for these children. Yet, he now saw that Mengele had no feelings at all. He could easily have them killed without a thought. Bile rose in Ernst's throat, and he wasn't even able to speak to excuse himself. Instead, he had to run outside and vomit. When he'd returned Mengele was laughing. The smile on Mengele's face, and the twinkle in his eyes was so wicked that it made Ernst tremble. And it was then that Ernst discovered that Mengele was a sadist. Since that day, he'd seen that smile and that twinkle many times, and each time he saw it he felt like spiders were crawling all over him.

Now as he stood watching Shoshana as she sat like a young mother surrounded by all the twins, Ernst wished he could do something, anything, to help her and her sisters. His thoughts turned to the red-haired boys and what had been done to them that day. Ernst knew that soon one of those boys would be very ill; the child would suffer terribly. But the other would not be spared. He would suffer too; he would be overcome with guilt. And if Mengele allowed him to live, he would carry that guilt for the rest of his life.

Ernst wished he could have found a way to convince Mengele to spare the boys, but he was powerless. If he had tried, he was afraid Mengele would turn his experiment on Shoshana's sisters, and that would be far worse. Mengele's experiment wasn't about finding a cure for typhus. Ernst was certain of that. It was about Mengele exercising his power to play God with these unfortunate prisoners. Mengele greatest pleasure lie in his power to decide who lived and who died.

Ernst had not become immune to this cruelty as Mengele had assured him he would be. Mengele promised him that after a time, Ernst would not care about the prisoners. He would see them as the vermin that they were. But it had never happened. A true healer at heart, Ernst suffered with every death he was forced to witness. This time, he'd been able to spare Shoshana's sisters. But there was no way to determine what would happen in the future. And he was worried about it, even now as he watched the twins sitting on the floor with their sister.

"Will you sing us another song?" Ernst asked Shoshana. Her voice soothed him. He needed to hear her sing a sweet gentle lullaby.

"If you want me to," Shoshana said. "Of course I will."

He nodded. "Yes, please do."

She sang. This time she did not sing a children's lullaby. This time she sang a love song. The song was about a man who left his lover and now she had a broken heart. Shoshana's voice penetrated deep into Ernst's soul. It brought back all the pain he was feeling due to his wife's fascination with Otto. Tears began to form in the corner of Ernst's eyes. Shoshana saw a tear roll down Ernst's cheek and she stopped singing.

"I'm sorry, Herr Doctor," she said, her voice trembling. He knew she was terrified. "I didn't mean to upset you."

He knew she was afraid he would punish her. He hated that she was afraid of him; he would never do such a thing. "It's all right. It's not your fault. I am just having a difficult day today," he said.

Then in a small voice, she asked, "Is there anything I can do for you?"

He walked over to her. The children were sitting on the floor gathered around her. Their faces were upturned looking at him, their eyes filled with terror.

"Go on and play," he said to the children. "Go, now. I would like to speak to this young lady alone."

All of the children quickly stood up. Bluma took Perle's hand. They started to walk away, but both were staring back at Shoshana, their eyes wide with fear.

"It's all right. I promise you. I won't hurt your sister," Ernst said as if he knew what Shoshana's twin sisters were thinking. "Go on and play."

After the children were gone, Ernst said. "I probably shouldn't be talking to you. But I need a friend. I desperately need a friend."

Shoshana nodded. Then treading carefully, the way one does when one is confronted by someone with absolute power over their lives, she said, "I will listen. And I promise you that no matter what you tell me, I will never tell anyone else."

"I believe you," Ernst said. "Somehow I see a lot of myself in you."

"Oh? How so?"

"You have a deep soul," he said. "I'm sorry. I know this is rude, but I forgot your name."

"I'm Shoshana. You're Dr. Neider, aren't you?"

"Yes," he smiled. "But you can call me Ernst." Then he took a deep breath. "But only use my name when no one else is around. It wouldn't be safe for either of us for you to call me Ernst when any of the other staff could hear you."

"Of course, I understand. When anyone is around I will call you Dr. Neider," she said.

Ernst smiled at her. He could see that her hands were shaking. He wanted to hold them in his own to stop their trembling. But he didn't. Instead, he began to tell her all of his fears and worries about Gisele and Otto. She listened quietly, nodding her head in sympathy. It felt good to talk to someone. He needed this. He needed to unburden himself. Ernst talked for almost an hour before he realized how much time had passed. "I should be going now," he said. "Thank you for listening."

She nodded.

Ernst left the twins' room feeling a little bit lighter. Talking things out had made everything seem less horrible.

As Ernst was walking through the hallway, Mengele stopped him. "Neider," Mengele patted him on the shoulder. It seemed like a friendly gesture, but Ernst didn't trust him. Mengele smiled and the space between his teeth caught Ernst's eye. Then Mengele continued speaking. "So, you're a married man now. Good for you. And surprisingly, I like your wife. She's quite the looker. I was hardly expecting that from you. I thought you would marry some intellectual girl with a face to match." He let out a short, wicked laugh, "Someone more like yourself. Anyway, I'm feeling generous today, so I've decided to put in a request with the party to award you and your new bride a house to live in. In fact, the house I am requesting is located right here on the grounds of this camp, and it should be ready for you in about six months or so. I figure that if you are right here on the grounds, you will have no reason to come in late to work all the time. And of course, your pretty young wife should be quite grateful to have a house of her own."

"Thank you," Ernst said. But he wasn't happy with the idea of living within the camp. Not even if it meant having a house of their own. He was afraid of what Gisele would think of the camp and, even more importantly, what she would think of him once she had a better idea of what he was doing at work. *Mengele knows that if we live on the grounds she will see everything that is going on here at Auschwitz. And he wants her to see it. He wants her to question me and to find me vile. Everything he does, although it seems like he is being kind, comes from cruelty. Mengele wants me to lose Gisele. He knows she is the only happiness I've ever had in my life, and he wants to watch me lose her.*

CHAPTER TWENTY-SIX

♊

That evening, Ernst gave Gisele a kiss on the cheek when he walked into their apartment after work. He was sure he felt her tense up when he kissed her. *Maybe I am just imagining it,* he tried to tell himself. "I'll get ready for dinner," he said. "I have some very good news." *I wish it were better news. I wish the house was far away from the camp. And I wish my job was far away from here too.*

He went to the bathroom and scrubbed his hands and face. Then he sat down at the table. Gisele sat across from him. She had prepared a light dinner. He was hungry and could have used something more substantial, but he didn't complain.

"So, you said you have good news. What is it?" she asked.

"Dr. Mengele liked you a lot. In fact, he liked you so much that he has put in a request with the authorities to give us a house to live in. Would you like that?"

"You know I would. I'd like it very much," she said.

"He says it will be about six months before we can move in."

"Even so, that is good news," she said.

After that, she was quiet. He knew something was wrong, and he was afraid that it had to do with Otto. Ernst wished that Gisele would just talk to him. He wished she would open up and tell him what she was thinking. He tried to think of things to say to start the conversation, but he couldn't think. His mind was consumed with the fear of losing her.

Their marriage had always been a physical one. She was young, and although he was quite a bit older than her, they made love almost every night. So he figured that after they made love, when they were lying in bed together, he would try to speak to her. He would tell her how much she meant to him. And he would do his best to make her see that a man like Otto wasn't worthy of her.

They sat quietly for a couple of hours, she working on her embroidery, he reading a book, before Ernst said he was going to get ready for bed.

Gisele sat down at her dressing table and combed her hair. Ernst lay in bed watching her. She rubbed cream into her face and neck, and then she got into bed beside Ernst. He leaned over and kissed her. She responded but much less passionately than she usually did. Gently, he smoothed her hair out of her face. Outside, a large full silver moon threw light at them through their bedroom window. "You are even more beautiful by moonlight," he said. Gisele's breathing was soft. Ernst kissed behind her ear and her neck. He could feel her pulse through her skin. It was a soft thump, but it was always there when he kissed her neck. He ached with love for her as he leaned down and kissed her lips again. Then he moved to her neck and down to her breasts. Then for the first time since they had become lovers, Gisele pushed him away.

"I'm tired, and my head is aching. I am not feeling well," she said. He thought her voice sounded as if she felt pity for him.

I could be wrong. Maybe I am just imagining all of this. It's possible that she is really feeling ill. "I'm sorry. Let me get you something to help."

"No, I don't want to take anything. I just want to sleep," she said, then she turned over so she was facing away from him.

Ernst wanted to believe that nothing was wrong. He wanted it in the worst way, but in his heart he knew that his wife was not feeling ill. He knew this was not something he could cure with medicine. Gisele, his precious and beautiful Gisele, was losing interest in him. And he was quite certain that it was because Otto had caught her eye. Hearing her breathing slow down, he knew she'd fallen asleep. *I must try to rest*, he told himself, but he couldn't sleep. When he closed his eyes, he thought of his wife with Otto: Otto who was so handsome and debonair. Otto, the man who had made his childhood a living hell. Gisele, perfect and beautiful. Together they would look like the ideal couple. But he knew better. If there was one thing that Ernst had an uncanny sense of, it was human nature. And deep in his gut, he felt certain that Otto would never take a woman like Gisele seriously.

Ernst had suffered because Otto was a tormentor when they were children, and he was certain that Otto's cruel streak had not disappeared. When they were children, Otto was openly vicious, poking fun at Ernst and causing the other children to do the same. But now that Otto was older, his viciousness had grown into something more sophisticated. Ernst had met men like Otto when he was at the university. He'd been careful to stay far away from them. But what he observed was that they had grown up and stopped targeting weaker men. Instead, they had turned their interest to women. They bedded and collected girls as a hobby.

I am helpless to stop this runaway train. I am losing Gisele. Since the day I met her, I have felt like I was living a dream. I never felt like I was good enough for her. She was more than I could ever have wished for. And deep in my heart, I never really believed that she would stay with me for very long. But I didn't think it would end this quickly. I thought that if I did everything I could to keep her happy, I would have a few years with her before she left me. And to make matters even worse, she is fascinated with a man whom I truly hate. I don't know what to do. I feel so broken.

He poured himself a glass of whiskey and drank it slowly, sitting by the window. His mind drifted to the redheaded boy Mengele had injected that day. *He is probably starting to feel very sick right now,*

Ernst thought, and he shook his head. His poor brother is probably distraught. *I can't believe this terrible job I have. Well, if Gisele leaves me, and I hope with all my heart that she doesn't, but if she does, I am going to quit this job. I will be heartbroken to live without her. I know that there will never be another woman for me. Gisele will always have my heart. But even if I don't have love, and even if I must live a lonely life, I will use my medical license as I had always planned to do, to help and to heal. So, I will go away from this horrible place, away from Mengele and all of his sadistic plans, and I'll go to some small village in the country where I can live a quiet life as a country doctor.*

CHAPTER TWENTY-SEVEN

Ⅱ

Ernst was sad to discover that he had been right about the red-haired boy. Before he began his rounds the following morning, he went into the hospital to check on him. The smell at Auschwitz was already a terrible one. But the odor of sickness and misery surrounding this young boy was even more pungent. He was lying in his own vomit and diarrhea. *This boy is sick, very sick.* Ernst touched the child's forehead and found that he was burning up with fever. *Terrible shame that this poor child should be suffering so,* Ernst thought as he got a cool rag and washed the boy's face. *If I don't clean this boy up, the nurses won't do it. They will leave him like this.* The last thing Ernst wanted to do was clean up a mess like this one. But he had such compassion for the dying boy, that he did it. Once he'd finished, he walked quickly to Mengele's office.

"The b-b-boy who was injected w-w-with typhus yesterday is dying. If you plan to test a cure, I w-w-would hurry and do so."

"You would hurry and do so, now, would you?" Mengele said mockingly. "You have some nerve, Neider. I find it rather hard to believe that you are trying to tell me what to do."

Ernst sucked in his breath. *I forget myself. I must tread very lightly.*

I've made him angry. Now I have to find a way to get back on his good side, or I could be his next victim. He might not kill me, although he might, but he would think nothing of punishing me by hurting Shoshana and her sisters. "I'm s-s-sorry, Dr. Mengele, if it s-seemed that I w-w-was trying to give you orders. I w-would never attempt to do such a thing. I just wanted t-t-to inform you that the disease had t-taken hold, in case you w-were not aware. I know you w-w-wanted to test a cure, and s-s-so I thought th-that perhaps th-this might be a good time to test it."

"Hmm. I see," Mengele said, yawning. "Yes, I'll see about that later this afternoon."

Careful, be very careful, Ernst told himself. "I understand. But, with all due respect, this afternoon might be too late. It seems he has a very bad case of typhus. I went in to see him this morning, and he looks very bad."

"Yes, well, I might just have to euthanize this one. We have plenty more. I'll just use another set of twins. I did have Otto tell the boy's twin brother that his brother was dying. I watched him through a glass. He seemed to know already, even before Otto told him. In fact, Otto said he was getting phantom symptoms. Can you imagine? Fascinating, isn't it? I must admit that it always amazes me how even if they are separated, twins always seem to feel it inside themselves when their twin is sick or dying."

"Yes, fascinating," Ernst said without enthusiasm. He didn't mention the red-haired boys again, but he was feeling sorry for them. However, he couldn't escape the nagging worry that one of Shoshana's sisters might be next.

CHAPTER TWENTY-EIGHT

♊

Gisele searched through her closet anxiously. She wanted to be sure she wore the perfect dress, one that showed off her ample breasts and accented her curves. Today she was going to meet Otto for lunch, and she had to look her best. *Even if I am planning on staying faithful to my husband, I still want Otto to think I am stunning.* She'd set her long, golden hair in pin curls the night before. As she removed the pins and let the curls fall to her shoulders, she smiled at her reflection. Then she pulled her hair back on one side with a pearl comb that Ernst had given her. With a light touch, she applied some rouge, mascara, and lipstick. Once she finished, she studied her reflection in the mirror and said aloud to no one but herself. "I am gorgeous." Then she winked at herself in the mirror and giggled.

The color of the dress she'd chosen was perfect. She stood up and slipped it over her head. It fell like waves gently caressing her body. The deep shade of midnight blue complemented her eyes. Gisele ran her hands over the material, feeling the texture of it. It was a garment of good quality, something she could never have afforded before she met Ernst. This was the kind of dress she'd admired in store windows but had never imagined owning. She twirled around like a ballet dancer. Wearing this dress made her feel like she was born to be one of the wealthy German wives and not a poor French girl, which she actually was, from a conquered country.

Gisele sat down on the bed and rolled her silk stockings. She was careful not to run them on her nails which she'd filed and painted red the previous evening. Then, one stocking at a time, she placed her foot inside and pulled the silk carefully up her leg. As always, when she wore these stockings, she marveled at the rich feeling of silk against the skin of her legs. Then she slipped on her black leather high-heel pumps, grabbed her handbag, and headed out the door to catch the bus.

She arrived at the restaurant where she and Otto had agreed to meet. Glancing at her watch she realized she was ten minutes early. Her heart beat faster when she thought of how handsome he was. *I should wait outside for a few minutes, so I can be a little late. I don't want him to think I am overeager to see him. After all, I've agreed to this luncheon with him in exchange for his arranging a private meeting with Dr. Mengele. He must think that I am doing him a favor and that I am not attracted to him at all. If he knows how I feel about him, he will take advantage of me. And I am not sure I will be able to resist him.*

Gisele left the front of the restaurant and took a walk up the street where she gazed in the windows of the shops. There was a dress shop that caught her eye. She gasped when she saw a suit in the window that was the height of fashion. If she'd had more time, she would have gone inside and tried it on. But as it was, although she knew it was unwise to be too early, she also knew it was not a good idea to be too late, just in case Otto might think she wasn't coming and leave. The suit was a dark navy-blue wool, that looked very chic on the mannequin in the window. Sighing, Gisele made a mental note to ask Ernst for some money. Then she would return to the store and try it on.

Glancing at her watch, Gisele saw that it was five after eleven. *I am a few minutes late.* They'd agreed to meet at eleven. *By the time I arrive, it will be almost ten after. I think that's perfect. I'll head over to the restaurant now.* It surprised her how nervous she was. Most men had no effect on her. What they said or did had never mattered to her. *What is it about this one that makes my heart beat faster? He's handsome, it's true. But I have encountered handsome men before, and they haven't had this effect on me. I have to stay in control of my feelings. I hope I can do it.*

She'd expected to see Otto waiting when she walked into the restaurant. But he wasn't there. *I hope I haven't missed him. Could he have come and left so soon? I'm only ten minutes late,* she thought, feeling anxious. Then she told herself, *Perhaps it's better if he left. I won't have the opportunity to get into trouble. But, I also won't have the opportunity to meet with Dr. Mengele—*

"May I help you?" a young female hostess asked, interrupting her thoughts.

"Yes, I'd like a table for two," Gisele said.

"Of course. Follow me, please."

"By the way, I am meeting someone here, and I am a bit late, I'm afraid. I was wondering if a man has been here and left. He is a tall, blond man. He would have been alone. And he might have told you that he was waiting for someone."

"No, I'm sorry, Fräulein. There was no one like that here."

"Thank you," Gisele said, and she sat down at the table to wait. She watched the hostess go back to the front of the restaurant and thought, *She called me Fräulein. How funny. Looking at me, she doesn't realize I am a married woman. But I thought I looked so mature.*

The small restaurant catered primarily to a German clientele. This didn't surprise Gisele at all. The finer restaurants, hotels, and shops in Poland were reserved for their German conquerors. The Polish people had been pushed aside. Their needs were secondary. Gisele never said anything about this, but she felt sorry for them. The Germans treated them the same way they treated the French, like they were of a lesser race. She glanced around the restaurant. It was not as nice as most of the places Ernst took her, but she'd made it clear to Otto that she wanted to go somewhere out of the way where they were unlikely to encounter anyone who knew her as Ernst's wife. She didn't want this meeting to get back to her husband.

There are no white tablecloths or candles. No flowers, nothing fancy. Just good, solid German food, she thought as she watched steaming plates of sauerbraten and sausages coming out of the kitchen.

Time was ticking, but Otto had still not arrived. By eleven thirty, Gisele was ready to cry. She'd never been treated so poorly. Most men jumped at the chance to talk to her. She couldn't understand it. Otto had called her twice begging to see her, and now he wasn't showing up. *Why would he have done this? Just to humiliate me?* With trembling hands and trembling lips, Gisele gathered her handbag and got up to leave the restaurant. She began walking toward the door just as Otto came strolling in. His golden curls framed the handsome chiseled bone structure of his face as he sauntered over to the table.

"I'm sorry I'm late. I got stuck at work. I had to find a way to talk your husband into taking on my afternoon work so I could leave."

"Oh?" she said, sitting back down. "What did you tell him?"

"That my mother was ill. He's a sucker for things like that. When we were children, he was a real mama's boy. I mean he had a very good, strong relationship with his mother," Otto corrected himself. Then he smiled, and Gisele melted.

What do I see in him? He is handsome. So what? Plenty of men are handsome. Why is this one different?

He sat down across from Gisele and smiled at her. "You look lovely," he said.

"Thank you." She blushed.

"Let's order. I'm starving."

They ordered the sauerbraten. While they waited for their food, Otto bragged about his bravery as a doctor on the front lines of battle. "I saved so many lives." He sighed. "That's why I received a promotion and was able to come to work with Dr. Mengele. It's quite an honor."

"Yes, I know," Gisele said, but she thought, *He is so arrogant. And he brags about himself so easily. I should find him repulsive. Yet I don't. I am more attracted to him all the time.*

Otto talked about himself the entire meal. He told her about his years in medical school, and the women he dated and how they could not keep his interest. "That's why I never married," he said. "Of course, there was no one like you. You are a very special girl, Gisele. You're not only beautiful, but you're graceful, and smart."

Gisele listened. She knew she was blushing. "So, you really think I am different than the others."

"Absolutely," he said. "I've never met a girl like you."

She looked at him as he spoke and studied him. *I wonder what he would be like in bed. His body is so perfect. His face, his eyes. I would love to feel his arms around me. I would love to feel him inside of me.* She knew she was blushing. So she looked away and tried to think of something else. But before she could, she caught him smiling at her. His smile was so compelling that it made her wish he would kiss her.

The food arrived. Steam rose from the plates and the aroma was wonderful. But Gisele had no appetite. She was far too attracted to Otto to think about food. However, she didn't want him to know just how taken with him she was. So, to prevent herself from staring at him, she moved the food around on her plate with her fork.

He ate heartily and while he was eating, he didn't speak. She waited, trying to think of something to say once he was finished. Finally, he patted his lips with his napkin and smiled at her. "You hardly ate," he said as if he was first noticing her.

"Oh, I did," she lied. "I never eat much."

He smiled at her. "I hope you liked the food."

"Yes. I did," she said.

"Glad to hear it."

"By the way, Otto, have you arranged the meeting with Dr. Mengele for me?"

"I haven't had a chance," he admitted. "But I won't have any trouble. Dr. Mengele favors me. And, of course, why wouldn't he? I am the perfect Aryan."

"You mean he favors you over Ernst?" she asked.

"Yes, exactly. I know Ernst is your husband. And, of course, I would never want to say anything derogatory about him. But quite frankly, Gisele . . ." He reached across the table and took her hand. Her skin burned where he touched her. Then looking into her eyes, he said, "I can't see how a woman as beautiful as you could be married to him. You must admit, he is rather clumsy and awkward. Of course, if you try, you could find that endearing. However, no one would ever say that is the perfect Aryan man."

Gisele knew that what Otto was saying about Ernst was true. But it hurt her to hear him say it out loud. She wasn't in love with her husband. But she cared for him. He'd always been kind to her. And although her body cried out for Otto, she still couldn't bear to hear anyone speak unkindly of Ernst. "Please, I don't want to offend you. But I would appreciate if you didn't talk that way about my husband," she said.

"Did I offend you?"

Suddenly he looked very concerned, and that made her melt. *He cares about me*, she thought. "Well, yes. Ernst is my husband. And I do care for him very much."

"I am truly sorry. I would never want to offend you," he said.

She managed a smile. "I understand, but please don't do it."

"Of course I won't," he said, "But, may I say something?"

She nodded, looking down.

"You said that you care for him, your husband, I mean. But you didn't say that you love him."

"Of course I love him," she argued.

"Do you? Do you really, Gisele? Or do you long for passion and romance?" Otto asked.

"I can't answer that."

"You don't have to answer it to me. These are questions you

should ask yourself. We only live once, my dear. Do you want to waste your youth? Your beauty? Your life? On a man like Ernst?"

She looked away. "This conversation is making me uncomfortable."

"I'm sorry," he said. "Let's talk about your meeting with Dr. Mengele. Can you tell me what it is you want to talk to him about?"

"I'd rather not. It's very personal."

"I understand. Well, it seems that every subject I try to discuss about is off limits. But it's all right," he said, then he waited a few moments. "So, I'll just sit here and look at you. I find you so attractive. I am drawn to you like no other woman I have ever known."

She felt her face grow hot.

"I think of you all day and all night," he said. "I wonder what it would feel like to hold you close to me and feel your silky skin against mine."

"You shouldn't talk like this. You know I am married." She gasped.

"Another subject that's off limits?"

"Otto, I don't mean to be so difficult."

"Don't you like me? Perhaps we should just leave. Just go home."

"No. No, let's not. I do like you. Yes. I do. Oh yes," she blurted her answer and was immediately sorry. *We should go home. I should leave here and forget this man forever. What am I doing?*

"Gisele, Gisele." He said her name in a deep, breathy voice that made her entire body tingle. "I know you are married. However, I am a man who has been around a bit, and so I also know you are attracted to me. I can see it in those magnificent blue eyes of yours. I'll guarantee you that you have never had a lover like me. Once you and I have been together, you will be hungry for more. And a woman like you shouldn't waste herself. These are the best years to enjoy your body. You won't be young forever, Gisele. Seize this opportunity. I promise you will feel things you've never felt before. I promise you won't regret it."

"But what about Ernst?"

"He need never know anything about us if you don't want him to. Our affair will be our little secret," Otto said.

She knew her face was as red as a ripe strawberry. She looked away from him, embarrassed by his boldness. Her body was responding to his words. She felt warm and wet between her legs, and she longed to feel his touch. In a small voice she said, "Excuse me, please. I'll be right back."

She was headed to the bathroom. *I need to get away from him for a moment. I must splash my face with cold water. I need have some time alone to gather my thoughts, or I am going to lose control and fall into his bed. I have never wanted any man the way I want him.*

But as she walked through the crowded restaurant, she saw a familiar face. Terror struck her. It ran through her veins. She was unable to move, glued to the floor. The man she recognized was staring directly at her. *I would know those eyes anywhere. It's him.*

CHAPTER TWENTY-NINE

In the morning, Naomi woke up alone in the barn with a wool blanket covering her. *He's gone. That German soldier is gone.* She wrapped the blanket around her shoulders and sat up. *But before he left, he covered me with this blanket. I wonder where he got it and why he would leave it behind. It must have been his. He's going to be cold tonight. He'll need a blanket. Yet, he left it for me.* Her stomach ached with hunger; she searched for the bag of food, but then she remembered that they'd eaten it all the night before. Her head ached, and she felt like crying. *I am going to starve to death out here in this forest,* she thought. *I know Herschel meant well setting me free. He was trying to make up for the rough marriage we had. And he was willing to sacrifice himself to save my life. I am surprised he turned out to be so noble in the end. But even so, he's made things even harder for me, because now I am alone. My children are somewhere; I don't know where. But I do know that they are on their own. And I am here in the forest, freezing without food or water. At least if I had gone with Herschel, we would have died together. But now, I must fend for myself, and I don't know how.*

Then she heard stirring outside the barn. She trembled with fear. But when she turned, she saw Friedrich walk in. He shook a dusting of snow off his coat. "I went ice fishing," he said almost cheerily. "Have you ever eaten raw fish?"

She shook her head.

"It's not the best-tasting thing. But it will keep you alive. We can't build a fire because the smoke could attract enemies."

She nodded, determined to eat whatever he'd brought. "Thank you for the blanket," she said.

"You were shivering in your sleep."

"It's very cold."

"Yes, it sure is. But I've gotten used to it. I was in Russia. So, this weather is nothing to me. Now, if you want to feel true cold, you have to go to Russia. When I was there I felt like my blood had frozen in my veins. It was that cold."

"You were fighting in Russia?"

"Yes, our glorious führer sent me and my troop there. He wants to conquer the Russians. Good idea, no?" he said cynically. Then he let out a short, bitter laugh. "But he forgot to give his soldiers coats and boots that were warm enough to face the Russian winter." Sarcasm dripping from his voice, he then continued. "That's the great Adolf Hitler. Some leader, huh? He's so drunk with his own power that he doesn't care about his men. All he knows is that he's determined to rule the world."

Friedrich sliced a piece of raw fish and handed it to her. It didn't smell fishy. In fact, it had no odor at all. She thought about how careful she'd once been to keep a kosher home, and she let out a short laugh. Friedrich looked at her puzzled as to why she was laughing. But he didn't ask her anything. He watched as she put the fish in her mouth. It tasted strange, but it wasn't nearly as bad as she thought it would be. It wasn't slimy. Naomi chewed quickly and swallowed.

"Good girl," he said, then he handed her another slice. "Watch out for bones."

She nodded, then she ate it.

"While I was out this morning, I looked in the windows of the house. I didn't see anyone. I think this place might be abandoned. At least I am hoping so. We can try to stay here for a while. It could be risky. But it might be worth it. At least it gives us some shelter until the weather warms up a little."

She nodded. "Do you think we could dare go inside the house?"

"Not yet. I want to watch it for a while to be sure that no one is living there. I mean, I am fairly certain right now. But if we go in and find someone there, we will have to kill them."

She looked at him in surprise. "Kill them?"

"I'm afraid so. We can't risk having someone turn us in, now, can we? You know what the Germans will do to us if we are caught. Don't you?"

She nodded.

"So, to be safe, we're going to have to do it my way. All right?"

"Yes," she said. "Thank you for going fishing for us."

"Of course." He smiled. Then he leaned against the wall and lit a cigarette.

The smell of smoke made her cough, but she didn't tell him to stop. Neither of them spoke. He was clearly enjoying the cigarette, and she didn't know what to say to him. *I'm glad he's here with me. I never thought I would say that about a German. Especially a soldier. But he's not really one of them. He seems like a good man. I hope I am right because I can't survive this forest in the winter on my own. In fact, I doubt I could survive it at any time, even during the summer. I don't know how to hunt or fish. I could search for wild mushrooms.* She smiled inwardly at the thought as her mind drifted back to her lover, Eli, and how they'd spent lazy days searching for wild mushrooms in a field of fragrant wildflowers.

It had been years since she had last seen Eli. But her memories of him were still vivid. And even the thought of wildflowers and wild mushrooms brought back every emotion she'd felt on that last day they said goodbye forever. It was only right. She was married to another man. Eli deserved a life of his own. And even though he was her eldest daughter Shoshana's father, she could not leave her husband and marry him. They'd been broken up for five years but still living in the same small shtetl, running into each other occasionally before he decided to marry a girl from their small village and then move with her to Britain. One of his future wife's relatives had a possible position for Eli and so they had left the shtetl. It had been terrible for Naomi, because it had only been a few years earlier that her twin sister had moved east with her husband, first to Lithuania and then to Romania. At the time, when her sister, Miriam, left, Naomi felt abandoned. Then she felt even worse when Eli moved away. Not that they ever spoke, but it gave her a strange sort of comfort to see him every so often in town. However, once the Nazis had taken Poland, she found that she was glad that Eli and her sister had escaped before this nightmare had begun.

"So, why don't you tell me a little bit about you? I mean, after all, we are stuck here in this barn together. We need something to do," Friedrich said.

"What do you want to know?"

"Whatever you want to tell me."

"All right. I come from a little village outside of Warsaw. I am married. At least I was married. But I don't know anymore, whether my husband is alive or dead." She hesitated. " I have three children, all girls." She sighed softly.

"Hmm, all right," he said, exhaling a wave of smoke that lingered in the cold air for a moment. "And how is it you ended up here, all alone in the forest with a German soldier?"

"It's a long story," she said.

"We have plenty of time." He smiled. "But if you don't want to tell me, that's quite all right."

"I'll tell you, if you want to know."

"Sure, I want to know." He smiled.

She told him about the ghetto and how Herschel had bargained with the guard. He listened quietly. Then he said, "You know, we soldiers didn't know anything about the camps and the ghettos until recently. At least I didn't."

"How could you not know?"

"Because I was at the Russian front, fighting a war for a man who I really didn't know much about. Adolf Hitler. I believed his lies. He said he was going to make Germany great again. He promised to restore the world's respect for the fatherland. I knew how broken my father was after the Great War and how defeated everyone felt because of the treaties of Versailles. I guess I wanted to believe Hitler. I admit, I heard all the crap he was spewing about Jews. But I didn't know any Jews personally. I mean, the doctor who treated my leg when I broke it as a kid was a Jew, but I didn't really know him. So, I wasn't worried about the Jew-hating stuff. I wanted my country back."

"Interesting," she said.

"I mean, Germany was a mess when I was a boy. My father came back from the war injured and angry. My mutti had a job, but she was struggling. And there was crazy inflation. Do you know what that means?"

"No," she said.

"It means that it cost a small fortune to buy food. We couldn't afford to live. German money was dropping in value every hour. My mutti would work, and by the end of the day, her money was almost worthless. Sometimes it took more than an entire day's pay to buy a loaf of bread. And that's no exaggeration."

"It sounds terrible. Food was never plentiful in our village, but we did have local farmers," she said

"It got even worse. Then came the unemployment. That's when I lost my job at the factory where I worked. My mother lost her job too. The factory where she worked closed down. And my father who was a cripple from his injury began to drink."

"So now you had no income?"

"That's right."

"And were you married?"

"No, I was engaged when the country went to war for the second time."

"Is your fiancée waiting for you?"

"Who knows. I haven't heard from her in over a year. It could be the mail, or she might have given up on me." He shook his head and pulled the last puff out of the cigarette. Then he put it on the ground and smothered it with the toe of his boot.

"I'm sorry," she said sincerely.

"And, I'm sorry for what Hitler and his party have done to your people. I have heard about the ghettos and the camps and the murders of Jews. It's horrible," he said.

"How did you find out about these things?"

"You're not the first Jew I've met since I deserted my platoon. I met another one. A young fella. He told me a lot. In fact, he spoke Yiddish. That was how I recognized the language as Yiddish when you were speaking. Anyway, the things he said that the Nazis were doing to the Jews were barbaric. And I want you to know that not all the Germans agree with such treatment of the Jews. I don't."

"I am glad to hear that. It would be terrible if you did. Especially since I'm here with you in this barn."

He let out a laugh. Then she laughed too.

"So," she said boldly, "perhaps you would be willing to tell me a little bit about you? I already understand that you are a German soldier who left his platoon for moral reasons. And that you are engaged."

"I didn't leave for moral reasons alone. I wish I could say I was such a good man. But, I left because I felt that Hitler cares more about conquering the world than he does about his soldiers. So, I suppose I am a selfish man. I wasn't willing to die for a leader who didn't give a damn if my platoon was freezing and starving to death on the Russian front."

"What do you think will be the outcome of all of this? I heard that Germany is fighting two different wars. Is that true? How is such a thing possible?" Naomi said as she leaned back against the wall of the barn.

"Well, yes, sort of. Germany is fighting the Russians in the east and the British in the west. Until the winter, my troop was holding its own in Russia. But the winter knocked us out. We weren't prepared. And then, two months ago, in December, the Americans entered the war. That sealed the deal as far as I am concerned."

"What do you mean?"

"I think it's only a matter of time before Germany loses the war."

"Do you really think so? I mean, I truly hope so," she said excitedly, then she wished she hadn't sounded as gleeful as she did. *After all, he is a German, and I don't want him to get angry and leave me here in the forest alone.*

He nodded. "It's bittersweet for me. I don't want to see Hitler win. But I don't want to see Germany lose either. I know that probably doesn't make sense to you. But although I hate Hitler and everything he stands for, I still love my country."

She didn't answer. Instead, she looked away from him so he wouldn't see the joy in her face.

Outside, the snow had begun to come down heavily.

"Looks like we're in for a storm," he said. "Good thing we have shelter."

She nodded.

The wind howled, and the sound it made was like a banshee's wail, or maybe the snarl of a wild dog.

She didn't say anything, because there was nothing to say. But inside she was rejoicing at the idea that Hitler might be defeated. This was the first time she could see a light in all this darkness. *Oh, Hashem, let it be so. Please let Germany be defeated soon. But most importantly, I beg you to please watch over my family and keep them safe until we can be reunited.*

Naomi and Friedrich sat together in silence and listened to the wind. Then he said, "Before I became a soldier, I was just an average fellow trying to get by. I lived in a small town outside of Frankfurt. I met Gerda, my fiancée, at the factory where we both worked. She was a typist. A good one too. We dated for about a year before we became engaged. She was disappointed when I told her that I wanted to enlist. She wasn't enthusiastic about the idea. But she knew it meant that I wanted to better myself, and that was important to her. After all, I had lost my job. I needed an income if we were ever going to start our lives together."

"So, I am sure she is waiting for you."

"I'm not. I have to admit I heard rumors about her. People told me that before the Nazis took over in Germany, she was a bit of a wild girl, if you know what I mean."

"I'm sorry, I don't exactly."

"Well, you see, before Hitler took power, Germany was governed by the Weimar. During this time, there was a lot of promiscuous sex and drugs going around. Gerda took classes in typing and shorthand, but she really wanted to be an actress. So, she moved to Berlin for a while. From what I heard from people who knew her then, she ran with a very experimental crowd. They tried drugs of all kinds and overindulged in alcohol. And, of course, there was the rampant sex. Then when the Nazis came to power, she returned home to live with her parents and start over. I tried to ask her questions about her life when she was in Berlin, but she refused to discuss it."

"I am shocked that as a man you would agree to marry a girl who had such a past."

He laughed. "Most of the girls I knew had a pretty sordid past right after the fall of the Weimar. You must have come from a very sheltered life not to have known about all of this going on in Germany. It was quite a wild time."

"I didn't know. And yes, I grew up in a very sheltered place. I was not permitted to read books other than religious books. And certainly not newspapers. But I must admit, I was not without sin. I did some bad things in my life."

"May he who is without sin cast the first stone," Friedrich said.

"I'm sorry? What did you say?"

"I didn't say it. Jesus did. I don't follow his word as much as I should. I stopped going to church years ago, but as a boy, my mother took me to church every Sunday. My folks were Lutheran."

"I'd like to hear more about your religion," she said.

"Only if you promise to tell me about your sins," he said, smiling.

She blushed. "I can't. I'm sorry. I just can't."

"Maybe in the future when we know each other better," he said. "Do you smoke? I mean, I hate to share my cigarettes. They are so damn hard to come by, but I will share one with you if you'd like."

"Oh, no, thank you. I don't smoke."

"I'm glad to hear it. I won't have to feel like a louse not sharing my cigarettes with you."

She smiled, a sad, wry smile. "Fredrich, can I ask you a question?"

"Of course. Anything."

"Why do people hate the Jews so much?"

"The truth is, folks just need someone to blame for their misery. The Jews are always an easy target. I grew up hearing how Jews were rich and how they stole from other people to get that way."

"So, it's strange that you could see through all of this and that you don't hate Jews too."

"Me?" He pointed his thumb at himself. "Funny thing is, I don't hate anyone unless they give me a reason to hate them. And all this stuff about the Jews ruining Germany. You know what I am talking about; the stuff Goebbels and Hitler talk about all the time. I don't know that any of that is true either."

She looked at him and cocked her head. "I never read a newspaper, and I don't listen to the radio, so I have no idea what they said about Jews."

"Do you want to know?"

"Yes, I want to know everything. I want to learn," she said.

"Well, we have plenty of time. I'm no genius, and I have to admit, I haven't spent all that much time reading the papers or listening to the radio for news. But I'll tell you what I've heard and what I've read. How's that?"

"Yes, I would like that."

CHAPTER THIRTY

Ernst walked back to his desk. He sat down and leaned on the desk with his elbows, then he put his head in his hands, and he thought about Shoshana. She was so good with the children. And she was so kind to him. He wished he could do something for her. In fact, he wished he could do something for all of them. When he thought of the children that Mengele had imprisoned in his rooms awaiting his next experiment, Ernst felt sick to his stomach. He saw their young, innocent faces, wizened by what they had been forced to endure. *No child should go through what these children go through. No adult should either. I sometimes feel as if I am in hell. If I leave, I may lose my wife, but more importantly, these innocent children will lose the only person who might try to intervene with Mengele on their behalf. Even so, eventually I will be forced to go. I can only take so much.*

Outside his office, he heard two nurses; they were talking and laughing together. He wondered how they could carry on as if this place were a normal hospital. A shiver ran down his spine. *I wish I could kill Mengele. If only I had the nerve. But I am a coward; I've never killed anything in my life. He hates me because he thinks I am weak. Perhaps he's right. But if I were stronger, I would kill him, not innocent people. So, he should be glad that I don't have it in me to be violent because if I did, he would be dead already.*

It was lunchtime, but Ernst had no appetite. He couldn't stop thinking about the boy that Mengele had given typhus. In his mind's eye, he could see the boy and his twin brother. In his heart, he could feel their pain, and he wished that he could run away from his thoughts. Mengele had gone to see the child earlier that day, to administer his experimental cure. But it came as no surprise to Ernst that the cure had no effect on the disease. *When I overheard him and Otto discussing the fact that Mengele's attempt at a cure failed, Mengele just laughed. The man is less than human. And now that young boy is dying. And for what reason? A perfectly healthy boy is now dying. This whole hospital is a travesty. In fact, this entire camp should not exist. It is here for the sole purpose of killing innocent people. How did I ever get involved in this?*

The air itself seemed too close, like a living thing pressing against his face. It had a sharp, musty scent. Outside his office window, Ernst watched the ashes falling like snowflakes. *A transport came in yesterday. I know Otto and Mengele did the selections. And now, the ashes of the burned bodies cover the ground. It's like a nightmare, except it's real.*

Mengele walked by Ernst's office and knocked on the door. Before Ernst had a chance to tell him to come in, Mengele had already entered.

"Heil Hitler," Mengele said.

Ernst went through the motions of standing up and saluting, "Heil Hitler."

"So, I wonder where Otto has gone off to this afternoon. He made up some story about his mother being ill. I don't believe him, do you?" Mengele said, smiling that wicked smile again.

"Yes, I believe him. He has no reason to lie," Ernst said.

Mengele had a twinkle in his eye when he said, "I am not sure if he does, or he doesn't. However . . ." He hesitated for effect, then continued. "Otto did mention something rather odd to me before he left."

"Oh?" Ernst said, a little annoyed. *He's playing some sort of cruel game. I can feel it. I just don't know what it is yet.*

"Yes, in fact, he asked me not to tell you what he said. However, I think it's only right that you should know."

Now Ernst was a little curious. *What would Otto be hiding about his mother?* "What is it?"

"It's rather odd, actually. But I found it interesting. He asked me if I was willing to meet with your wife. Apparently, she has something to speak to me about. I can't fathom what it could be, can you? And why would she contact Otto? I would think that if she wanted to speak to me, she would go through you. Do you have any idea what is going on here?" Dr. Mengele sat back in his chair and looked directly at Ernst.

At the mention of Gisele, Ernst sat up and looked at Mengele nervously. He hadn't heard anything about her wanting to speak to Dr. Mengele alone. And he was wondering how and why she would contact Otto. The very idea of Gisele and Otto talking together behind his back unnerved Ernst. "Actually, I don't know anything about this," Ernst said, his heart in his throat as he looked at Mengele. Mengele's voice was sympathetic, but his eyes were twinkling with delight. *He knows that he is hurting and worrying me, and he is enjoying it,* Ernst thought.

"Well, we will have to see exactly what Otto has in store now, won't we? If I were you, I would keep that wife of yours on a very tight leash. After all, Otto is a handsome man, and he is the type that women fall for. Just a friendly suggestion."

"Thank you," Ernst said. "I'll keep it in mind. But I trust my wife," he lied. *I wish I did.*

"Oh yes, I almost forgot to tell you this, but I do have some rather disappointing news," Mengele said, his voice almost mocking now. "The red-haired boy with the typhus . . ."

"Yes." Ernst nodded.

"He died this morning. So, the cure I have been working on was ineffective. But no need to feel disheartened. I have another one. So, I am planning to use another set of twins to try it out," Mengele said calmly.

Ernst felt dizzy but he held back the urge to vomit. *That boy is dead. At least his suffering is over,* he thought. *And now, I have to hope he isn't going to use Shoshana's twin sisters next. But I dare not let him know that I care about those girls, or he will definitely use them.* Ernst didn't say anything because he was afraid his tone of voice, or his expression, might betray his fears about Bluma and Perle or his feelings of disgust. Instead, he turned away and gazed out the window.

The ashes were still falling. That meant the crematoriums were still burning bodies.

"So, if you're not busy, I'd like you to come with me to the twins' room so we can tell the red-haired twin that is still alive, that his brother is dead," Mengele said. "After we've finished there, perhaps we can go out and have a beer and some lunch. I'd like to discuss this situation between Otto and your exceptionally beautiful wife." Mengele stood up.

Ernst got out of his chair. His legs felt like rubber. With a heavy heart, he walked beside Mengele toward the twins' room. When they arrived, Mengele turned to Ernst and said, "Having a beautiful wife is a joy, but it's also a burden. Men will always be trying to undermine you. And, quite frankly, with your looks, you're in for a very difficult time, my boy."

Before Ernst could say a word, Mengele had opened the door to the twins' room. They entered. All of the prisoners inside grew quiet when they saw Mengele. Ernst's eyes darted around the room as he searched for Shoshana and her sisters. They were sitting on Shoshana's cot. For a second, a very brief second, his eyes met hers. Ernst looked away quickly, not wanting Mengele to notice the connection between Shoshana and himself.

"Come here, all of you, and greet your Uncle Mengele. I have candy for you," Mengele said, his arms stretched open.

The children gathered around Mengele. He reached into his pocket and pulled out pieces of candy which he distributed to them.

The children were laughing and giddy as they ate the much-coveted sugar. Once they'd all received and eaten their candy, Mengele said, "Now, quiet down. I have some sad news I must share with all of you."

The room grew silent. Ernst saw that Mengele's gaze was fixed on the red-haired twin. "I am afraid the young red-haired boy became ill the other day with typhus. I'm sorry to have to tell you that he died."

"No," the red-haired twin yelled out. "No. It can't be. It can't be. My brother was fine. He wasn't sick. You did this. You and Dr. Otto. You gave him a shot of some kind. Don't you remember? I saw you do it. And now he's dead. My brother is dead."

"I'm sorry. I truly am. But the injection we gave him had nothing to do with typhus," Mengele said, smiling. It was that sadistic smile Ernst had come to recognize. He shuddered as he watched Mengele enjoying the boy's pain at losing his brother. "We don't know how he contracted the disease. But as all of you know, typhus is rather common in the camp."

The red-haired boy threw himself down on his cot and wept.

Mengele turned to Ernst and said, "Let's go. We're done here for now."

Ernst followed Mengele, but as he was leaving, he caught a glimpse of Shoshana. She was crying. She looked at him for a second, then turned away. Ernst thought he saw disgust and hatred in her eyes. He wished he could go to her and tell her that he had not wanted this to happen. He had been against it from the start. In fact, he wanted to say if it weren't for him, Mengele would have used her sisters for this experiment. And now one of her sisters would be dead. But he said nothing. Instead, he followed Mengele out of the room. Once they were outside and the door to the twins' room was closed and locked, Mengele walked up to the nearest guard. "Heil Hitler," he said cheerfully.

"Heil Hitler," the guard replied.

Then Mengele sighed and shook his head. "It seems we must

send that red-haired boy in the twins' room to the gas. Do it as soon as possible. His brother died. And now he's weeping. I am afraid that he is just upsetting the others. The best thing to do is to dispose of him."

"Of course, Dr. Mengele," the guard said. "I'll take care of it right away."

"And don't tell the others where he is going. If they ask, just say that since he is no longer a twin, he is not going to be in the twins' room anymore."

The guard nodded.

Ernst trembled. *Mengele decides who lives and who dies. And now two boys are dead and for no reason. So many people die in this place every day. Every day.*

"You don't look well," Mengele said to Ernst. "You're rather pale."

"I'm not feeling well," Ernst said. "Would you mind if we rescheduled our lunch date?"

"Of course not," Mengele said, smiling that same wicked smile, then he hurried away, leaving Ernst standing in the hall alone with his thoughts.

CHAPTER THIRTY-ONE

♊

Gisele was trembling as her eyes met the eyes of Marcel Petoit. He looked exactly the same. His wild, wavy dark hair was pushed back from his face, and he was smiling broadly. It was hard to believe he was real. *How did he find me?* she thought. *I can just imagine how many people he has murdered by now. It would be so easy for him to kill me.* Petoit lifted his beer mug and toasted her. She felt cold all over. The hair on the back of her neck stood up. *I am in danger,* she thought. *I must get out of here. I must get away from him. He won't try to do anything to me with Otto around. Otto is too big and muscular. Petoit would be afraid of him.* She turned and ran back to the table. She could hear Petoit laughing like a madman behind her.

"Please, can we go?" she said.

"What is it? Are you ill?" Otto asked.

"No, I just want to leave. Now."

"Of course," Otto said. He stood up and helped Gisele with her coat. He put several reichsmarks down on the table and then, linking his arm under hers, he led her out of the restaurant.

Gisele looked behind her. Petoit was no longer sitting at the table where she'd seen him. Her eyes scanned the restaurant. He was nowhere to be found. But she knew him, and she knew he was following her, hunting her like a predator. She had seen him kill before. The man was not human; she was certain of it. He'd murdered young children without any remorse. And now he'd disappeared from that restaurant like a ghost. *I can't go home. He'll follow me, and then he and I would be alone in my apartment. But I dare not bring Otto to my apartment with me, just in case Ernst comes home early from work. I am going to have to go to Otto's apartment. I'll be safe there.* "Can we go to your flat?" she asked.

"Of course we can. In fact, I'd love that," Otto said, smiling.

With Otto's strong arm around her waist, Gisele felt safe. They walked to the bus stop and waited. Otto was making light conversation. But Gisele wasn't listening. Her senses were on high alert. She was watching, listening, and waiting in case something might happen.

"What is it? You aren't yourself," Otto said. "Something is wrong. I can tell. Did you see Ernst at the restaurant or outside?"

"No, it's not Ernst. It's something else. Someone else. A man who is planning to do me harm. But I can't talk about it here in the street. I'll tell you when we get to your flat," she said.

"All right. But you needn't be afraid. I am here with you. And no matter what happens, I will protect you," he said.

They rode the bus in silence. He held her hand and every so often he squeezed it. "Don't you worry. Everything is going to be just fine. I'm here, and I promise to protect you," he said softly into her ear. She forgot about Ernst being her husband, and as the rickety old bus navigated its way down the snow-filled street, she began to wonder what it would be like to be married to Otto.

She let herself believe that Otto had the power to protect her from anyone and anything. Feeling safe and sheltered, she lay her head on Otto's shoulder. Even though she was fearful of Marcel Petoit, the feel of Otto sitting so close to her set her on fire. When she looked up into his handsome face, she felt overcome with desire. *How can I be feeling all these wonderful things toward Otto even though I am horrified at seeing Petoit today? It makes no sense. I should be thinking about a way to escape from Petoit. Yet, I can't even focus on him. All of my thoughts are of Otto. He is like a drug to me. I am lost in his strong arms and the depth of his eyes. I have never felt this way toward any man before. And the fact that I can feel safe when I am with Otto only makes him even more appealing.*

The bus smelled of sweat, garlic, and sauerkraut. Gisele found the odor nauseating. *At least it's cold outside. The smell would be worse if it were the middle of summer.*

They arrived at their stop. Otto helped Gisele down the stairs of the bus.

His strong arm was around her shoulder, and she felt like she was wrapped in a cocoon of his warmth and safety. Her body was pressed against his, her breath fluttering against his coat. She burned and tingled where his arm touched the skin on her neck.

Together, wrapped up in each other, they walked two streets until they came to a tall building. "This is it," he said. "This is where I live."

She smiled. He took out his key and opened the door. She followed him inside. The door closed behind her, and she felt an overwhelming sense of relief. For the moment, no one—not Petoit, not Ernst, not the Gestapo—no one could get to her. But even so, her body still trembled with a mixture of emotions, fear, relief, and desire. Otto took her into his arms. A shiver ran down her spine. His eyes locked with hers, and she felt herself vanish into him. Gisele no longer felt like a single human being; it seemed that she had melded into Otto, and without him she would never be whole again. His lips tasted faintly of mint and honey, and in that moment, Gisele felt something stir inside her. He carried her to his bed, and slowly, he made love to her. It was like she'd never made love before. Everything felt new. In his arms, it was as if she were floating. As if they were floating together. Although she felt it only in her mind, she was bound to him. If she let go, she might fall. And so she could no longer separate herself from him.

He played her body as if he were a master of music and she a fine violin. But after he finished, he turned away from her and faced the wall. Gisele didn't understand why, but she felt abandoned. He was suddenly cold. And at that moment, she knew that this was nothing more than sex for him. She had been falling in love, but he didn't love her. She could feel it somehow. Trying to believe that she might be wrong, she reached over and rubbed his back. He pulled away. There was a part of him that was unreachable. The sex had enhanced her desire for him, but it had snuffed out his desire for her. She reached for him again and rubbed his neck, but again he pulled away. Otto was closed emotionally.

"Was it all right for you?" she asked tentatively, almost afraid of his answer.

"It was quite wonderful," he said, but his tone of voice was disinterested, cold, not caring.

"Are you sure?" she pressed, hoping he would say something warm and loving.

"I am quite sure. You are a beautiful woman, and you are a wonderful lover." He smiled, then he got out of bed and walked into his living room, leaving her lying there naked on his bed. Naked and alone.

Oh, he is charming. He says the right things. He called me beautiful and said that I am a wonderful lover, she thought, but because she had the instinct of a woman in love, she knew he was not feeling the same things she was feeling. *I know I should not have expected more than just sex. But I did. I really did. I was starting to see myself divorcing Ernst and marrying Otto. I feel like a fool.* Her heart was breaking. She felt lost and rejected. *I should get up and get dressed. I should go home. But what about Petoit? I am afraid of Petoit. And what about Otto? I can't just walk out of here as if this meant nothing to me. I love him. I can't just walk away. What can I do to make him want me again?* Gisele got up and wrapped the sheet around her. Then she walked into the living room where Otto was sipping a whiskey and smoking a cigarette. "Would you like a smoke or a drink?" he asked.

"Yes, that would be lovely."

He stood up and poured her a glass of whiskey and handed her a cigarette. She didn't smoke. But she wanted him to think she was sophisticated, so she allowed him to light it for her. When she inhaled, she began to cough, but instead of rushing to ask her if she was all right, Otto just laughed.

"You don't smoke, I take it?"

She shook her head.

"Don't start. It's an expensive habit," he said.

She nodded. "I don't like it much."

A few silent, awkward moments passed, then Otto said, "Well, it's late. I am tired." He yawned and then smiled. "You should probably be on your way home. Ernst will be getting off work soon."

"But what about Petoit?" she asked.

"Who?"

"Don't you remember I told you that a man was following me? His name is Marcel Petoit. You said you would protect me?"

"Oh yes, I suppose I do remember. However, I wouldn't worry too much about him. It's still light outside, and I highly doubt he would do anything to you on a crowded bus."

"Do you want to know all about it? I said I would tell you once we were alone," Gisele said.

"No, not necessary. You'll be all right. Just take the bus and go on home, so you can get there before your husband does."

She wanted to cry. It was as if he was not the same man she'd had lunch with a few hours ago. That man had been attentive and kind. This one was cold and cruel. Yet the more distant he became, the more she wanted him to love her.

"I'll go," she said, trying to hide the hurt in her voice. "But, I hope you intend to keep your promise about arranging a meeting for me with Dr. Mengele."

"Of course I intend to keep my promise. What kind of man do you think I am?"

"A cad," she said simply. She hadn't wanted to say it, but the word just slipped out of her mouth.

He laughed heartily. "Yes, that's what all the girls say," he said.

"Bastard," she whispered under her breath. "So, you'll call me to tell me when you've arranged for me to meet with Dr. Mengele?"

"Of course I'll call you, luv," he said. "And perhaps we can even make another lunch date. Would you like that?"

Her heart leapt with hope, and she hated herself for how vulnerable he made her feel. But she couldn't deny it. She wanted to see him again. "Yes," she said in a small voice. "I would like that."

"I knew you would." He winked.

CHAPTER THIRTY-TWO

♊

Ernst was already at home when Gisele arrived at their apartment. When he heard her key in the door, he felt sick. He was pretty sure that he knew where she'd been, but he didn't know how to talk about it with her. When she walked in, her hair was messed up and her silk stocking twisted. Her eyes were sad. He studied her for a moment, and he could see all of the signs. His beautiful, precious wife had been with Otto. And she'd made love with him.

"I'm sorry I'm late," she said without looking at him. Gisele began talking fast, much faster than usual, and he knew she was lying. "I was shopping, and I got carried away. I was trying on dresses. You know how much I enjoy that. Then"—she laughed a little—"well, I missed my bus."

He nodded. *How I wish it were true*, he thought sadly.

"I stopped on my way home and picked up some food for dinner. I'm sure you're probably hungry."

Ernst didn't feel much like eating. But he said, "Yes, I am hungry. So, I'll set the table."

"Thank you so much. Let me wash up, and I'll be right back." She walked quickly to the bathroom. He watched her go and felt a deep emptiness growing inside of him as if he knew he had already lost her.

They sat across from each other. Ernst pushed the food around on his plate as he observed the subtle way Gisele avoided his gaze. It made his heart ache. *This marriage is over. It's only a matter of time now. I've lost her*, he thought. There was so much he wanted to know but didn't ask her any questions. In fact, they ate in silence. She gobbled her bread and cheese, and once she'd finished, she said, "You haven't eaten. Didn't you like it?"

"I had a big lunch," he lied. Then he stood up and began to carry the dishes to the sink to be washed.

Ernst didn't try to make love to Gisele that night. He wanted to hold her and tell her how much she meant to him. He yearned to make love to her, to somehow win her back. But he knew deep inside that it was futile. So he leaned over and gave her a soft kiss. "Good night," he whispered. "Sleep well."

"Yes, good night," she answered in a shaky voice.

She turned away from him and faced the wall. He felt hot tears forming in the corners of his eyes. Ernst hoped and prayed that somehow, Gisele would have a change of heart. He wished that by some miracle she would turn toward him and tell him she loved him. If she had just told him the truth about Otto and asked for his forgiveness, he would have granted it willingly. But she didn't. Soon she was breathing softly and deeply, and he knew she had fallen asleep. But Ernst couldn't sleep; he lay awake the entire night.

CHAPTER THIRTY-THREE

♊

Gisele found herself thinking about Otto constantly. First she was angry, then she was hurt. He'd used her and thrown her away like a dirty rag. She cursed him, and yet she still found herself waiting by the phone for a call from him. Days passed without a call from Otto. Gisele couldn't understand it, but the more he avoided her, the more she wanted him. She became so obsessed with thoughts of him that she pushed her fears and worries concerning Petoit to the back of her mind.

As far as Dr. Mengele was concerned, she decided that she could have asked Ernst to arrange the meeting with Dr. Mengele, so she could talk to him about her mother. It didn't matter to her anymore if Ernst thought that Dr. Mengele was the only reason she'd married him. At this point she didn't care what Ernst thought. In fact, she was so fixated on Otto that she wasn't thinking straight. Besides, she was certain that no matter what she did, Ernst would always forgive her. She felt sorry for him because he loved her so much. His puppy-dog love for her was written all over him. She'd always pitied Ernst, but since she'd met Otto she understood him better. Because now, she, too, knew how it felt to love someone and not have that love returned. She found herself biting her nails and twisting her hair so hard until she broke off several strands.

Gisele hardly left the apartment these days. She was glued to the phone, waiting anxiously for it to ring. However, once a week, she had to go to the market to purchase food, and when she did, she had to remind herself to keep watch behind her to make sure Petoit wasn't lurking in the shadows. All of this stress was taking its toll on Gisele. Her lovely peaches-and-cream complexion had broken out in an ugly red rash that stretched from her chin all the way down to her collarbone. The lovely golden locks which she had always worn in curls around her face now hung limp and greasy. *I am falling apart. These feelings I have for Otto are destroying me,* she thought sarcastically. *Well, if Petoit wants to see me dead, he doesn't have to kill me. All he has to do is keep watching. I am dying a little more every day.*

Gisele no longer went out even to the dress shops, which had always been her favorite pastime. Finally, she couldn't bear it anymore, and she went downstairs and out to the store to purchase a package of cigarettes. She didn't smoke. In fact, when she tried it with Otto, it had hurt her throat. However, everyone who she knew that smoked said that smoking calmed their nerves. And she was desperate to find something to calm herself. At first, the hot smoke made her cough until she felt like her lungs were going to come up through her throat. Then she felt nauseated and vomited. But a few hours later, she tried again. She lit a cigarette, and finally smoking had the desired effect. She felt a little calmer. But she still spent hours staring at the phone. And still, Otto did not call. She didn't have a number to reach him at work. So she decided she would go to see him at his flat.

When he returned home from work, she planned to be there waiting for him. *He promised to arrange this meeting with Dr. Mengele. It's the least he can do for me. He is treating me like a pariah. How dare he treat me this way. I'll show him. When he sees me again, I'll make him want me again. I will look my best. I'll be coy, just like the girls at the brothel. He will want me. I know this will work.* She was young, and her youth made her enthusiastic. A strategy began forming in her mind, and the very idea that she had a plan that could win him back made her feel hopeful and giddy. *I know how men are. They can't control themselves around beautiful women. So I must tend to my looks and make myself gorgeous again. And this time I won't give him what he wants right away. I won't let him bed me. I'll make him wait. I'll make him fall in love with me first.* She smiled to herself. It was the first time she had smiled since that afternoon she'd had lunch with Otto.

With newly found enthusiasm, Gisele took a shower and washed her hair with the special shampoo she'd brought with her from France. This perfumed shampoo was a luxury that she saved for special occasions. When she opened the bottle, the fragrance made her feel like she was surrounded by a garden of roses. Closing her eyes, she inhaled the scent. It was sexy and it was sensual, and it made her feel beautiful. She poured a small amount into her hair and lathered it up. The suds ran down her body as she massaged her breasts and thought of Otto. *He will want me. I know it.* Allowing the warm water to rinse the shampoo out of her long locks, she felt her old confidence returning. Once her hair was clean and soap free, she got out of the shower. Next, she sat down at the dressing table Ernst had given her and began to set her hair in pin curls. It would take a few hours to dry, but that was all right because she had plenty of time before Otto would be home from work. *My hair is so shiny. I know once it's curled and dry, it will be stunning. I am certain of it,* she thought as she wound each curl around her finger then secured it with a pin.

Once her hair was dry, she planned to carefully apply her makeup until her eyes were dark and sultry, her lips as red as blood, and her cheeks no longer pale. Then she would walk to the bus stop to catch the bus that would take her to Otto's flat. She was so wrapped up in her plan that she forgot to remind herself to watch for Petoit.

CHAPTER THIRTY-FOUR

The following day, Shoshana noticed that Ernst looked very sad when he came to make his morning rounds. His eyes were surrounded by dark circles. It looked as if he hadn't slept. His hair was greasy and unwashed, and his clothes were wrinkled.

"Good morning," Ernst said, his voice soft and sad as he prepared to do his required blood draws from Perle and Bluma.

"I hate these needles," Bluma complained. She wrapped her arms around her chest.

"But at least Dr. Neider is gentle," Shoshana said.

"Yes, that's true. Dr. Mengele and Dr. Otto are rough. It's like they want to hurt us," Bluma said.

"She's right. Dr. Otto and Uncle Mengele always hurt us," Perle said.

"I'm sorry that they do," Ernst said sincerely. He gazed at the two little girls who sat side by side on the small cot in front of him, and his heart hurt for them. *It is very likely that they will never marry, never have children, or live to see old age. They will probably never taste another steak dinner or go to see a film or a ballet. Chances are they will die young, never facing adulthood. They will be children forever.*

Perle reached out her hand and placed it softly on Ernst's wrist. "You're crying, Dr. Neider," she said.

He hadn't realized it, but he was crying. Quickly, he wiped the tears from his cheeks with the back of his hand. "Oh, no, I'm not crying," he said gently. "It's just the cold air. Sometimes my eyes tear up from the cold."

"You were crying," Perle said. Then she looked directly at him. Although she was only eight years old, she had the eyes of an old sage. "It's all right to cry when you are feeling sad. Are you sad?"

He was sad. He was sad for so many reasons. And even though he'd tried to hide it, this small child saw right through him. Ernst couldn't lie to her. "Yes, I am," he said. "I am very sad."

"For us?"

"Yes, for you. For all of you. I would change things if it were in my power. But I am no one here at Auschwitz. I am powerless." Then in a small voice, he added, "And I am sad for me too."

"You don't have any good reason to feel sad. You are a German, not a Jew," Bluma said boldly. "If you were a Jew, you would have a good reason."

"Quiet. That is not nice. Dr. Neider is always kind to you girls," Shoshana said. "He isn't like the others."

"That's right, he isn't. He is different than the others, and that's why I know I can tell him how I really feel. I would never say these things to Dr. Mengele or to Dr. Otto," Bluma said.

"But you shouldn't punish Dr. Neider for what the Nazis are doing to us. It's not his fault," Perle said.

"But even though he is nice, he is still one of them," Bluma said.

"Well, Bluma, to some extent you are correct," Ernst said. "It's true. I am a German. And I wear the symbol of the Nazi Party. But believe me, little girl. I don't agree with the Nazi doctrine."

"Then why do you follow them? Why do you wear their uniform

and say 'Heil Hitler'? Why do you do it if you don't agree with it?" Bluma asked.

"I'm sorry. My sister talks too much. She asks too many questions. Please forgive her. It is very kind of you not to punish her for being so outspoken," Shoshana said, giving Bluma a reprimanding look. Shoshana's hands were shaking. She folded them to keep them still.

"You don't have to be afraid of me," Ernst said. "I don't believe in punishing children for speaking the truth." Gently, he drew blood from each of the twins. Then he turned to look at Shoshana. She was beautiful. Not in the same way that Gisele was beautiful. Gisele was wild, sexy, and exhilarating, like climbing to the top of a mountain on a crisp, clear day. Dangerous and breathtaking. While Shoshana's beauty was warm, glowing, and beckoning. It was deep and comforting, like a roaring fireplace on a cold winter night.

Shoshana studied Ernst for a moment. Then in a soft voice, she said, "You really are not like the others."

"No, I promise you, I am not," he said, "but I am working with Dr. Mengele, and your sister is right: I should probably leave here and find a job as a real doctor. However, if I go, I can't be of help to anyone, not to you or your sisters. As long as I am working here at Auschwitz, I can try my best to do some good whenever I can."

She looked into his eyes. *He's so sincere, I wonder why he ever accepted this job in the first place.*

It was as if he'd read her mind. He gave her a sad smile and then gazed out the window. "After I graduated from medical school, I joined the army. I didn't know what the Nazis stood for. I only knew that I wanted to help the wounded men at the front. That was how I met Mengele. He was wounded. I helped him. Then, I was wounded and forced to leave the army. I returned to Berlin and got a job, but soon Dr. Mengele contacted me. He said he wanted to help me, because I had saved his life. That was when he offered me this position. I took it not knowing anything about Auschwitz. I was flattered —honored, in fact. I never expected to work with a famous doctor.

But then"—he sighed—"I arrived here at Auschwitz, and when I saw what was happening . . . well, I knew I had made a mistake. I thought of quitting.

"I am ashamed to admit it, but the money was very good, and I didn't come from a rich family. When Mengele saw that I was struggling with the ethics of working in a place like this, he told me to take some time off. He said I needed a holiday. I was glad to get out of here. I went home to Germany, not to where I was born, but to Berlin where I had attended the university. That's when I met Gisele, my wife. She was so pretty, far too pretty for a man like me. And she was so impressed with my job that I felt that if I wanted to keep her interest, I had to stay here and continue working with Dr. Mengele," Ernst said, his shoulders slumping, and his head hanging down.

Shoshana gasped. "Has she ever been here to Auschwitz? Does she know what goes on here?"

"She doesn't know." He shook his head. "I'm glad she doesn't know. I would be so ashamed."

"But I believe you told me that she's met Dr. Mengele and Dr. Otto?"

"Yes, actually, she has. But, Mengele is charming when he is out in public, so she has no idea that he's a monster here at work. And . . . to make matters worse, I believe I am losing Gisele anyway. She seems to be very taken with Dr. Otto."

"Oh." Shoshana gasped. "I don't know what to say."

"It's all right. There's nothing to say. I am an unattractive man. Not to mention that I am clumsy and awkward. While Otto is handsome in that special Aryan way. Blond, blue eyed, strong bone structure, athletic. He is everything I am not. I can't blame her." *Shoshana is so easy to talk to. She is so warm and kind. I have never met a girl who I feel so comfortable with.*

"I blame her. I think she is wrong. How can she find another man attractive when she is your wife?"

"Marriage is just a piece of paper."

"Do you really believe that?"

"I do." He sighed sadly. "Gisele is attracted to Otto. She can't help herself."

"You forgive her, don't you?"

"I do. I understand her too."

"Well, I don't understand her at all. In fact, can I be so bold as to say that, if you were my husband, I would be proud of you. I would be proud that you aren't cruel like these other Nazis. I would be happy to tell people that you actually want to practice real medicine. And . . . I don't think you're awkward or ugly."

He smiled at her. *Shoshana is such a special young woman. I don't know what I can do for her, how I can help her, but I must find a way.*

CHAPTER THIRTY-FIVE

Ⅱ

O tto had just returned home from work when he walked into the lobby of his apartment building to find Gisele waiting for him. He groaned. "What are you doing here? I'm a bit tired, and not in the mood for company."

"I'm sure you feel that way," Gisele said, but she was hurt. Then she wrapped her arms around her chest and in a bold voice filled with false confidence, she said, "However, you did make a promise to me. You do remember, I am sure. Now, I must see Dr. Mengele. You said you would arrange it."

"And if I don't?"

"You are a bastard, aren't you?" she said angrily. "Why would you make a promise you had no intentions of keeping?"

"I have to go. I don't feel up to discussing this with you right now. I'm exhausted. Go home to your husband. That's where you belong. Now, good night," he said as he turned to walk up the stairs.

Gisele reached up and grabbed his arm. "Otto, you used me. You toyed with my feelings."

"Don't be such a child. We had fun. Now it's over."

"And you refuse to keep your promise."

"Didn't your mother ever tell you that a man will promise you anything when he wants to get you into his bed?"

"So, I was a conquest?" she shrieked. "That's all I was to you?"

"Call it what you like." He tried to pull free of her grasp on his jacket, but she held on tightly.

"You put my marriage in jeopardy for your own pleasure. You really are a bastard."

"I didn't jeopardize your marriage, Gisele. You did. You could always have said no. But you fell right into my bed. Admit it; you wanted it as much as I did," Otto said, then he pried her fingers off his sleeve and walked up the stairs. She stood watching him, tears falling down her cheeks. Her fists clenched with anger. She ripped at her hair. She bit down on her hand until it hurt. "You bastard. You dirty bastard," she yelled, but he didn't hear her. He was already inside his apartment.

CHAPTER THIRTY-SIX

♊

Gisele hated Otto. She hated him so much that she wished she could kill him. All the way home on the bus she thought of ways she would like to torture him. But by the time she arrived at her own apartment building, she was crying again. *I think I might be in love with him,* she thought. *Because I can't get him out of my mind. I want him so badly. I want him to want me again the way he did.* As she fumbled through her handbag for her keys, she broke one of her fingernails. Frustrated, she sank down onto the stoop and put her head in her hands.

"Gisele," the voice said in a whisper. "Gisele." *Did I hear that, or did I imagine it?* She felt a chill run through her. "Gisele," the man said again. *I know that voice.* She felt her heart race. She looked around, but she saw no one. Then she began to run.

CHAPTER THIRTY-SEVEN

♊

In the morning when he awoke the following day, Ernst found himself looking forward to seeing Shoshana. She was sitting on the twin's cot when he entered the room. He smiled at her. She returned his smile, but her lips trembled. They always did. He knew she was still afraid of him. He wished he could somehow change that. But as he approached her, he saw her face light up, and his heart melted. *I wish I didn't have to keep sticking these healthy children with needles every day. I know it's painful for them to have their blood drawn. And there is no reason for it. But even so, I find that I am certainly glad to see Shoshana. She's even prettier when she smiles.*

"Good morning, girls," Ernst said to Shoshana and her sisters.

"Good morning," Perle and Shoshana said, but Bluma just looked away.

Ernst didn't say anything to reprimand Bluma. He felt sorry for her, but he hoped she remembered to hide her defiant attitude when she was around Mengele and Otto because they would not treat her as kindly. He sighed as he began to take his syringes out of his bag and lay them out on the table. Then as he looked at the syringes he made a decision. "How would you girls like it if I didn't draw your blood today?"

"I would like it a lot," Bluma said.

"Me too," Perle admitted softly.

"Then I won't. But it will have to be our secret. If either Dr. Mengele or Dr. Otto ask if you had your blood drawn this morning, you must say yes. Can you do that?"

"Yes, of course," Bluma said.

But Perle eyed him skeptically. "Won't they see that you don't have our blood for today?"

"Don't you worry about that. You leave that up to me," he said. "And by the way, I brought you some paper and pencils to draw with. And, I also brought a children's book that I think you might enjoy. Your sister can read it to you. However, you must be sure to hide these things when any staff come in here. Make sure Dr. Mengele and Dr. Otto never see them."

"I'll make sure that no one ever finds these things," Shoshana said. "That was very kind of you."

He smiled. "I wish I could do more."

"I believe you," she said. Then she said to her sisters, "Why don't you two go and draw some pictures while I speak to Dr. Neider."

They walked to the end of the room and sat on the floor with the pencils and paper. When they were gone, Ernst said, "Thank you for talking to me yesterday. I was feeling rather sorry for myself. And you made me feel better."

She smiled, but then her face cracked, and tears began to flow down her cheeks. For a moment, neither of them said anything. "I'm so sorry. I'm so sorry. I can't help myself. I didn't mean to . . ." Shoshana whispered.

"It's all right. I understand."

"It's just that I am scared. I am terrified for my sisters and for myself. I don't know what's become of our parents or what's become of my friend Ruth. I think she may be dead. I don't know for sure. But what I do know is that our lives are so uncertain. I am afraid all the time."

"I know, and that's why I am going to do what I can to help you." He was moved by her tears. Without thinking of the consequences, forgetting for a moment that she was a Jew and he was an Aryan doctor and that this was forbidden, he reached up and gently touched her cheek. "I promise you. I will try to do what I can."

"Dr. Neider," she said, then hesitated for a moment. "Can you find out if Ruth is alive?"

"Give me her name, and I'll see what I can do," he said, handing her a pen and paper.

Shoshana wrote down Ruth's name and handed it back to him.

Ernst stood up to leave. But as he did, he caught the eyes of the other young prisoners in the room. They were all looking directly at him wide eyed and wondering. As he gazed about and met the wondering stares of the children, he could see they were terrified of him. And it made him feel bad. *This was not what I went to medical school for. I went to become a doctor. A healer, not a sadist who uses medicine as a way to torture children.* He bowed his head and looked away from them.

"I'll see you tomorrow," Ernst said to Shoshana who was watching him intently. Then he slowly walked out of the room and closed the door behind him. His hands trembled as he turned the key in the lock. *I've locked them in, imprisoned them because Mengele demands that I do. What kind of man am I to willingly do Mengele's bidding?* Ernst thought as he walked toward his office. He dropped the blood samples he'd taken from the other children off at the lab, then he quickly went to his office and locked the door. Once he was alone, he sat down in his chair then pulled a syringe and tourniquet out of his bag. He tied the tourniquet around his forearm. Then with a needle, he drew blood from his own arm. He filled the tubes and then marked them with the same numbers that were tattooed on Perle's and Bluma's arms. He knew Mengele never checked the blood. So he would never know that this was not the children's blood. Quickly, he took the vials and went back to the lab where he placed them in the container with the others. Then he returned to his office and collapsed into his chair. No one had seen him, and no one knew what he'd done.

Leaning back in the chair, he thought about Shoshana and her sisters. She'd admitted to him that she was afraid, and that made him long to protect her. The fact that she had been so open with him brought out hero qualities in him that he never knew existed. *She sees me as a human being. She knows I am different than Otto or Mengele*, he thought. *I will not disappoint her. I must find a way to help her and her sisters.*

CHAPTER THIRTY-EIGHT

♊

S hoshana took the book that Ernst had brought for them out from under her pillow. "Would you like me to read to you?" she asked Perle and Bluma.

"Yes, please," Bluma said.

But Perle ignored Shoshana's question. Instead, she smiled. "He likes you," Perle said. "I can tell."

"What are you talking about?" Shoshana asked.

"Dr. Neider. He's different than Dr. Otto or Dr. Mengele. He's more like a Jew. But you already know that, don't you?"

"I don't think he's different," Bluma said. "I think he is just like the rest of them. The only difference is that he likes Shoshana, so he's nice to us. But I think he's a Nazi all the same. And I hate them all."

Shoshana shrugged. "I don't know what to think," she said. "All I know is that he is kind to us. He brought you some things to do. And you both have to admit that you were getting bored. So, this book and the paper and pencils will help."

"Do you think he can keep the Nazis from killing us?" Bluma asked.

It broke Shoshana's heart to hear her sister, who was so young and should be far more innocent than she was, say those words as if it were natural for her to expect to die. But then again, how could she not expect it. Death was all around her. *Bluma and Perle are just children, but they have already seen things that no child should ever see, no person should ever see. They've lost their parents. We are hopeful that it's not true, but we strongly suspect they may be dead. And we are afraid Ruth is dead too.*

My poor sisters watched that young, red-haired twin boy suffer after losing his brother. And we are all unnerved by the piles of dead bodies right outside our window. Everyone here says that the smell and the ashes from the crematorium are from the burning of bodies. This place is so horrible, it hardly seems real. My sisters are so young and because they are, they seem to accept that this is a way of life. It's not fair. They should be playing and singing and eating good food like the soup our mama used to make. Instead, we are grateful that because we are Mengele's chosen, we have a little more to eat than the others here at the camp. But the food is not decent. There are insects in it, and it's not nourishing. Hashem, if you are here and you can hear me, help us, please.

Shoshana could not answer Bluma's question. She did not know the answer. So she just pulled her sister into a hug and held her tightly.

CHAPTER THIRTY-NINE

Ⅱ

When Ernst arrived at home after work, the apartment was dark. He thought perhaps Gisele was in the bedroom taking a nap. So he walked quietly to the bedroom and looked at the bed. It was empty, still neatly made. He turned on the lights. The apartment was empty. Then he walked to the kitchen and found that nothing had been prepared for dinner. His heart sank. *She must be with Otto. In the past, Gisele would have prepared food for us; now she no longer cares.* He sighed. *I assume she will be home late. I know Otto left work at the same time I did, so he should be getting home about now. Or perhaps they are meeting somewhere for dinner. I know I should speak to her and tell her what I know about her and Otto, but once I tell her, there is no going back, and that will be the beginning of the end for us. Then she will feel free to tell me what I already know: that she no longer loves me, and she wants a divorce so that she can be with him. I don't know if I can bear that.* He poured himself a glass of whiskey. *All my dreams are going up in smoke.*

CHAPTER FORTY

♊

Gisele ran. "Gisele," he whispered. She turned around. A scream escaped her lips. He was right behind her, mocking her. It was Marcel Petoit. She ran faster until she reached the building where she lived and breathlessly ran up the stairs as quickly as she could. Her chest was heaving, and she could hardly catch her breath. All the while, she was watching the door to the building, hoping he would not follow her inside. Then the door creaked open, and he entered. She dropped her handbag and let out a scream. Petoit began to run up the stairs two at a time. Gisele screamed again, a bloodcurdling scream of terror. Her handbag fell to the ground. She pounded her fists on the door. "Help me. Ernst, help me." The door to her apartment opened. Ernst stood there looking bewildered. She fell into his arms. "He's following me," she said. "He wants to kill me."

"Who?" Ernst asked, looking around the empty hallway.

"Him," Gisele said, turning around, but Petoit was gone.

"Come inside." Ernst picked up Gisele's handbag and then took her arm. Holding her tightly, he led her inside the apartment. "What is going on? Are you all right?" he asked.

"Yes, but there is something I must speak to you about."

He felt weak and cold. "All right," he said as he locked the door behind her. Then he poured himself another glass of whiskey. "Please tell me what is going on."

Gisele was trembling. "Can I have a glass too?"

"Of course," he said, reaching for a shot glass. He poured the golden liquid into the glass and handed it to her. She drank it in one gulp.

"Take it easy with that. You should sip it, or you're going to get sick," he said.

She nodded.

Ernst looked her over. Dark mascara was smeared under her eyes. Her deep-red lipstick had spread around her mouth, looking almost clownish. Her hair was a mess. "What happened to you?" he asked. "Who was following you? And for that matter, where were you?"

She sank down into the chair next to the table where he'd placed her purse. Nervously, she fumbled with the handle.

Gisele could not look at him. She stared at the table and her handbag, and then she began to weep. Heart-wrenching sobs sprung from her throat. Ernst could see that she was in real pain. And for the first time since he'd known her, he really looked at her. What he saw was beyond her beauty. She was little more than a teenager, just a child playing at being a woman. For a moment he thought of Shoshana. Shoshana was a few years younger than Gisele, but she was far more mature. Or at least that was the way it seemed to him. Ernst remained quiet. He knew from his medical training not to press Gisele to talk. The best thing to do right now was to wait patiently until she was ready to speak. He handed her the handkerchief he carried in his breast pocket. She thanked him.

Several moments passed in silence. Ernst poured himself another glass of whiskey.

Then in a small voice, Gisele began to speak. "It all began when I was living in Paris."

He nodded.

"In a brothel."

He cocked his head, trying not to look shocked.

"But I wasn't a whore. I was the cleaning woman."

He didn't say a word. She took a cigarette from her purse and lit it. Gisele inhaled deeply. He'd told her that he didn't like this new habit she had taken up of smoking. But right now, he said nothing about it. He waited for her to continue.

"One night, the madam sent me out to the store, because we ran out of beer. On my way I was raped."

"Yes, you told me."

"But what I didn't tell you was that I got pregnant by that man who raped me. I couldn't have that baby. I didn't want a child by a man who had forced himself on me. I would have resented the baby forever. I had to get rid of it." She sucked in a deep breath. "I never wanted to tell you this. I thought you would hate me."

"I don't hate you. I could never hate you," he said, and he began to wonder if he'd imagined this whole thing between Gisele and Otto. He began to think that maybe there was another reason she had been acting so strange lately. *Perhaps what she is about to tell me is the reason she has been so distant.*

"The cook at the brothel was my friend. She was an older woman, like a mother to me. When I told her that I was pregnant, she said she knew of a doctor who had gotten rid of pregnancies for other girls at the house. I told her that I wanted to see him. So, she gave me his address. I went to see him." A sob choked out of her, and she stopped for a moment. Then she went on. "I went to see him, and he agreed to help me get rid of it. But he was expensive. I couldn't afford to pay him. But I had to get rid of it. I had to. So, when he proposed that I work for him in exchange for this abortion, I agreed."

"And you worked for him?"

"Yes."

"In his office?"

"No, not like that."

"How then? Prostitution?" he asked.

She shook her head. "Worse."

He refilled his shot glass. "Go on," he said softly, trying not to sound at all judgmental.

"He hired me to recruit Jewish families to pay him to help them get out of France. But they never got out. He even named this mission of his. He called it Fly Tox."

"Fly Tox? I believe that's an insecticide company."

"I don't know what Fly Tox means. But this mission of his had nothing to do with any insecticide company. It was all about money. He charged these Jews a lot of money. And he promised to help them escape." She lit another cigarette. Then she was silent for several moments.

"All right, go on, tell me the rest," Ernst said.

"His name was Dr. Marcel Petoit." She sucked the cigarette smoke in deeply, then she continued. "He told me that I was to promise the Jewish families that he was going to get them out of France and save them from the Nazis. He said they would be going to a settlement in South America. They were required to pay a large sum of money for his services. But he explained that they would pay it if they could because this was their only chance of survival. He told me that the Jews knew that Hitler was going to have them murdered," she said, looking at Ernst, then quickly looking away.

"Like I said, I took the job. And I went to the Jewish neighborhood where he sent me. I found a family that was desperate." Her voice cracked. "I did what Petoit told me to do. I told them that if they could get their hands on the money to pay, they could be saved. The husband agreed. He said he would have the money." Gisele put out her cigarette in the ashtray. Then she sucked in a deep breath and continued. "I arranged for them to meet with the doctor and myself. They arrived on time. Petoit took their money. Then he sent me home. The next day he took care of my pregnancy. I had no idea what he was going to do. I swear I never suspected," she said, and tears began to run down her cheeks. "So, I did it again, thinking I was actually helping these Jews get free from the Nazis.

"The second time I brought him another Jewish family, things were different. This time he didn't send me home. He made me stay. He told the family that they were going to need vaccinations because vaccinations were required to get into South America. And he said that was where he was sending them because that was where they would be safe. As we were all climbing into his car, he gave the husband the first injection. He made me watch, because he wanted me to give the injections to the rest of them. I did it." She let out a short wail. "I did it, Ernst. But I didn't know. I swear I didn't know."

He looked at her but stayed silent. It seemed for several moments that she was not going to continue. But then she said, "The vaccination wasn't a vaccination at all. It was something that killed them. I didn't know it, but he planned to kill them all along. In fact, I didn't even realize they were dead until we arrived at an old farmhouse, and I looked in the back seat of the car. I was horrified to see the whole family dead. But not Petoit. He wasn't affected at all. He must have been doing this before he recruited me, because he had installed ovens in the farmhouse. And he made me help him burn those dead bodies. It was terrible, Ernst. Terrible. And then, this time, he paid me. It was blood money, Ernst." She shivered.

"I will never forget the smell. Oh, the smell." She trembled. "I was horrified by what I had done. I couldn't do it again. I just couldn't. And he expected me to. He was making a lot of money doing this. And he felt that I still owed him. I had to get away from him and from all of it. I tried to avoid him, but he came to the brothel looking for me. When he found me, he threatened me. He said that if I didn't come back to work for him, he would kill me. I knew he was capable of it. I saw him kill that whole family without blinking an eye. I was afraid of him. So, I tricked him. I made him believe that I cared for him. And then I ran away during the night. I escaped from him and went to Germany hoping he would never come looking for me. But he did. He's here. And, he's going to kill me."

"Hmm," Ernst said, clearing his throat. "You said his name is Marcel Petoit?"

"Yes. That's his name. He is a doctor."

Ernst took a sip of whiskey. *I was so concerned with Gisele finding out about the horrors I've taken part in at Auschwitz, while it seems she has not been the innocent girl I thought she was.* Until now he'd thought of Gisele almost like a Madonna. Even though he'd been certain that she was cheating on him with Otto, he never blamed her. He thought Otto was responsible. But now he was seeing Gisele in a different light. "Where were you going at this time of the evening? You know this is when I come home from work. And it is getting dark. I've told you it's best that you should be inside after dark."

"I had forgotten something at the store," she lied.

He cocked his head. "Forgotten?" That sounded untrue. "What were you doing all day?" Ernst had never questioned Gisele before. He'd always just been grateful that she was with him, but now he wanted explanations.

"I was napping."

"All day?"

She shrugged.

"Gisele, are you lying to me?" he asked.

She nodded.

"Why?" he asked.

"Because I've made so many mistakes. That's why."

"I think you should tell me everything," Ernst said sadly. "I think I need to know. I need to hear it from you."

She began to cry again. But then she blew her nose and wiped her eyes. "I'll tell you," she said, hanging her head. Gisele sighed. She told him all about how she was also running from the Gestapo for the murder of the man who raped her. And then she hesitated, but she looked into his eyes and began to cry as she told him all about Otto.

CHAPTER FORTY-ONE

♊

I t was difficult for Ernst to sit and listen quietly while Gisele told him that she had been intimate with another man—not just any man—but a man who had once tormented him. Every word she said felt like a dagger through his heart.

Then she said, "I wasn't in love with you, Ernst. I care about you, but it was never love. I married you because you were successful, and I wanted to meet Dr. Mengele. I think he may be my father."

The words stung.

"I am not proud of what I did with Otto. You didn't deserve that."

"I loved you. It's hard for me to understand how you could have had sex with him."

She nodded.

Ernst nodded. He poured another glass of whiskey. It felt warm as it slid down his throat. "Is there anything else you want to tell me?" he asked.

"I am sorry. I should not have done these things."

"You never loved me," he said in a small voice.

She shook her head. "I was never in love with you. But I do love you, Ernst. And I should never have done these things. I realize how important you are to me." Gisele began weeping hard.

If he had not been so filled with hurt and anger, he would have felt sorry for her. He would have taken her into his arms and held her. But he couldn't. Ernst studied his young, beautiful wife. "You never loved me," he repeated the words that were so hard for him to accept. "I would have done anything for you. I would have given you the world."

"I'm sorry. Can't we try again? Please, Ernst. Can't we try again?"

He shook his head. "I don't know. I need time to think this all through. I feel betrayed, used."

"I don't want you to feel that way. That's a terrible way to feel. I know, because that's how I feel about Otto."

Ernst looked at her, and the love he felt for her seemed to dissipate like water boiling into steam. "Ahhhh, well, sometimes you are such a smart girl. And other times, like now, you are a poor fool. I suppose it's because you're young. Maybe, maybe not." He was talking more to himself than to her.

Gisele looked at him; her face was filled with panic. "What are you going to do? Are you going to throw me out? If you do, Petoit will find me. I need help. Perhaps I should meet with Dr. Mengele and tell him about my mother. Perhaps he will help me. Perhaps he will protect me from Petoit and from the Gestapo."

Ernst gave a harsh laugh, then in a cynical voice, he said, "You don't know the wonderful, famous Dr. Mengele the way I do. He is not the man you think he is. I sincerely doubt he will help you."

"So, what, then? What is to become of me?"

"I don't know, Gisele. I need time. I need time to think," he said in a voice that was detached. "I love you. I still love you. Love doesn't just disappear. But I can't trust you. And that leaves me with an important decision to make."

"You are going to decide what to do with me?"

"I'm going to decide what I want to do about myself. I don't know if I can stay married to you or not. I don't know if I can stay at this horrific job. I just don't know right now," he said. Then he got up and walked out of the room.

CHAPTER FORTY-TWO

♊

Ernst slid his arms through the sleeves of his overcoat. He wrapped a scarf around his neck, and then he went outside. He needed to walk, needed the fresh air to help him sort out his thoughts. *She never loved me.* The words rolled around in his head, over and over again. *She never loved me.* When he thought of Gisele lying naked in Otto's arms, he felt the bile rise in his throat. A quick glance around told him that the streets were empty. Everyone else is probably at home enjoying their dinners with their loved ones. *Not me. I am alone, because I chose to love a woman who cannot love me. A woman who finds me repulsive.* He felt dizzy. Then he ducked between two buildings and vomited in the alleyway.

He held on to the side of the building and heaved until his stomach ached. Then he turned his head to look up at the sky filled with stars. The tiny flickers of light in the otherwise dark sky were so beautiful that they intensified his pain. Hot tears spilled down his cheeks. He slammed his fist against the bricks of the building and felt searing pain in his hand. He was angry, very angry. He wanted to punish Gisele for hurting him. *She is not the sweet, inno-cent girl I thought she was. Is it possible that she is nothing but a liar and murderer after all. What kind of monster did I marry? It seems I am surrounded by monsters. I should throw her out and let that man, that Petoit, find her. I should let him kill her the way she murdered that innocent family.*

Ernst was trembling with rage. He bit his lower lip. He pushed himself away from the building and began walking. A half hour passed. Then forty-five minutes. The fresh air filled his lungs and slowly cleared his head. *I am hurt. But it isn't in my nature to hurt anyone else. The truth is, I will always love her, and I refuse to believe that she is a horrible person. She didn't realize what she was doing. I must believe that to be true. I am a forgiving person. I always have been. However, the truth is, things between us have changed, and now I don't know if I can spend the rest of my life with her. Even so, I couldn't live with myself if I didn't protect her from this man who wants to murder her. I must find a way to stop him. At the same time, I must be careful to leave her out of it. If the Gestapo even suspects that she was involved with this murderer, this Petoit fellow, they might put two and two together. They might even find out that he frequented the brothel where she worked as a maid during the time when that German officer was killed. I think perhaps the best thing to do is find a way to inform the French police of this Petoit's crimes without using her name at all.*

He sucked in his breath. *Yes, the best thing to do is involve the French police.* He continued to walk, and as he did, a plan formed in his mind. *The information should come from a neighbor, someone who lives near the farmhouse. Anyone living close would surely smell the burning bodies. The first thing I must do is to find out the address of this farmhouse. Then I will go to visit with the neighbors. I will offer them a nice sum of money to turn Petoit in to the police. I am sure they will want to get rid of the terrible smells, so they should be agreeable.*

Finally at peace with his plan, Ernst walked back to his apartment. When he entered, he found Gisele sitting on the sofa; her face was red, and tearstained. "You came back," she said in a soft voice. "I was afraid you wouldn't."

He nodded. "Yes, I came back." *She looks so small and sad.*

"Write down the full name of the man who is chasing you. I need the correct spelling."

"Marcel Petoit," she said, then she got up and took a pen from his desk and wrote down the name.

"And do you know the address of the farmhouse?"

She nodded. "Yes, I do. It's twenty-One Rue LeSuer, Paris."

"I am going to call Dr. Mengele in the morning and tell him I am feeling ill. I am going to tell him that I need to take a few days off. Then I am going to Paris to take care of this problem for you. While I am gone, you must promise me that you will not leave the apartment. It is not safe for you to be out yet. Petoit is still here in Poland. You must do as I say until I can be sure he has been arrested. Do you understand me?"

"Yes," she said. "And thank you for helping me."

Ernst nodded. "It's all going to be all right," he said.

"Do you still love me?" she asked in a small voice.

For a moment, he didn't speak. The silence was deafening. Then he looked into her azure-blue eyes and nodded his head.

A long sigh came from Ernst's lips. "Yes," he said sadly. "Yes, I still love you. I will always love you. But I just don't know if I can be your husband anymore."

She began to weep. He wanted to take her in his arms and tell her that he loved her and that he would stay with her. But he couldn't. So he stood up and went into the bedroom and closed the door.

CHAPTER FORTY-THREE

♊

Ernst drove to Paris. It was a long, tedious drive. But he found himself thinking about Shoshana rather than thinking about Gisele. He was worried about Shoshana. He prayed that she and her sisters would be all right until he was able to return.

The farmhouse was easy to find. The strong, hideous odor lingered in the air.

Ernst knocked on the neighbor's door. A man answered. He was obviously a farmer. A calm and gentle man.

Ernst smiled and introduced himself as Pierre Leclerk, a wealthy businessman who was interested in purchasing Petoit's farm. "Do you know Monsieur Petoit?" Ernst asked the farmer in perfect French.

"I don't know the man who lives there," the neighbor said, "but he is always burning something over there. The smoke and the smell are overpowering. It's terrible. I sure would be glad if he sold the place and moved away."

"What would you say if I told you that he is a very bad man. What if I told you that he was killing people and burning bodies there?"

"Murdering people?" The neighbor's eyes flew open wide.

"Yes," Ernst said. He was careful not to say that the murdered people were Jewish. He had come to realize that Jewish lives had no value since the Nazis had come to power. If he'd said that Petoit was killing Jews, there was a possibility that no one, neither the neighbor or the police, would pay any attention.

The neighbor looked frightened. "So, you're saying that a madman lives next door to me?"

"Yes. That's right. He poses a constant danger to you and not only to you but also to your family."

The neighbor rubbed the stubble on his chin. "That's pretty scary."

"It sure is," Ernst agreed. "But, what would you say if I told you that you could earn some extra money by turning this Petoit fellow in to the police? I would do it myself, but no one would believe me. They would think I was making it all up to force the price down, because I want to buy the farm."

"But what if they told Petoit that I turned him in?"

"The police wouldn't tell him. You could ask them to protect you until they arrested Petoit."

The neighbor considered this for a moment. Then he nodded and asked, "Just how much money are you willing to pay?"

"More than enough to make it worth your while. Let's put it this way. If you have a bad crop this year, you will still have enough money to get you through the winter," Ernst said, smiling.

"I'll do it," the farmer said.

"Good. And when you tell the police to check out the farmhouse, you must also tell them that they can find Petoit in Poland. I know that he is there; he has been there for a while. If they hurry, they will find him in a little town called Brzezinka. It's close to Oswiecim. Do you want me to write this down for you?"

"No, I can't read. But I will remember it. A town called Brzezinka, near Oswiecim."

"Yes, that's right," Ernst said, then he smiled at the neighbor and said, "And by the way, what's your name?"

"I'm Andrée Marcais."

"Nice to meet you, Andrée."

"Nice to meet you too."

"I am an honest man. I believe you are too. So, here is your money," Ernst said. "I trust you will do as you say."

The neighbor nodded.

CHAPTER FORTY-FOUR

♊

Gisele wished Ernst hadn't left for France. Since she'd been followed by Petoit, she was nervous about being alone.

When the phone rang in her apartment, Gisele jumped. She ran to pick up the receiver, certain it was Ernst telling her that he'd taken care of things with Petoit and that she was finally free.

"Hello," she said breathlessly.

"Hello." It was Otto.

When she heard his voice, all of the feelings she had for him returned. She was excited that he was calling. *Perhaps he has changed his mind. Perhaps when he saw me the other night he realized how much I meant to him.*

Her heart fluttered wildly. She wished she could say she had lost all desire for him. But she hadn't, and hearing his voice only reinforced her feelings. *Stay calm. Don't let him know how much you care for him,* she thought. "Who is this?" she said as casually as she could.

"You don't recognize my voice?" he said, not waiting for an answer. "It's Otto. I'm calling because I decided that I owed you. So, I arranged that meeting for you with Dr. Mengele. He was actually quite receptive to the idea of meeting. He said he would be more than happy to speak with you. Can you meet with him this afternoon at the restaurant where you and I had lunch, say four o'clock?"

Ernst said I must not leave the apartment, she thought. But she had to speak to Mengele. She had to find out if he was her father. *And perhaps Otto will be there too. I would love to see him again.* "All right. I'll be at the restaurant at four," she said.

His voice grew heavy with desire. "And when you've finished speaking with Dr. Mengele, why don't you take the bus over to my apartment. I know your husband is not feeling well. So, I am sure he will be resting."

He won't be at the restaurant. But he wants to see me. He must have realized he cares for me. Of course, he thinks Ernst is not feeling well. That's what Ernst told Dr. Mengele. But it's even better for me that Ernst is out of town, she thought. Then she remembered what the girls at the brothel used to say: *Sex, for a man, is like being hungry for food. Once they are satisfied, they lose interest for a while. The same way we lose interest in food once we are full after eating a big meal. But then as time passes, the hunger returns, and we must eat again. The same hunger returns for a man when he wants sex again. But this time will be different. This time I will not give in to him so easily. I will make him yearn for me until he falls in love with me.*

She was so lost in thought that she didn't realize she hadn't answered him.

"Are you there?" Otto asked.

"Oh, yes. I'm sorry. I'm here," Gisele said.

"So, you'll come to my apartment?"

"I will," she said. "As soon as I finish speaking with Dr. Mengele."

The phone line went dead. She placed the receiver down in its holder and ran to the bathroom to style her hair and apply some makeup.

CHAPTER FORTY-FIVE

Ⅱ

Mengele was tapping a pen on the table when Gisele arrived at the restaurant. He smiled at her as she walked over to the table and asked, "Would you like a beer?"

"Yes, please," she said as she sat down.

He motioned for the waiter. "Bring the lady a beer," he said.

The waiter nodded.

"So, you wanted to speak with me?" Dr. Mengele said casually. He was still rhythmically tapping the pen.

"Yes, I have something important I need to tell you."

"Important." Mengele sounded as if she had said something that amused him. "And what, may I ask, could be so important?" He smiled at her, giving her his most charming, winning smile.

She returned his smile.

"I don't know where to begin," she said. "I don't know how to tell you this."

"Then let me help you. I can see you are attracted to me. I am the kind of man who knows how to treat a beautiful woman, and I can be very discreet. You are quite lovely. Like a breath of spring."

She looked down at the table. She was confused. *How did this get so out of hand? He thinks I've come here because I want to have sex with him, perhaps be his mistress.*

"I'll be blunt," Mengele continued. "As you know, I am a married man. However, I do find you appealing and I would be willing . . ."

She stopped him in mid-sentence. "I think I may be your daughter." She blurted out the words. "My mother's name was Simone Lenoir. She met you when she was a teenager, fourteen or fifteen perhaps. You were on holiday with your parents in France. Do you remember this?"

CHAPTER FORTY-SIX

♊

Mengele was silent. He glared at Gisele. Then his face went dark. "I don't recall anything like that happening. My family did not go to France. I didn't impregnate some French girl. You are a conniving little thing, aren't you? Looking to cash in on my name and my fine reputation. What do you want—money? I have no intention of giving you any. I am not your father."

"But . . . it's not money I am after."

"I don't believe you. I believe you are trying to blackmail me. It won't work. I am a high official in the Nazi Party. If I wave my hand, I could have you killed. Do you realize that? Keep your mouth shut about such lies, or it will cost you. This I promise you."

She was bowled over by his response. Gisele could hardly breathe. "I don't want anything from you. All I wanted was to find my father. My mother died, and I have always longed for a family . . ."

"You have Ernst. Be happy with what you have." Mengele's tone was menacing, and his eyes were threatening.

She knew that it was best to assure him that she'd been wrong, even though she still believed he was her father. "I'm sorry. I-I must have been wrong," she stammered. "I just thought . . ."

"There is nothing for you to think about. I am not your father."

"No, you're not. I made a mistake," she said. "I made a mistake. Please forgive me."

He seemed to calm down. "Yes, we all make mistakes." He smiled, but there was a warning in his smile. "Just make sure you don't make the same mistake twice."

"Yes, of course. You're right," she said.

Mengele laid a few reichsmarks down on the table. Then he stood up and walked out of the restaurant.

Gisele was trembling. She stood up and straightened her skirt. Then she left. Out on the street, the tears began to flow down her cheeks. *My mother hated Germans. Now I can see why. I am not sure, but I have a feeling she might have told Josef Mengele that she was pregnant with me, and he rejected her. He left her to fend for herself. When her parents found out, they were ashamed. They threw her out of the house, and then she was on her own. My poor mother,* she thought as she crossed the street, realizing what her mother must have gone through. She walked to the bus stop and sat down on the bench. *I shouldn't go to Otto's apartment. I should go home. Ernst might just be the only good German, and I am fortunate enough to be his wife. So, why can't I love him? I care for him, but I just don't feel the things a wife should feel for a husband when I am with him. He is more like a father to me than a lover. And Otto, everything about Otto excites me. I want him to love me the way I love him. But I am afraid that if I go to see him, I'll make love with him again, and then he'll spurn me like he did before."*

In spite of her fears and misgivings, Gisele still believed that there was something special between her and Otto. Or at least that was what she wanted to believe. So, she boarded a bus to Otto's apartment. When she arrived at his building, she went inside and sat on the stairs in the hallway by the mailboxes waiting for him to return home from work. When he arrived, he looked her up and down and smiled. "You look like a piece of cake. Come on in. I am craving sugar."

She ignored his reference to sex. "I want to talk to you," she said.

"Come on in, and I promise you we'll talk." Otto smiled.

"No. I want to talk here. I can't trust myself alone with you."

"Am I that irresistible?" He laughed.

"Otto. Please be serious. You mean a lot to me. And I need to know what you feel about me. About us."

"What do you mean? You are a married woman. How serious do you want me to be? You want me to tell you to leave your husband and marry me?"

"Yes," she said firmly.

"All right. Then come inside, and we'll talk about it."

She walked into his apartment feeling hopeful. He closed the door behind her. Once the door was closed, he did not hesitate for a second. Otto pushed her up against the wall. Then he pulled her dress up and without even a kiss, he took her hard. There was no affection in his eyes. By the time he'd finished she was crying. Otto pushed away from her.

"You hurt me," she said softly. "I wasn't ready."

"I'm sorry," he said, but he didn't sound sincere. "You should be going now. Your husband is going to be home waiting for you."

"How can you treat me this way? You show me no respect at all."

"How can I treat you this way? Because you allow me to treat you this way, Gisele. You want me to respect you, but you don't respect yourself."

"What do you mean by that?" She was almost screaming now. "You have become so rude. I don't even know you anymore."

"Come on, you are a married woman. Why would you come to a single man's apartment if you weren't looking for passion? I gave you what you wanted. I gave you good sex. I gave you what your worm of a husband can't give you."

"How dare you talk that way about Ernst. He is a good, decent person."

"Too good for you. I feel sorry for him."

"I hate you," she said.

She was screaming so loudly that the neighbor knocked on the wall. "Be quiet in there," the neighbor yelled through the paper-thin walls.

"Go home, Gisele," Otto said. "Go home before Ernst realizes you're gone."

Tears ran down her cheeks as she turned and walked out of his apartment. He closed the door behind her. But once she was in the hallway, she cried out, "You are a terrible man, Otto Schatz. You are the kind of man who takes advantage of women. You treated me like a whore. Like a whore!"

The young woman who lived next door, the one who had been pounding on the wall, walked out of her apartment to see what the commotion was about. She carried a young toddler in her arms. At the same time, Otto walked out the door of his flat. His face was red with anger as he raced quickly over to Gisele and slapped her across the face. "Yelling and screaming in the hallway is not permitted here. You are going to get me kicked out of my apartment. Is that what you want? Is it?"

"I don't care." She was still screaming. "You deserve it."

Otto turned to the neighbor. "Get back in your flat, or I'll slap you next." The young woman, clutching her child, ran back into her apartment and slammed the door. They heard her turn the lock.

Then Otto turned toward Gisele. "Get out of here. Go home."

Gisele began running away from Otto's apartment and toward the bus stop where she could catch the bus that would take her back to her apartment. It was several streets away. She hurried along, wanting to be on the bus, away from Otto and all the pain she was feeling. Gisele was drowning in her own misery. Forgetting the danger that lurked in the shadows, she crossed the street and made her way through a deserted alleyway as she took a shortcut to the bus stop. Strong arms that felt like bricks fell upon her shoulders. A large male hand covered her mouth. She felt herself being pulled down to the ground.

"I told you I would find you," Petoit said. "You didn't make it easy. But, I am a master at this sort of thing."

She struggled against his hand covering her mouth. He looked into her eyes. Something softened in his face, and then he loosened his grip. She broke free. There was no one around. It was not worth trying to scream. He could break her neck in a second. Instead, she tried to reason with him. "Marcel, it wasn't you that I was trying to escape from. It was Annette. She was trying to pin that murder on me. And I had to run away. I couldn't risk telling anyone where I was going, not even you."

He looked at her for a moment; his gaze was unfocused. Then his eyes hardened; they didn't even look like human eyes. He began laughing softly. "You expect me to believe you?" He covered her mouth again; this time his grip was harder. It was so hard, she felt like he might break her jaw or her neck. "Gisele." Then in a soft growl, he said, "You ran from me. No one runs from me. I am sure that you were aware that the Gestapo came and questioned everyone the morning after you and I had our romantic evening together. They left, but they returned a few hours later and arrested Annette. I heard about it from one of the whores that came to see me about an abortion. As soon as I heard what had happened, I went directly to the brothel to find you. I was going to help you. What a fool I was. I thought you and I had something special between us. I thought you might be falling in love with me. I was wrong. You didn't care for me. You were already gone. You'd left a few hours before. I felt so betrayed. How dare you treat me this way when I was nothing but kind to you."

He wouldn't release her. She kicked and struggled, but her mouth was still covered, and she couldn't answer him. Petoit's face was contorted. Gisele's eyes were wide as she was battling to get out of his grip. But he was strong. Very strong. And she knew that he was not going to release her. "You are a little fool. We could have been happy together. We could have been lovers and earned plenty of money together. But you ran. And now . . ." She tried to bite his hand.

This angered him even further. He took his other hand and bashed her head against the side of the building. White-hot pain seared through her. Then everything went dark. In the distance, a white light appeared, and Gisele's mother reached out her hand. The pain ceased.

"Come with me," Simone said. "Don't be afraid. I am here with you now."

Gisele gave her mother her hand, a warmth came over her as her blood pooled on the pavement in the alley. Gisele was dead.

CHAPTER FORTY-SEVEN

Ⅱ

Marcel Petoit was finally satisfied. He wasn't at all worried about getting caught for what he'd done. Gisele had been punished for the shabby way she treated him. Without turning back to glance at her even once, he walked away, leaving her dead body in the alley.

Marcel thought of himself as a clever man. He had been committing crimes since he was just a young boy, and he had not been caught. He took the gold pen out of his breast pocket that he'd stolen from the poet that first time he had gone out to dinner with Gisele. Looking at the detail in the metal workmanship, he smiled. *I have always been able to steal anything I wanted*, he thought. And even committing murder had long ago ceased to frighten him. He just wished that Gisele hadn't ruined their partnership. *It could have been very lucrative for both of us*, he thought as he sighed aloud.

He walked for a while until he arrived back to the hotel where he was staying under an assumed name. After gathering his belongings and packing them carefully, he took his suitcase and left his room. Careful to avoid the woman at the front desk, he strolled out of the hotel without paying his bill. Marcel Petoit boarded the next train back to Paris where he had a new female employee waiting for him to return. He had recently hired her to recruit Jewish families, and she seemed very eager to begin working.

Petoit felt no guilt about killing Gisele. In fact, he felt nothing. It was rare that he had any feelings about anything. But if he did, they were never feelings of remorse. He was tired, and he slept for several hours. When he awoke, he ate the sandwich he'd purchased before he left Poland. While he was eating, he thought about the new girl who would be working with him. He hadn't told her exactly what was going to happen to the Jews she recruited. Not yet. She would find out soon enough. Still, she was a bit of a disappointment. He didn't think she had as much potential as Gisele. After all, she wasn't as pretty or innocent looking as Gisele had been, but she would have to do until he could find someone better. And once he found someone better suited, he would think nothing of silencing her forever. *People are disposable,* he thought. *Once I am done with them, and they don't serve a purpose for me anymore, it is best to get rid of them, so they don't have an opportunity to talk.*

When Petoit arrived back in Paris, he took a taxi to his apartment. He carefully unpacked his things. Then he went out to a nearby restaurant to have something to eat. When he returned home, he telephoned his new employee: "Chloe, it's Marcel. I've returned to Paris. Are you ready to start working?"

"Actually, yes, I certainly am," Chloe said.

"Good. Well, why don't you go out, and see if you can find me some Jews tomorrow?"

"I've already found some. I went to the Jewish neighborhood last week. They have been waiting for you to return to Paris."

"That's wonderful news. Good job. How many of them are there?"

"Four. A husband, a wife, and two teenage children."

"Did you tell them the price?"

"I did."

"And do they have the money?"

"They do. They are in hiding right now. But I know how to find them. They are very scared. So, I know they would like to get out of France as soon as possible."

"Tell them I will meet with them tomorrow night. Inform them that their journey will begin immediately. They are to pack lightly, only what they will need and also their most valuable possessions. Tell them that they should bring anything that they think they can sell if they need to once they get to South America," Petoit said, yawning. He was ready to take a shower and get some rest. But he was also glad that she had taken care of business even when he was away. *Perhaps she will be better at this then I originally thought.*

"Shall I give them the address of the apartment that you gave me?" she asked.

"Yes."

"What time?"

"Tell them nine o'clock tomorrow evening."

"I'll take care of it," Chloe said. "See you tomorrow."

CHAPTER FORTY-EIGHT

♊

The family of Jews consisted of a young husband and wife with two shy teenaged girls. They were trembling and anxious. The husband handed Petoit an envelope. "You'll find all of the money you requested in this envelope. Do you want to count it?" he said.

"Of course not. I trust you. You need my services. You would be a fool to do anything that would cause me to send the Gestapo after you," Petoit said confidently.

"I assure you that the money is all there," the man repeated.

Petoit looked at the worried faces of the couple. "Relax." He smiled reassuringly. "You have nothing to worry about," he said calmly. "I have been doing this for a long time now. I have perfected a route that is very safe. You will be settled in a community of other Jewish people in Argentina. That's in South America, in case you didn't know."

The wife's lips quivered as she smiled at him. Then in a soft voice, she said, "Thank you for helping us." A tear fell down her cheek "We are not wealthy people, but everyone we knew gave us money so we could get out. My husband has always been a beacon of light in our community, and we've been blessed to have a lot of good friends."

"Well, now you have two more friends, Chloe and myself," Dr. Petoit said. "We are going to help you get out of France and away from the Nazis. But first, it is required that you take a vaccination in order for the government to allow you to enter Argentina."

"Is the vaccination safe for our daughters?" the father asked.

"Of course," Petoit said. "I would not accept your family for this program if the vaccination were not safe for young people. Now, let's go to the car, but first roll up your sleeves . . ."

CHAPTER FORTY-NINE

Ⅱ

"You can go home," Petoit said to Chloe. "Come back tomorrow morning, and I'll pay you."

He started to get into the car.

"I can come with you," she said.

"Not tonight. There will be plenty of times in the future when you can come with me." He smiled. "Tonight, we will be meeting with a special agent who is going to help me. He doesn't want me to bring anyone else along with us. So, I'll see you in the morning."

She nodded. "Yes, of course," she said, looking at him skeptically. "You will give me my money, won't you?"

"Of course. I need you to continue working for me. So, I would not think of treating you so poorly. I am surprised that you don't think more highly of me," he said, then he got in the car and drove away, leaving her standing on the street.

CHAPTER FIFTY

♊

When Petoit arrived at the farmhouse, he left the bodies in the car and went into the house to fire up the ovens. But before he had the chance to take the bodies out of the automobile, two French policemen entered the house. They found him busy with the ovens. "Are you Marcel Petoit?"

Petoit looked around nervously. He tried to run outside, but a large policeman caught him just outside the door and held him in a strong grip.

Another police officer was standing next to Petoit's car. "There are four dead people in this auto," the policeman said to the other officers. "A man, a woman, and two young girls."

"Oh my gosh," the other officer said.

"Well, at least we caught him in the act," the large policeman who had Petoit in his grip, said, then he turned to Petoit. "Marcel Petoit, you're under arrest."

CHAPTER FIFTY-ONE

Ernst's hands trembled as he gripped the steering wheel on the way home from France. *This is the end of my dream, my dream of spending the rest of my life with Gisele. And now that it's ending, I might as well leave Auschwitz and find a small town that needs a local doctor. Leaving Dr. Mengele will be a good thing. But it is also a disappointment. Before I arrived at Auschwitz, I believed that this job was going to be a wonderful learning experience for me. I had hoped it would be a magnificent period of time in my career. Instead, it turned out to be a horrific unveiling of the workings of a sadistic mind.* He shook his head.

For several miles, as he drove through the countryside, he entertained the idea of working in a small town. He visualized the weak and sick coming to him for help. Ernst wasn't interested in earning a lot of money. *I want to help people. I want to be a real doctor.* The daydream he was having of being a real healer felt good. For a while he allowed it to entertain him.

Then his thoughts turned to Shoshana and her sisters. *However, if I leave, Mengele might decide to hurt them. He probably would choose*

Shoshana's sisters just because he senses that I care for them, and he would want to hurt them to punish me. I can't go, not without doing something to help them. I must find a way to get Shoshana and her sisters out of Auschwitz. But how?

CHAPTER FIFTY-TWO

♊

Fredrich held the two dead squirrels by their tails when he entered the barn. "I went hunting. We'll have meat tonight," he said to Naomi who was sitting on the ground looking out the window.

"Oh." Naomi glanced at the squirrels in Fredrich's hand.

"You've never eaten squirrel?"

She shook her head. "Never."

"Neither have I." He smiled. "But I'll tell you what, it's better than starving."

"You can say that again." Naomi sighed, then she added, "Please don't tell me we have to eat that raw. I don't know if I can."

"First of all, you could if you had to. But no, we aren't going to eat them raw. I have an idea. A way we might be able to cook them without sending up too much smoke into the air."

Fredrich walked over and tugged at the wood that comprised one of the horse stalls. It was dry and brittle. Some of it fell apart in his hands. "Just as I thought," he said. "The wood is dry and old. It will be good for making a fire."

"But what about the smoke? How are we going to keep the smoke from wafting up into the air? You said that we must be careful because the Nazis will find us if we make a fire because they'll see the smoke."

"I am going to try something," he said.

It didn't take much strength for Fredrich to break off a few pieces of wood. He lay the two squirrels down on the ground and began to dig a hole with his hands in the corner of the barn. He dug until he was able to build the sides up surrounding the small pit he'd dug. Then he placed the wood in the pit.

"Should I gather leaves?" Naomi asked.

"No, leaves will create too much smoke. We want to have as little smoke as possible. That's why I wanted to be sure that the wood was dry."

"Is it safe to make a fire inside the barn?"

"I hope so. I've never done it before. But we're going to try. I think the main thing is that we don't let the fire burn too long. Just long enough to cook this meat quickly."

"A crackling fire would be lovely for warmth too." She sighed. "But you're right. We don't want to set this barn on fire. Or kill ourselves with smoke inhalation."

"No, we don't. But at least we have openings that are like windows in each of the stalls. So, although it might be a little smoky, we'll be able to breathe. I'm going to take these squirrels outside and skin them. I have a knife. There's no reason you should have to watch that. I can imagine it might make you sick."

"Thank you," she said. "But I'm stronger than I look. I used to have to kill my own chickens and pluck them."

"Did you really?" He smiled. "I'm impressed. So, you came from a farm?"

"Not exactly. I came from a very small village. I suppose you might say we were a little backward in comparison to the cities. Would you believe I didn't even realize how backward we were until my family and I were sent to live in the ghetto in Warsaw."

"The ghetto?"

"Yes, after the Nazis took Poland, they made all the Jews register. It was a law. And then once they knew where to find us, they sent soldiers with guns to gather us up. All of our possessions were stolen from us by the Nazi soldiers. Then they transported us to a small area in Warsaw where we were imprisoned. We lived in terrible conditions. Overcrowding, disease, no food. It was very bad. So, that's why, when they offered us a better life if we were willing to work, my husband and I jumped at the opportunity.

We were sent to a transport station where they loaded us onto a train with so many other people that we could hardly breathe. In fact, we couldn't sit down; we had to stand up the entire journey. While we were on the train, my husband overheard some guards talking. They said they were planning to murder all of us. When he heard that, he made some sort of deal with one of the guards to let me go. The guard agreed, and I was sent out alone into the forest. And so, here I am."

"Your husband stayed behind? He stayed on the train?"

"Yes, he traded his own life for mine. I am sick about it. I feel so guilty."

"You realize that the best thing you can do to honor him is to make sure you survive this. You must live. That's what he would have wanted."

Naomi looked into Fredrich's eyes. She saw kindness there, and it made her want to cry. "I know you're right. But when I think that I might never see my daughters again, I don't want to live. I don't want to go on without them."

"It's understandable, Naomi. But because of the sacrifice your husband made for you, you must live. Living is your revenge on Hitler."

Her shoulders slumped. She turned away from him and began to cry silently. Naomi was weeping so hard that her back was rocking.

Fredrich put down the squirrels and walked over to her. Gently, he put his hand on her arm. She looked up at him. In another time, in another life, the life she lived before Hitler, she would have cringed at the touch of a strange man, a man she hardly knew, and a goy too. It was forbidden in her world for a man to touch a woman who was not his wife. But she'd broken that law long ago when she'd fallen in love with Eli. *Perhaps it was my sin of loving Eli while I was married to Herschel that has caused me such misery in my life. My sister, Miriam, was convinced that my relationship with Eli was the reason our parents died. Perhaps Hashem is angry with me. But if that's true, then why are all of the Jews suffering? Not everyone broke the commandments. There were plenty of good, frum, religious people in that ghetto, starving, and dying for no good reason at all.*

And now as she sat on the dirt floor in a barn on the outskirts of a forest, all the laws she'd grown to believe were so important didn't seem to matter at all. The only thing that mattered was taking her next breath and somehow finding a way to get back to her daughters. "My husband is probably dead," she said more to herself than to Fredrich. "Poor Herschel. Things were not always perfect between us. But his life should never have ended this way. When I think that he is dead, it makes me hurt all over."

"So, the best thing to do is not think about it. Don't think of the things that make you sad. You desperately need to keep your spirits up. You must stay strong. That is the only way you will survive. That is how you will find your children again," he said.

"Do you believe they are still alive?"

"Yes. I do," he said encouragingly. "And, I believe you will find them again."

His hand was still on her arm. But she didn't mind it. She was glad for the human contact. She needed his strength, his reassurance. "Thank you," she said.

He nodded. "Of course, I am that type of fellow who prides himself on his charm. And so I make it a point to be of service to pretty ladies." He laughed a little. "I'm just joking. I'm really a rather shy fellow." Then he laughed again. "All right. So that's a lie too. I'm not shy. I'm outspoken. But I am not a charmer, and I am no ladies' man. The real truth is, I am rather boring. In fact, you might say I'm just an ordinary fellow."

"I am glad you're here with me," Naomi said. "You make me laugh, and you make me feel a little safer."

"We're in this together, you and I." He looked into her eyes. His face grew soft. She thought he might kiss her. And somehow she didn't think she would mind. Then he took a deep breath and looked away. He didn't kiss her. Instead, he said, "All right, I'll be right back with clean meat ready to cook."

She nodded and watched him walk outside. It didn't take him long, about twenty minutes before he returned. When he walked in, he was smiling. "Everything is ready to go. Now, let's try to cook this food without burning this place down. What do you say?"

Naomi nodded.

Fredrich took a match out of his pack and lit it. Next, he carefully started a piece of wood on fire. Then he placed it on top of the pile of wood which he'd loaded into the pit he dug. It took a few seconds. Then there was a fire inside the pit. He'd already driven a spit made from a wet tree branch through the meat. And he quickly began to cook the kabobs, turning them slowly over the open flame.

Once the meat was cooked, Fredrich put out the fire with his coat and then carefully pulled the meat off the stick and lay it on the ground to let it cool.

"Well, I've never eaten squirrel before, so this should be a new experience for both of us," Fredrich said, and then he smiled at Naomi. She let out a laugh.

"What's so funny?"

"All the years before the Nazis came, I was so careful to keep kosher. We didn't eat this, and we didn't eat that."

"I don't know what you're talking about."

"Keeping kosher is a Jewish religious law. Pork was not allowed. Shellfish was not allowed. I had two sets of dishes, one for milk, one for meat. All meat had to be blessed and declared kosher by a rabbi. We never mixed milk and meat. And when the Jewish holiday of

Passover came around, I changed both sets of dishes to special Passover dishes. Ahhhh..." She sighed. "We were so particular about what we ate, and now here I am about to eat squirrels. And would you believe that I am looking forward to it? I am so hungry that the smell of this meat is making me salivate."

He smiled. "Yes, I understand. The army taught me that when you are in a desperate situation, and your stomach is empty, you'll eat just about anything. I don't want to tell you some of the things I've eaten."

"Yes, it's probably best that you don't," she said, and they both laughed.

"The meat should be cool by now. I'm sorry, I know it's still smoky in here."

"It's all right. At least the windows in the stalls are open. The air will clear in time."

"Well, at least those open windows are good for something, right? I've been wishing that there were no open windows because it's so darn cold. But, you see, we found a reason to be happy about something that was previously an annoyance. So, that's a good thing."

She nodded, shivering a little from the cold.

"And soon it will be spring," she said, smiling.

"Yes, soon it will." He smiled back. Then he handed her a piece of cooked meat. As he did, his hand brushed hers.

Naomi felt a bolt of electricity flow through her. He must have felt it, too, because he looked into her eyes, and for a moment, they both stopped everything they were doing and stared at each other. Naomi was aware of him in ways she'd never been aware of him before. His manly fragrance—he smelled like the outdoors mixed with just a tinge of sweat. His large, capable hands were calloused but strong. It had been a long time since she'd felt a man's arms around her, and she found herself longing for Fredrich to hold her. As the thoughts entered her mind, she felt suddenly ashamed. Looking away, she tried to focus her attention on their meal. She took a bite of the meat. It was not what she had been expecting. It was light and nutty, and most of all, delicious. She closed her eyes and chewed. It had been a long time since she'd eaten meat. "It's good," she said.

"It is," he answered.

She opened her eyes and glanced up at him to find that he was still staring at her, and he was smiling.

CHAPTER FIFTY-THREE

♊

When Ernst returned home, he entered his apartment and searched for Gisele to tell her what he had done while he was in France, but she was not there. He was tired as he sank down into his favorite chair and sighed. *I told her not to go out. She went anyway. I just hope she is all right. She knew, just like I know, that our marriage is over. I wonder if she packed her things and left me.*

Ernst went to look in Gisele's closet to see if she'd taken her clothes. But they were still there. *I have no idea where she is, but I hope she is all right.*

He walked back into the living room and poured himself a glass of whiskey, which he drank with one gulp. Then he went to bed and slept a deep and dreamless sleep.

In the morning, he woke up feeling empty as he glanced over at the side of the bed where Gisele had slept. He leaned over and sank his face into her pillow. He smelled the fragrance of her shampoo, and a sadness came over him. *It's hard to say goodbye to a dream,* he thought. He felt spent and lazy and would have lain there all day and felt sorry for himself had it not been for Shoshana. He forced himself to get out of bed and get dressed.

CHAPTER FIFTY-FOUR

♊

There was a firm knock on the door. Ernst ran to open it. He thought it might be Gisele. It was not. Instead, he found two policemen standing there.

"Are you Dr. Ernst Neider?" one of them asked.

"I am," Ernst said.

"May we come in?"

"Of course," Ernst said.

Ernst opened the door wide, and the police walked inside.

"Do you work at the Auschwitz camp with Dr. Mengele?"

"Yes," Ernst said. He was nervous. He could not imagine why the police were at his home so early in the morning.

"And do you know a person by the name of Dr. Otto Schatz?"

"I do. He is a colleague of mine. We both work under Dr. Mengele."

"I see," the policeman said, then he cleared his throat. "Were you aware that your wife, Gisele Neider, was involved with Dr. Schatz?"

Ernst looked away. "I wasn't sure. But I thought it was possible."

"I'm sorry we must inform you that your wife's body was found in an alley. She's been murdered. Prior to her murder, Schatz's neighbor reported witnessing Dr. Schatz and Gisele having a fight in the hallway of his apartment building. We believe Otto Schatz killed your wife. We have arrested him."

Ernst was stunned. It was one thing for his marriage to be over, but it was altogether another thing for him to learn that Gisele was dead. He felt a deep ache in his chest. Tears flooded his eyes. "She's dead?" he asked in disbelief.

"Yes. I'm sorry."

Ernst nodded. Then the two policemen left his apartment. He sank down onto the sofa and wept. He acknowledged that she had not been a good wife. *But she still did not deserve to die*, he thought. Then he remembered Petoit and wondered if it had been Petoit or Otto who had killed Gisele. *Either way, I am not going to say a word to anyone. If Otto takes the fall, then so be it.*

Ernst felt sick. But he decided that he would rather go to work and see Shoshana than sit at home and mull over the miserable events of Gisele's death in his mind. So he gathered himself and went into work. As he drove toward the camp, he found he was looking forward to seeing Shoshana. He wanted to talk to her, to tell her everything that had happened. Somehow he knew it was safe to tell her. And it gave him comfort to know that he could trust her.

Ernst drove up to the gate at Auschwitz. The guard saluted him. "Heil Hitler, Dr. Neider," he said.

"Heil Hitler," Ernst responded, trying not to sound annoyed.

"Welcome back."

"Thank you," Ernst said as he maneuvered his automobile through the gate and down the path to the hospital. He was excited. In fact, it surprised him how much he couldn't wait to see Shoshana.

When he walked into the hospital, he was greeted by the nurses at the desk. "Welcome back. I hope you are feeling better," said a young, blonde nurse with her hair in two braids that wrapped around her head. "Dr. Mengele said you were ill."

"Yes, thank you. I am feeling much better," Ernst said as he picked up the tray of tubes and syringes that were to be used for the morning blood draws. Then he headed into the twins' room. He went to Shoshana's cot immediately and was shocked to find that Shoshana and Bluma were lying on Shoshana's cot curled up into each other like two abandoned kittens. His eyes searched the room for Perle, but she was nowhere to be seen.

"Where is Perle?" Ernst asked.

Shoshana raised her head. Her eyes were red, and her face was blotchy from crying. She looked at Ernst and shook her head.

"Dr. Otto gave her typhus. She died. And you weren't even here to help us," Bluma said angrily. She was bolder with Ernst than she was with the other doctors. It was as if she knew he would not turn her in no matter what she said. Bluma's face was red with anger. Her small fists were clenched as she went on to say, "My sister Shoshana told us that you were our friend. But you aren't. You're just like the others. You let them kill my sister."

Ernst was so stunned, he could not speak. His face fell. He shook his head and said, "No. It can't be. I am so sorry. No."

"Yes, my sister is dead. I was with her when she died. Mengele wanted to watch me suffer, and he got his wish. Now the other twins in this room are saying that Shoshana and I had better stop crying, or Mengele is going to send us to the gas. I don't care. I am not afraid to die. But I swear that if he doesn't kill me, someday when I am older and bigger and stronger, I will kill him. I will make him pay for what he did to Perle," Bluma said.

Ernst looked down at Bluma where she lay beside Shoshana. *She is so small and helpless, but so darn brave that it makes my heart ache. The poor child has just lost the most important person in her life, and of course she is angry and lashing out. It's to be expected. But it's dangerous for her to do that here in Auschwitz. I must silence her, because if Mengele hears her, he will think nothing of killing her.* "You mustn't speak like that. I know how much this hurts you, and I don't blame you for being angry. But I am trying to help you and your sister, and I can't protect you if you make Mengele angry. Please, Bluma, you must try your best to keep these thoughts to yourself."

Bluma sneered. "I hope Mengele does hear me. I want him to know how much I hate him."

"Please don't say these things out loud. I know you don't care what happens to you right now. But what about Shoshana? You wouldn't want Mengele to hurt Shoshana because he was angry at you, would you?" Ernst said gently.

This seemed to stop Bluma's outburst of rage. Her shoulders slumped, and tears began to flow down her cheeks. "No. I wouldn't want that. I wouldn't want that at all."

Shoshana didn't say a word. She didn't try to stop Bluma from speaking so harshly. Ernst studied her, and he knew that she had given up hope.

"Shoshana," he said, then in a voice that was barely a whisper, he continued. "I should have been here to stop this. I am sorry. I am truly sorry." Tears burned his eyes. "I didn't become a doctor to torture and kill. But I am stuck in this terrible place right now because I want to save you and Bluma. If it weren't for you two, I would leave Auschwitz and find another job far away from this place. But I can't leave you behind."

Shoshana looked at him blankly. "Perle was just a little girl. She was just a child. How could her existence have hurt men like Dr. Otto or Dr. Mengele? Why did they have to kill her? She had no power to hurt them, none at all. And you know how mild she was; she was just a gentle little soul. She would never have hurt anyone."

"But I would," Bluma declared. "I would kill them all if I could."

"Shhh, please, Bluma." Ernst's voice was commanding. "Now listen to me. You must keep those thoughts to yourself. I can't help you unless you work with me." He took a deep breath. "I know it's hard, but you must stop crying. You must. Unfortunately, now that you no longer have a twin sister, Mengele will probably have you transferred out to one of the blocks. I am going to do what I can to stop him from transferring you and Shoshana. But I can't guarantee that he will listen to me. If he doesn't, I will see to it that you both still get extra food. I will sneak it to you myself every day after I finish working. And I will make sure you both get decent job details. Then as soon as I can think of a way to help you escape, I will help you."

"That would put you at risk. You mean to tell me that you would put yourself in danger for my sister and I?" Shoshana asked.

"I plan on it," Ernst said.

"If you get caught, what will become of you?"

"Nothing good," he said, then he smiled. "But that won't stop me from trying."

Shoshana looked at him, and for a moment, a very brief moment, he thought he saw a light in her eyes. And from that moment, he had no doubt in his mind that he would risk his own life to help her and her sister. *I have done bad things working here with Mengele. But this is my opportunity to be the man I always wanted to be. And if I am caught and punished, it will be worth the pain and suffering to know that in the end my parents would have been proud of me.*

CHAPTER FIFTY-FIVE

♊

Bluma dreamed of Perle's final hours each night when she tried to sleep. Often she awoke screaming. Shoshana, lay beside her trying to quiet and comfort her. Other times she would wake up weeping fiercely.

Tonight was no different.

Bluma fell asleep beside Shoshana. But she dreamed that she was back in bed lying beside Perle in the hospital on the final night of Perle's life. Bluma knew that Perle had typhus. She'd heard Dr. Mengele talking to Dr. Otto when they gave Perle the injection. She had kicked and screamed and tried to stop them, but they tied her down with restraints. Mengele told Dr. Otto that he wanted to see how long it would take before Bluma caught the disease from her dying sister. "She heard you. Now she will be afraid," Dr. Otto said, referring to Bluma. She wanted to spit at him. She wasn't afraid of catching typhus. In fact, she almost wished she would so that she and Perle could die together. After all, they were born together, it seemed only right to Bluma that they should die together. But for some odd reason, Bluma seemed to be immune. She never showed a single symptom.

But she suffered nonetheless. Every ache and pain that ravaged Perle's small body was felt by her sister. Bluma saw Mengele watching her and Perle, and she could see in his eyes that he was enjoying her agony. However, nothing mattered to Bluma at that time but Perle. She hated to see Perle in pain. And she was angry with herself because she wasn't even able to offer Perle some water when Perle grew very thirsty. For three miserable days, Perle suffered in silence. Perle stopped communicating with Bluma. All she did was cry. And then after three days, in the middle of the night, Perle awoke. Bluma was lying beside Perle unable to sleep.

"Bluma," Perle said. Her face was lit as if she were illuminated by a candle. But there was no light in the room.

"Yes," Bluma responded, taking Perle's hand and holding it close to her heart.

"I had a dream." These were the first words Perle had spoken in three days.

"Yes. Tell me all about it." Bluma was relieved to see that Perle was speaking. It gave her a glimmer of hope that Perle might recover.

"It was about you."

"Me?" Bluma asked. "What did you dream about me?"

Perle cleared her throat. "You were swimming in the ocean. Do you remember how we always said we wanted to see the ocean? We said that someday we would swim in the ocean together."

"Of course, I remember. We saw pictures of it in books, and we used to say that someday when we grew up, we would take a trip to the ocean," Bluma said. "And someday we will. We will survive this place, Perle. I promise you, we will."

Perle smiled, and with a trembling hand, she touched her sister's face. "The ocean was beautiful, Bluma. The water was so blue. It was as blue as that robin's egg we found once a long time ago. Do you remember?"

"Of course. I remember everything we ever did together," Bluma said.

"And you should have seen the sky in my dream. It was so bright.

The sun was shining on your hair. And you were happy. You were so happy, Bluma. You were free from this place and alive and . . ." Perle closed her eyes. She reached over and took Bluma's hand. Perle squeezed Bluma's hand one last time. Then she said, "I love you."

"No," Bluma said, but she knew Perle was gone. And she began to weep. Bluma looked at her twin sister's small, lifeless body and swore that someday she would avenge her sister's death.

CHAPTER FIFTY-SIX

Ernst tried very hard, but he could not convince Mengele to keep Bluma and Shoshana in the twins' room. Mengele planned to send Bluma and Shoshana to the gas. So in pure desperation, Ernst took another approach, one he thought would appeal to Mengele. Ernst explained to Mengele that he wanted to keep Shoshana and Bluma where he could watch them so that he could calculate the amount of grief that the two sisters would suffer while in mourning over Perle. Mengele considered this and decided that this was a good reason to keep the girls alive. He liked the idea that Ernst would continue to observe them in their misery, so he agreed to have the sisters transferred to a block rather than sent to the gas.

"You are going to have to conduct your experiment with these two on your own time. When you are at work, you will do as I expect. Is that understood?"

"Yes, of course," Ernst said.

"Good, then let me know how long two young women will go on grieving over the death of an insignificant child. Won't you?"

"I will give you a full report," Ernst said.

CHAPTER FIFTY-SEVEN

⠈⠒ ⊓

Shoshana and Bluma were sent to live in a crowded, dirty block with other female inmates. Ernst brought them food the first night after they'd been transferred. When he saw Shoshana, he couldn't hide the horror in his eyes when he saw that her hair had been shaved. He reached up and touched her newly shaved head. Then in a soft voice, he said, "I'm so sorry."

In a small voice, she said, "It's all right. You know what I was thinking? I was thinking that if I had gotten married, my mother would have come to see me the day after my wedding, and she would have shaved my head. Of course, that would have been very different circumstances." She sighed wistfully. "Sometimes I regret not getting married. Not because I wanted to marry my betrothed, but because it might have given my parents some nachas to see me wed."

"Nachas?"

"Joy," she said. "I didn't know that they would be gone from my life so soon. I always thought that there would come a time when my father would forgive me. Now, it's too late. And that breaks my heart."

"So, you were engaged? Did you love him?"

"It was an arranged marriage. I hardly knew him."

"I understand," he said. "May I ask you a question?"

"Of course."

"I know it's probably none of my business, but I can't help but wonder why your mother would shave your head."

"Well, you see, once a woman is married in my religion, she should not show her hair to anyone but her family. So, as her hair is growing back, she wears a shatel, which is what we call a wig. Or she wears a head covering."

"That's interesting. But why?"

"Because hair is beautiful; it's a big part of a woman's beauty, and a married woman shouldn't want to attract the attention of men other than her husband. And also we cover our heads out of respect for God."

"Why did you choose not to marry him? I am assuming arranged marriages were common in your community. Was it because you felt you were too young?"

Shoshana let out a short laugh. "No, not at all. Girls marry very young in my community. I am not married because I refused to get married. I rebelled against my father and our traditions. It caused a lot of problems between my father and me. He was so angry that I defied him. He'd made a good match for me with a good man. And he felt I was ungrateful. He didn't speak to me for a long time. He sat shiva for me, mourned for me, as if I were dead."

"That had to hurt you," Ernst said.

"It did. My father refused to let my sisters and my mother associate with me. I was really heartbroken. But, I couldn't help my feelings. I wasn't ready to accept the marriage. I wanted something more. I wanted love, I guess."

"I can understand that." Ernst sighed. "Everyone wants to love and be loved. It's a human need."

"I suppose it is. But in my religion, we don't grow up to believe that. We marry for reasons other than love. And I just couldn't do it."

"I married for love," Ernst admitted sadly, "but I found that I was the only one in love. She never loved me."

"Do you really believe that?"

"I know it for a fact. She told me as much."

"I know she hurt you."

"She hurt me in so many ways," he said.

"I'm sorry to hear that. You are a good person. You deserve to be treated better," Shoshana said.

"I suppose."

"Are you still married to her?"

"No. She was murdered." *Someday, perhaps, I will tell Shoshana about Gisele and Petoit. And all about what the police said about Otto too. But not now. For now, I will keep it to myself. I would rather not risk anyone hearing the truth. It could bring the Gestapo to my door with questions.*

"I'm sorry," Shoshana said.

"It's probably for the best. It's sort of like a deep cut. Until it forms a scab, you can't start to heal. So, I bled when I found out she didn't want me. Then she left and my heart formed a scab. Now, I am healing." He smiled.

"You sound so much like a doctor." She returned his smile.

"I am a doctor. Since I was just a boy, all I ever really wanted to do was practice medicine. I should never have been chosen to work with Mengele. I am not his kind of a doctor. But . . . I am glad I am here, even if this is a terrible place, because I met you."

"I am glad you're here too. And not only am I glad I met you, but I am grateful to you for helping Bluma and I."

"I only wish I could have done something for Perle."

"Yes, so do I. I miss her every day," Shoshana admitted.

"I know," Ernst said, and he touched her shoulder.

The touch of a man was a rare thing for Shoshana. It felt warm and electrifying. She looked up into his eyes. And although the world would not have seen Ernst Neider as a handsome man, to Shoshana he was perfect.

Each evening, as Mengele expected, after Ernst finished his duties, he went to check on Shoshana and Bluma. But unbeknownst to Mengele, Ernst hid extra bread In the pockets of his jacket which he gave to them when he was certain no guards were watching. He examined both Shoshana and Bluma just to assure Mengele that he was actually conducting an experiment. And because he was considered to be their doctor, he was able to have them placed in work duties of his choice. He knew that he must make sure they had jobs that made them indispensable. That way they would not be sent to the gas by someone higher up than Ernst. Ernst had Shoshana sent to work as a seamstress, and Bluma was sent to work as slave labor at a neighboring factory.

CHAPTER FIFTY-EIGHT

♊

In his own way, Ernst grieved for Gisele. He was sorry that she had come to a bad end. But he knew it was not his fault. Even after she told him that she'd never loved him, he had still gone to France in an effort to make things right for her.

Otto was arrested and charged with Gisele's death. Even though Mengele seemed to favor him, when the time came and Otto needed Dr. Mengele, Mengele did nothing to help him.

Only Petoit knew what truly happened to Gisele. But he was no novice to homicide, and Gisele was not his first or his only victim. Nor were the poor Jewish families that he slaughtered and burned. Marcel Petoit was a serial criminal who had begun as an avid thief and over time graduated to become a vicious killer.

Over his lifetime, Petoit had amassed a large sum of money. However, when he was arrested, the police found twenty-three dead bodies in the basement of his home in Paris. He was tried and convicted. On May 25, 1946, he was beheaded by guillotine.

CHAPTER FIFTY-NINE

1944

Even though they were both lonely and very dependent upon
each other, Naomi and Fredrich had not yet become lovers.
However, they were very good friends. They had plenty of
time to talk about everything with each other, and they did. They
foraged for food together and shared a single blanket each night. As
time passed, they found themselves growing more attracted to one
another.

Naomi was glad to have someone to lean on. And Fredrich was
always kind to her. And she was as happy as she could be in light of
the situation. Her face was radiant, out of place in this dirty barn in
the middle of a dark forest. If it hadn't been for her constant
worrying about her children, Naomi would have been happy. Unlike
Fredrich who, it seemed, was always happy these days.

Spring finally arrived, and the weather began to grow warmer. It
was a welcome relief from the miserable cold they'd endured. "I
know how to find wild mushrooms, the kind that are safe to eat,"
Naomi said. "Would you like to come with me?"

"I would," he answered, smiling. He'd gone fishing that morning, and they decided that it would be nice to have fish and mushrooms for their meal that day. They walked slowly until they were on the outskirts of the forest near a hill. Naomi climbed it easily. He followed.

On the hillside, Fredrich knelt at Naomi's feet and gave her a small bouquet of wildflowers. She smiled and kissed his cheek as she accepted the flowers. Tears came to her eyes. The smell of wildflowers and searching for mushrooms brought back memories of Eli, the only man she had ever truly loved. She was recalling how she and Eli had searched for wild mushrooms together. It seemed so long ago. Like a thousand years ago. But the smell of wildflowers would always take her back to those tender days when she and Eli were lovers.

She looked into Fredrich's eyes. *He is a special man, and I am very fortunate to have him here with me. He makes me as happy as I can be, considering the circumstances. I hope I make him happy too. I know he is falling in love with me. However, I can't return that love. I just don't think I will ever love anyone the way I once loved Eli. But I do care for Fredrich.*

"What are you thinking? I hope I didn't offend you by giving you those flowers," Fredrich said. "Please know that I would never want to make you uncomfortable. But the truth is, I have something to tell you. You have become my queen." He bit his tongue. "It has been a long time since I have been around a woman. And I know you and I are from very different religious backgrounds." He hesitated, then he continued. "I suppose what I am trying to say is please forgive me, but I think I am falling in love with you."

Naomi smiled. "I'm not offended about the flowers. I am touched by your kindness," she said. Then she touched his face.

"I feel so giddy around you. I feel like dancing and laughing. In the middle of this terrible war, I find I am joyful," he said.

Naomi laughed. Her laugh was deep and rich. It was like a song, a lullaby to Fredrich, and he smiled at the song of her laugh.

"You have a beautiful laugh," he said clumsily, drunk on the sunshine, his feelings for Naomi, and the promise of spring.

"A beautiful laugh?" she said. "I am not sure what that means."

"Me neither." He laughed.

Then they both laughed. Slowly he walked over to where she stood and leaned down to kiss her. Ever so softly he pressed his lips against hers. She sighed. It felt good to be so close to him.

"I was serious when I said that I am falling in love with you," Fredrich said.

She turned away. "I think perhaps you feel that way because we are here alone in this forest and so dependent upon each other for survival. I don't know if you really love me."

"But you don't feel the same way as I do, do you?" he asked.

"I feel something. Something wonderful and precious. When you and I talk, I feel warm and safe. I don't know if it's love. Maybe it is. All I know is that I am happy that you are here with me."

"I am happy too," he said. "It's very strange. We are in danger every day. In danger from starvation, from wild animals, from the weather, from the Nazis, and yet I am the most fulfilled I have ever been in my life. That's what love will do," he said, winking at her.

She smiled. Her hand was trembling as she reached up and touched his face. His beard was thick and long.

"I hope my beard doesn't hurt your skin," he said. "I wish I had a razor."

She laughed hard. "Where I come from, all the men have beards. They don't shave them. So, I suppose it's something very natural to me."

They both laughed. Then hand in hand, they walked back toward the barn.

When they got to the barn, Naomi put the basket down. "The weather is getting much better," she said. "Can we start walking toward Warsaw, toward the ghetto where I last saw my daughters? I pray that I will find them again."

"I did promise you that we'd go there, didn't I?"

"You did."

"Once we find them, we will have to think of a way to help them escape."

"Yes," she said. "I pray they are alive."

"I know. So do I," he said.

"So, we will leave tomorrow?" she asked.

"I think we might need to prepare a little before we go," Fredrich said, then he shook his head. "It sure has been nice having the shelter in this barn for a while. But I understand that you need to find your children. So, why don't we gather as much food as we can over the next several days. I'll go into the house and see if there's anything we can take with us on our journey."

"But we both agreed that we weren't going to go into the house."

"I know we said we weren't going to go into the house unless we absolutely had to. But if we are leaving this barn anyway, I'll see what kind of supplies I can find. Of course, I'll have my gun and whatever ammunition I have left. But before we leave, I think I should go hunting so I can get some meat for us. It'll take a couple of days to dry the meat because we aren't going to cook it. But, at least we'll have some food to take with us. I figure with all of that to do, we can leave by the end of the week."

"Thank you," she said.

CHAPTER SIXTY

♊

Fredrich slept like a cat. The slightest sound awakened him. He had come to know the familiar sounds of the forest. And even while he was asleep, he felt he could sense when something wasn't right. His time as a soldier had trained his ears to sift out unfamiliar sounds. That's why he was so surprised when he awoke the following morning to find himself surrounded by five German soldiers.

"Ein Deserteur. Ein Verrater, a deserter, a traitor," one of the soldiers said.

Naomi heard the strange voice. And immediately she was awake. She sat up quickly. Her dark hair spilled across her shoulders. Her black eyes stared at Fredrich wide with terror.

"And he has a woman here with him. Look at that black hair and those dark eyes. Do you think she's a Jew?" another of the soldiers asked.

"Might be. A deserter would take up with a Jew. She could be a Gypsy. He is a piece of filth just like her."

"She's not Jewish," Fredrich said quickly, hoping to protect Naomi. "I promise you that. She's not a Gypsy either. She's just a girl

I met who lives on one of the farms here. She's a Pole, but not a Jew. Let her go. Let her go home. Take me."

"And do you think we would take the word of a man like you? A man who would desert his fellow soldiers and disgrace the fatherland? You should be ashamed of yourself." The soldier pulled a gun.

Naomi screamed. But it was as if the soldier didn't hear her. He shot Fredrich in the face. Pieces of brain matter flew into Naomi's face. She was screaming hysterically now. When Naomi looked at Fredrich, he was unrecognizable. Another cry of anguish leapt from her throat. And then another. She was wailing like a dying animal when the oldest of the soldiers pushed her onto the ground and forced himself on her. Weeping, screaming, Naomi's entire body was trembling as the soldiers took turns violating her until they were spent. It took them almost an hour. By the time they had finished with her, she was no longer screaming. She was silent.

Naomi lay on the ground shaking so hard that she felt her body was going to break into pieces. Her dress was scrunched up around her waist, and blood pooled on the ground surrounding her naked thighs.

One of the soldiers, a young boy of no more than seventeen, pulled Naomi's skirt down and covered her. He ran outside the barn, and Naomi could hear him gagging and vomiting. Naomi lay there on the ground. She didn't move.

"Shall I shoot her?" one of the soldiers asked.

"Yes, why not?"

"We could take her along, use her again whenever we need a woman," another one of the soldiers suggested.

"That's a good idea. And we'll get rid of her when we've finished with her," the oldest soldier, the one who was obviously in charge, said.

Naomi heard their words, but they didn't register. She was in shock, traumatized by Fredrich's death and then the rape.

One of the soldiers picked her up by her arm. He was rough, and it felt as if he'd dislocated her shoulder. Pain shot through her, but her body was already hurting so badly that she didn't even respond. He pushed her forward with the butt of his rifle. "Let's get going," he said.

Naomi turned. She looked back and saw Fredrich's dead body. And once again, she began to weep. Softly this time.

"Don't start that again, or I swear I'll shoot you right here and now. I am allowing you to live for the moment. But if you make it hard for me to tolerate having you around, I can eliminate you just as easily," the leader said.

Naomi nodded. The reality of her situation was upon her. She wasn't ready to die. Not yet. Not if there was a chance her daughters were still alive.

The beauty of spring that Naomi had so marveled at the day before no longer seemed to exist. The sun shined, the trees were budding, and tiny wildflowers filled the open field, but she saw none of it. In her mind's eye all she could see was Fredrich, faceless, a mass of blood and tissue. He was gone, and she was at the mercy of the most horrible men she had ever known.

CHAPTER SIXTY-ONE

♊

The Nazi soldiers began walking toward the open road. As they walked along, they came across another platoon of German soldiers who were driving by in an open-air truck. They were on their way to deliver a group of prisoners to a concentration camp located not far from the forest. They were disappointed to see the truckful of soldiers because they had hoped to have their way with Naomi at least a few more times before shooting her and leaving the evidence of what they had done behind them.

"Heil Hitler." The truck stopped. The leader of the new troop of soldiers jumped down from the truck bed and saluted them.

"Heil Hitler," the other troop leader answered.

"I see you have a prisoner with you. A Jew, I am assuming."

"I don't know. But we found her in the forest. She had no papers, and she was running with a deserter."

"Since we are on our way to Auschwitz, we'll take the girl with us and leave her at the camp," the leader of the new troop said. The others who were looking forward to having more fun with Naomi hid their disappointment. By the stripes on the shoulder of the leader of the troop on the truck, they could see that he was of a higher rank than their leader. So they knew that his orders must be followed.

Naomi was pushed up onto the bed of the truck where she sat beside a ragged-looking man with a defiant face. The truck bumped and jerked along the rough terrain. Naomi had no idea where she was going, but she was relieved to be going away from that group of soldiers. She knew that if they still had her in their custody, they would rape her again and again until they killed her. She shivered at the memory of what they'd done to her. And what they had done to Fredrich. Not only did she remember the horror of Fredrich's death and her rape, but she also recalled the sweetness of the day before.

She thought about Fredrich's kindness and how hopeful she'd been when he promised that they would return to the Warsaw Ghetto to look for her daughters. It made her feel so sad when she thought about how he had said he loved her. *If I had known then that he would die this way, I would have told him that I loved him too. Even though it would have been a lie. I would have done it to give him that last final bit of joy. I cared for him, but I have only loved one man in my life and that was Eli. Still, Fredrich was so kind to me, and I will never forget him*, she thought. The three Nazi soldiers who were guarding the group were busy talking with each other. But even so, they never put down their rifles which were pointed directly at the prisoners. The ragged man with the sharp eagle eyes who sat beside Naomi watched the guards carefully. Then when the guards were busy talking among themselves, he whispered to Naomi, "When we get to our destination, make sure you look healthy like you can work. If you do, it will give you a better chance of survival."

"Survival?"

"Yes, they are killing people," he said.

"I've heard that."

"If you don't look healthy enough to work, you will be eliminated. It's that simple." His voice was barely audible, but she heard him.

She nodded. "Thank you for warning me."

"Bite your lip, and then take the blood and smear it on your cheeks so they look rosy."

"All right," she whispered.

He nodded and didn't say another word the rest of the trip.

When they arrived at Auschwitz, Naomi saw a sign that said, "Work Makes You Free." She glanced at the man beside her. He shook his head.

"It won't make you free, but it might keep you alive. At least until they don't need you anymore."

CHAPTER SIXTY-TWO

Ⅱ

The prisoners were forced to jump off the back of the truck. Then they were ushered into a line of other prisoners who had just arrived on a train. The guards were herding them to move forward like cattle going to the slaughterhouse. Naomi was frightened and confused. *Where am I? What is this place?* she thought. *Is this the same place the train was going? Is Herschel here? Is it possible he is alive?* A guard pushed her, and she moved up closer to the front of the line where she saw a smiling man with straight dark hair and a space between his teeth. Even though he was smiling, he looked evil. Naomi shivered. The man introduced himself to the group: "I am Dr. Mengele, but you can call me Uncle Mengele." Naomi couldn't believe what she'd just heard; she forced herself to stifle a scream. This man, this doctor, this "Uncle" Mengele, had been in Perle's dream. He was standing right in front of her, and he was exactly as Perle had described him. *Where am I? Where am I?* She wanted to cry out loud, *"Help me, someone tell me what is going on here."* But she bit her tongue and forced herself to keep silent.

"Left, right. Left, right." Uncle Mengele pointed his finger as he smiled at the new prisoners.

"You look oddly familiar," he said when he looked at Naomi. "Oddly familiar indeed."

"I am young, and I am strong. I can work hard," Naomi said.

"Oh?" He seemed amused. "And what can you do?"

"I can cook. I can garden. I can clean. And, I am a very, very good seamstress."

"Are you, now?"

"Oh yes, I have made wedding gowns all by myself. I've hand embroidered and sewn pearls on individually. I can make a gown that is so magnificent any woman would be thrilled to wear it." Naomi was talking fast. Her nerves were on edge. It seemed that this man was the person who would decide if she was healthy enough to work and make herself useful or if she was going to die today.

Uncle Mengele laughed. "All right. You are a very convincing Jewis. So, why not." He shrugged. "You can go to the land of the living, at least for now. Some of our officers might just be interested in sending their prospective brides to you to be fitted for their gowns. But . . . you had better be capable of what you say you can do."

"Thank you. Thank you," she said. "I promise you I won't disappoint you."

"Move along. Follow the line. Before I change my mind," Mengele said.

Naomi followed a lineup of women. Her head was shaved bald. Then she was showered and deloused. Once she was clean, she was given a uniform and a pair of clogs. And was sent into another line where she received a dark-greenish-blue tattoo of a number on her forearm. The pinpricks hurt, but she sat quietly.

Now she and the rest of the group were sent to their blocks. Naomi entered the dirty, overcrowded room filled with women, many of whom were scratching themselves. "There's lice in the straw," one of the women said almost apologetically. Naomi didn't answer. She searched for an open cot but found nothing until another woman, a young, pretty girl with a dark-blue eyes surrounded by worry lines, walked over to her. "Come, there is place for you right here by me," she said. Naomi followed her to a small opening between two other inmates. "Right here," the blue-eyed girl said.

Another woman who was standing nearby looked at Naomi and said, "You're in luck, Devorah died right there in that bed this morning. So that's why you have an open bed."

"A woman died here?" Naomi asked.

"Yes, I am afraid so. But don't think about that. You have a place to sleep. That's all you need to know." The blue-eyed young woman smiled at her. "My name is Leah," she said.

"I'm Naomi."

"It's nice to meet you."

"Likewise."

"And that one, the one over there who is always filled with gloom, her name is Zissel. I know Zissel means sweet, but she's not sweet. Are you, Zissel?" Leah indicated the woman who had just told Naomi that someone died in her bed.

"I'm sweet," Zissel said. "As sweet as I can be living in this hell."

"See, I told you. She's not so sweet. But you'll get used to her. And once you do, she's all right."

CHAPTER SIXTY-THREE

The following morning when the bell rang, Leah woke Naomi up. "Hurry, we have to get to roll call."

Naomi followed Leah outside where the prisoners were lined up. It had snowed the night before. It was an unusually late snow, and a light dusting covered the ground.

Two young women dragged a dead body out of one of the blocks and laid it on a pile of dead bodies.

A Nazi officer stood at the front of the lineup. He was surrounded by two armed guards pointing guns directly at the prisoners.

"Don't speak. Keep your eyes cast down at the ground; don't look directly at them. Answer when your number is called," Leah whispered to Naomi. Then she indicated the number that had been tattooed on Naomi's arm. "That's your number. You'll be referred to by the Nazis by that number from now on."

Naomi nodded. She felt the sweat beading on her forehead even though she was shivering from the cold.

The Nazi officer called the numbers of each prisoner. And although she was terrified, Naomi managed to answer when her number was called.

When the number of the dead prisoner was called, one of the young women who had brought out the body answered, "She died last night. Her body is on the pile."

The Nazi tapped his leg with what appeared to be a riding stick, and then he turned to a guard of inferior rank and said, "Go and check the pile. Make sure that the body with this number is there."

The inferior officer nodded.

Then the officer continued the roll call.

After the guard was satisfied that no one had run away during the night, Naomi was escorted to the sewing room.

"Three-seven-five-four-two," the guard called out when they entered the room.

A middle-aged woman stood up and quickly came forward. Her back was slightly hunched from years at a sewing machine. But she didn't complain. She just nodded and displayed the number on her arm.

The guard studied the number, then he indicated Naomi and said, "Three-seven-five-four-two, you will take this woman and show her what she must do. However, don't get any wise ideas about having a lazy day because you are training; you will still be expected to make your full quota today."

The middle-aged woman known as 37542 nodded. "Come with me," she said to Naomi.

Naomi followed her to a table.

"Sit here," said 37542.

Naomi sat down.

"We make uniforms for the German Army," she said. The guard walked away. The woman looked at him and whispered to Naomi, "Vi tsu derleb ikh im shoyn tsu bagrobn: that's an old Yiddish curse; it means, I should live long enough to bury him."

Naomi smiled and nodded her head. "I know," she said. "I speak Yiddish."

"It's nice to meet you, I'm Bashe," said 37542.

"I'm Naomi. Nice to meet you too."

CHAPTER SIXTY-FOUR

Ⅱ

S
hoshana hardly ever looked up from her sewing machine. She had never been a fast sewer like her mother, so she had a difficult time fulfilling her quota each day. But today she was hand stitching, tiny stitches, and she was feeling a little nauseated from staring at the needle. When she looked up, she could hardly believe her eyes. *I must be imagining it. Is that my mother? Could it be that my mother is here?* It took every ounce of restraint she could muster not to jump up and run to Naomi. But she knew that an action like that could easily get the two of them shot. She'd seen women shot for less. *I must force myself to keep up with my work and make my quota. I cannot slow down. But as soon as we are done for the day, I will go to her and hold her as I have longed to do. I will tell her that Bluma is alive and how much we both have missed her. And then . . . and then . . . I will have to tell her about Perle. We will grieve together. She will tell Bluma and I where Papa is, and I will ask Ernst if he can help us to see our father. It is a joyous day. I give thanks to Hashem.*

CHAPTER SIXTY-FIVE

$$\text{II}$$

Every day in the sewing room was long and difficult. Since she'd started working there, Shoshana had developed pain in her shoulders and neck. But today seemed even longer than usual. It was so difficult to stay in her seat and not stand up and run to her mother. She longed to feel like a child again. And even if she knew she wasn't safe, at least she could pretend to be in her mother's embrace. Shoshana couldn't concentrate on her work, and even though she was behind in her quota, it was impossible to take her eyes off her mother. *She's alive. My mother is alive.* She said the words over and over in her mind.

Bashe was busy teaching Naomi everything she would need to know to survive in the sewing room. As Shoshana watched them, she had no doubt that her mother could easily keep up with the quota. As a child she'd watched her mother make clothes for her and her sisters, and wedding gowns for friends who were getting married. She was fast on the machine and quick and efficient with her hand sewing. There was no garment she couldn't alter. No fabric or embellishment too difficult for her to handle. Her designs were always exquisite. *My mother will be all right here in this sewing room.*

The guards will learn quickly enough that she is a valuable asset, and that will be a good thing. It will keep her alive.

Finally, the bell rang. The workday was over, and it was time to eat. Bashe linked her arm through Naomi's. She was talking softly to her as she was leading her to the food area. Shoshana rushed up to them. "Mama," she said breathlessly.

Naomi whirled around and gasped. "Shoshana? You're alive. Oh, dear God in heaven. Gott im Himmel. My daughter is here. My oldest child is alive." Naomi caught Shoshana in a bear hug, and they both began to cry. "This is my daughter," Naomi said to Bashe. "We were separated. I didn't know if I would ever see her again." Tears spilled down Naomi's cheeks. "Are Bluma and Perle here too?"

"Bluma is here."

"Is she all right?"

"Yes, she works in a factory."

"Oy, she's just a little girl. Does she do all right?"

"Yes, she manages."

"And my little Perle? Where is my little Perle?"

Shoshana trembled. "Oh Mama," she said and shook her head. The words caught in Shoshana's throat. "Oh Mama, Perle died."

It was as if someone punched Naomi in the stomach. All the air left her lungs, and she bent over at the waist trying to catch her breath. She was panting. "No, no, it can't be. She was only a child. Just a child."

"Yes, I know. Bluma and I are heartbroken. I tried to protect her, but I couldn't. Little Bluma tried too. You know how bold our Bluma is . . ." Tears were falling down Shoshana's cheeks. "Mama. I am so sorry. I am so sorry."

"I have endured so much, and I haven't given up. But not this. Not the loss of my Perle. I can't go on."

"Mama. You must go on. You still have Bluma and I. We are still alive, and we have been praying every day that we would see you again. I need you. Bluma needs you. She lost her twin, her best friend. You know how close they were."

Naomi tried to pull herself together. "Where is Bluma? Can we see her now?"

"Yes, come let's go to the food area. She will be there waiting. She is going to be so happy to see you, Mama."

When they approached Bluma, she was already in line waiting for Shoshana. Her face lit up when she saw Naomi. "Mama!" she screamed. "Mama, you're here."

Shoshana pulled Naomi and Bashe into the line beside Bluma.

Naomi looked into Bluma's face and nodded. "I am alive," she said softly. Then she pulled Bluma into her arms. For several moments Naomi rocked her daughter slowly without speaking. Tears spilled down both their faces. Shoshana was crying too.

"Mama, where is Papa?" Bluma asked.

"I don't know. We were separated when we were on the train. It's a long story, and I am too tired to explain what happened right now," Naomi said. "Before I was arrested and brought here, I was living in the forest for months. I'll tell you more when I am rested."

"Is Papa here at Auschwitz?" Bluma asked.

"I don't know if he is or not. I haven't seen him since I left the train."

"You left the train without Papa?"

"Yes, like I said, it's a very long story," Naomi said.

"I told Mama about Perle," Shoshana said to Bluma.

"Oh, Mama," Bluma said. "I lost my sister, my twin. And for no reason. No good reason." Bluma's eyes were glaring with hatred, "Someday I am going to kill all of the Nazis."

"Shhhh. Be quiet. Do I constantly have to remind you of how dangerous it is here? You know better than to say what you think out loud like that. Whisper if you have something you feel you must say," Shoshana reprimanded Bluma. Then she turned to Naomi: "It's a good thing Bluma saved us a place in line. You are going to find that if you are not in line early, you won't get any vegetables in your soup. All that is left by the end of the line is broth."

When they got to the front of the line, they were served a single ladle of soup. Then they walked to an open space and sat down on the ground.

Naomi watched Bluma scoop an insect out of her soup and toss it on the ground. She shivered. *My girls used to be such picky eaters. Just look at what the Nazis have done to us.* It had been two days since Naomi's last meal, and her stomach was growling. A small bowl of broth hardly sufficed. But she didn't say anything

"Don't worry, Mama. I know you must be very hungry. I have a friend who will bring me some bread this evening. Don't tell anyone about it, because we are not supposed to receive extra food. But I know you are hungry, and I will bring bread for you to work with me in the morning."

"No, no, I'm not hungry at all," Naomi lied. "You eat it, you and Bluma. You two girls are growing; you need the food." She thought of Perle. *How am I ever going to get used to this? How am I ever going to get used to saying, I have two daughters, not three. Oh Hashem, why? Why did you take my sweet little Perle? She was such a guteh neshomeh, such a good soul.*

A loud bell rang. "That bell means we must go to our blocks," Shoshana said. "I'll see you tomorrow in the sewing room." Shoshana hugged her mother tightly. "I love you, Mama."

Naomi grabbed Bluma and pulled her into the hug. They were all crying. "I love you girls so much. So much."

CHAPTER SIXTY-SIX

♊

"My mother is here," Shoshana said in an excited whisper as soon as Ernst arrived. "I haven't seen her in so long."

He handed her the bread and smiled at her.

"It's bittersweet," she said. "I missed her so. And I am so glad she is alive. But I wish we were free, not here in this place. It's so terrifying."

"I know. And that's why I have decided that I am going to try to get you out."

"How? Where will we go?"

"I'm thinking Switzerland." His voice was barely a whisper. "It won't be an easy journey. But we can do it."

"Should we wait until later in the spring?"

"Ideally? Yes. But I can't trust the Nazis not to hurt you or your family. The sooner we can get you out of here, the better."

"But how?"

"I don't know yet. I am thinking about it constantly. I must find a way. I must. And I will," he said.

CHAPTER SIXTY-SEVEN

Ernst couldn't sleep that night. He had been having trouble sleeping since he returned from his trip to France and found that Perle had been murdered. He knew it was best not to ask Mengele why he had done what he did to Perle. If he asked Mengele too many questions that had to do with Shoshana and her family, it would pique Mengele's interest, and he would do horrible things to Shoshana just to watch Ernst's reaction. *He already has some idea that she and her family are special to me. But I must try my best to make it appear as if my interest in them is purely intellectual. He would have gassed Bluma if I had not convinced him that because she has such small but capable hands, she would be of use as slave labor in the munitions factory. I don't like her working there. It's far too dangerous for anyone, let alone a child. And the walk to and from the factory must be very hard on her. Her legs are short, and it's more than a couple of miles. No child should endure a place like Auschwitz.*

He was nervous. The lives of Shoshana and her family were at stake. Everything depended upon him and his making the right decisions. How he longed for another swig of whiskey, something to dull his senses.

Ernst had come to know his boss very well. He'd been observing Mengele since he began working for him. And because he knew Mengele, he was frightened of the future. *Mengele loves to play games, mean, cruel, sadistic games, where he earns trust and then breaks it. He enjoys hurting people, adults, but mostly children. And especially twins. I am convinced that Mengele is fascinated by twins because he knows they seem to have a special bond between them. And because they love each other so deeply, Mengele knows that they suffer deeply when their twin is hurt. And this fascinates the sadist in Mengele.*

The bottle of bourbon was almost empty. Ernst knew it was. He had planned to save it until the following day. But he couldn't. His nerves were on edge. He needed that dulling sensation that alcohol gave him. So he got out of bed to finish what was left. Ernst realized that he had been drinking too much lately, and yet it was the only thing that seemed to soothe his anxiety. Taking the bottle down from the shelf, he looked at the small amount of liquid that was left. Not bothering with a glass, he dropped into his favorite chair and took a swig. The heat of the alcohol warmed his throat. *I'm a smart man*, he thought. *I have never been a handsome man. But I've always been smart. Now is the time to use my brain. I must figure this out. I must devise a plan to save Shoshana and her family.*

He stayed awake searching for a solution until his head hurt and his eyes burned. But by morning, he had a solution.

CHAPTER SIXTY-EIGHT

♊

Ernst finished his morning blood draw in the room with the dwarfs. Then he entered the twins' room where he saw Bodo, Mengele's new assistant who had been hired to replace Otto, drawing a large amount of blood from the neck of a young child. Two guards were holding the child's arms and legs to restrain him. But the child was screaming in agony.

"What is going on here? I demand to know," Ernst asked.

"Dr. Mengele told me to draw the blood from their necks from now on. He says he needs larger amounts of blood."

"That is not necessary. Do you realize how painful that is?" Ernst said. "Even if you do it correctly. And my guess is, you are not doing it correctly."

"I am only following Dr. Mengele's orders." Bodo smiled, shrugging his shoulders. "He is planning to do some experimental work with blood transfusions, using the twins."

Ernst hated Bodo. But he knew Bodo was telling the truth. And it would do no good to say anything to Mengele. It would only anger him. Ernst shook his head and walked over to the set of twins in the next cot.

"I'll finish the blood draws today. Mengele wants you to remove the heart and liver from the dwarf he euthanized yesterday and then ship the body parts out to the Institute of Berlin Dahlem for examination," Bodo said.

Ernst couldn't speak. He just nodded. *So, that poor little fellow died.* Ernst had not become close to this prisoner, but he knew that although the man had been small, he had the heart of a lion. And he had stood up to Mengele on more than one occasion. Ernst admired the little man but also knew that Mengele had it in for him. *When I returned from France and saw that Mengele castrated the poor little fellow without anesthesia while I was gone, I knew the dwarf would die.*

"Did he die of an infection?" Ernst asked, not knowing why he wanted to know the answer.

"No, Mengele was hoping he would, but he didn't. So, yesterday Mengele gave him a fatal injection to get rid of him," Bodo said.

How did a man like Mengele ever get through medical school? How did a man like him ever become a doctor? And what about Bodo? Is he just an opportunist? Or is he a sadist, just like Mengele? I must stop thinking about this. I cannot allow myself to drown in the horror of this or I won't be able to help Shoshana and her family. I must keep my direction clear and focused. It is the only way my plan can succeed.

Ernst had an overwhelming feeling of sadness and disgust as he dissected the body of the little man Mengele had killed the day before. He carefully stored the organs and made them ready for shipping. Then he left the operating theater and went to his office where he took a swig from a bottle of schnapps that he kept in his desk drawer. He had no appetite for food, again, only for alcohol.

CHAPTER SIXTY-NINE

Ⅱ

Shoshana was sitting on the dirt floor telling Bluma a story, when Ernst came in that evening. "How is your mother?" he asked.

"She seems to be all right. Of course, she is very shaken up about Perle. We all are."

"I understand. I am too. I wish I had never left you. Perhaps I shouldn't have gone to France. But, even so, if I am being truthful, I am not sure I could have helped Perle, even if I was here. But you know that I would have tried."

"I *know* you would have," she said.

He handed her a loaf of bread. "I brought extra so you and Bluma would have plenty to share with your mother. I also brought you a blanket. It's freezing in here."

"You are kind," Shoshana said.

He smiled and nodded. "Now, I want to talk to you. I have an idea for an escape. But before I share it with you, you must promise me that you won't tell any of the other prisoners that you are planning to escape." He was close to her, whispering.

"But why?" she responded in a whisper. "They hate the guards as much as I do."

"Yes, they hate the guards. But remember, you haven't been out here in the general population very long. You are new to this. So, I am going to tell you what happens when a prisoner tries to escape."

"All right."

"If a prisoner attempts to flee, the guards torture all of the other prisoners in the camp. They make their lives miserable. So, when any of the prisoners find out that someone is planning to escape, they will do whatever they can to prevent it. That means that you cannot trust your fellow inmates. I promise you that if they know that you are planning to run, they will tell on you. And if we are found out, we will all be put to death. Even me," Ernst said, his voice barely a whisper.

"Do you think we should attempt to get out of here?"

"I think we must. Every day that you are a prisoner in this place, you are in danger. Bluma is in danger. Your mother is too. You are at the mercy of very cruel men with too much power. And, as much as I wish I could protect you, I am unable to protect you in here."

"So, you would risk your life for me and my family?" she said softly.

"Yes, Shoshana. There is a light that shines from your eyes. That light guided me through a very dark time in my life. You were the only person I could talk to about my wife. You are good and kind. And . . . well, I find that I care deeply for you."

"If we decide to do break out of here, are you going to come with us? Or are you going to stay here at Auschwitz working for Dr. Mengele? I know it's none of my business. But I care about you too," she said.

He didn't know what compelled him to do it, but he reached up and gently touched her cheek. "I would like to go with you. That is if you want me to. If not, I understand. And I will stay here, but I will help you as best I can to escape."

She was silent for a moment, looking down at the floor. Then she looked up at him. The light from a single overhead bulb reflected in her eyes. "I want you to come with us."

He smiled and took her hand in his. "I swear I will do whatever I can to get you to safety."

"Can I at least talk to my mother about it?"

"No, not yet. I don't want you to tell anyone. I understand that she is your mother. But she won't understand how it is in here, and we can't take the risk of her talking to any of the other prisoners. I think the best thing to do is tell her on the day we plan to leave."

"All right," Shoshana said. "I'll do as you say."

"I don't like to demand that anyone take orders from me. And in most cases, I wouldn't. Especially not you. I respect you, and I would never try to tell you what to do. However, because this is such a dangerous situation, I appreciate your cooperating with me."

She nodded. "I'm terrified. I am so afraid we will get caught . . ."

"I am afraid too. I won't lie to you. It's crossed my mind."

"My sister is just a child. I can't imagine the guards shooting her. My poor, brave Bluma. And besides, I have already lost one sister. I don't know if I want to risk everything trying to do this."

"We could stay here if you choose. I know you think it's safer to just stay where you are. But it's not. I promise you that, Shoshana. In fact, I know it would be a mistake. We are best off to try and get you out."

She shook her head. "I'm not sure, Ernst. I am afraid of the consequences."

"I'll do whatever you want," he said.

"For now, I don't want to take the risk. I know you mean well. But, everything is going along just fine and . . ."

"I'll respect your wishes," he said.

CHAPTER SEVENTY

♊

The following Monday, one of the low-ranking Nazi officers came to work in a foul mood. He'd had a terrible fight with his wife the night before and he was angry and sour. His wife was always making demands on him. No matter how much he gave her, she always seemed to want more. And when he was not able to provide it, she let him know that she thought he was a failure. She compared him to his superiors and declared that she didn't believe he would ever rise to their positions. For the first time last night, he had slapped her. It felt good, so he slapped her again. Then he continued to hit her until blood ran from her nose and mouth. When he looked at her and realized what he had done, he walked out of the house.

He got into his automobile and drove until he found himself at a hidden tavern. He had been there before. He went whenever he was frustrated and was able to escape the prying eyes of his wife. He went inside and searched for a discreet male companion. But the only other patrons in the bar were a couple. And so he was forced to drink alone.

When he arrived at the camp that morning to find that he was scheduled to participate in roll call, he was annoyed and angry. He'd only recently been transferred to the women's side of the prison due to an embarrassing indiscretion with a male prisoner in the men's camp. Of course, he had denied the entire incident, but his superior officer had not believed him. But he was lucky his superior officer had decided not to have him prosecuted for the incident. Instead, he kept his secret and opted to transfer him. The guard should have been grateful, but he knew better. He knew that his superior officer didn't do this out of kindness. He did it because he wanted to have something on him. Something he could use in the future to manipulate him if he needed to.

The morning roll-call bell rang, and the women lined up. They were on his nerves. Everything was on his nerves that day. He called out the numbers. The prisoners responded. But then he heard a young girl whispering something to another girl. *The audacity!* he thought. *How dare they speak when I am conducting roll call.* His anger and exasperation got the better of him. *I have the power to do what I please with them.* In a moment of rage, he grabbed one of the women by the shoulder and threw her down on the ground.

"Look, all of you. Watch this, and let it be a lesson to you never to speak when I am speaking," the guard said. Then he pulled his gun.

The young girl let out a scream. "No, please don't," she begged. But she was silenced by a gunshot to her temple. Then he turned the gun on the woman he'd thrown to the ground and pulled the trigger. In an instant her face was gone.

"Now, who else will dare to interrupt me when I am conducting roll call?"

No one spoke. In the silence, one could hear many things, but most of all the deafening sound of fear.

Shoshana didn't make a sound. But what she had just witnessed sent a shock through her entire being.

That evening when Ernst brought another blanket for Shoshana to give her mother and another loaf of bread for the three of them,

Shoshana was distraught. "Did you hear about the shooting at roll call this morning?" she asked Ernst.

"I tried to tell you. This kind of thing happens far too often," Ernst said.

"I think you're right about the escape. I was wrong. We must get out of here. We must take the risk."

"All right. Give me a few days to gather everything we will need." She nodded.

"I'll tell you as soon as I have everything ready," he said.

CHAPTER SEVENTY-ONE

rnst knew that the sooner they got out of Auschwitz, the better. So he got to work. Plenty of the guards smoked, so whenever he saw an ashtray with a cigarette butt in it, he grabbed the cigarette butt and the ashes which he wrapped in paper, then quickly, before anyone noticed, he put the paper in his jacket pocket. He picked up cigarette butts that he found on the pavement and stuffed them in his pocket, always careful to look behind him to be sure no one was watching.

Next, in order to facilitate his plan, he had to get into the office in the women's camp. It wasn't difficult for him to get in. Everyone knew he was Dr. Mengele's apprentice, and they allowed him in. Once inside, he stole two female guards' uniforms. He stuffed them into a bag, complete with boots and hats, and because he was a doctor, no one asked him what he had in his bag.

Early the following morning on his way to work, he drove to a local children's clothing store where he purchased a dress, stockings, and boots that he was pretty sure would fit Bluma. He wished they had attempted this escape before Bluma and Shoshana had been forced to shave their heads because bald heads would certainly attract attention. Ernst decided he would buy three wigs, one for Shoshana, one for Naomi, and a small one for Bluma. But he would not purchase them in town. Instead, he drove for several miles to buy them in a neighboring city so as not to spark any suspicion.

Once he had acquired all these supplies, he wrapped them in a blanket and stored them under the seat of his automobile.

A few days later, Ernst got up and got dressed very early in the morning. Then he drove to an open field several miles from the camp. He parked his car, and although it was a long and tedious walk, he made his way back to Auschwitz on foot. When he entered the camp, the guard at the gate looked at him suspiciously. "Where's your car, Dr. Neider?" he asked.

"It needed repairs," Ernst answered casually. "I had to leave it with the mechanic. You know how slow they are."

"I see. But you didn't have to use an outside mechanic. You could just as easily have brought it in here. Some of the other guards have used the Jew mechanics to fix their autos."

"I thought about it. But I don't trust those Jews, you know? They could loosen a wheel or something and cause me to lose control of my car," Ernst said, trying to sound convincing.

"I never thought of that. You're right. Better not to use them. Jews can't be trusted." The guard accepted his explanation.

Once inside the camp, Ernst knew where to look for the garbage trucks. He rushed over to several trucks parked in a line. Then he loaded one to full capacity with garbage. The keys were inside. He drove it to an area where he could easily access it later and then parked it.

Ernst was ten minutes early when he walked into the hospital to start work that day. Mengele gave him a quick nod of satisfaction and a "Heil Hitler."

"Heil Hitler," Ernst replied as he saluted. *He is pleased that I am early. And he doesn't seem at all suspicious,* Ernst thought. *Thank God.*

The day seemed never ending. Each hour that passed intensified the stress and worry of what was to come. By the time Ernst went to

Shoshana's block that evening, he was trembling with nerves and anxiety. Bluma was sitting on the floor playing a game with herself. "We're going to leave right now," he whispered in her ear. It's just getting dark outside. It's the perfect time to go. "Do you know where to find your mother?"

Shoshana nodded.

"Then go and get her quickly," Ernst said. "But don't run. Look as calm as you possibly can as you go through the camp. We don't want anyone to suspect anything. And hurry."

Within minutes Shoshana was back, and Naomi was with her. Bluma stood up and ran over to her mother. Naomi wrapped her arm around Bluma.

"Follow me. There is to be no talking. Do you understand?'

"I don't trust you," Bluma said.

"You had better trust me. I am your only chance at survival," Ernst said. His voice was commanding. "Now, be quiet and do as I say."

Shoshana nodded at Bluma. "Do as he tells you." She'd never seen Ernst speak so harshly to a child. But she understood how nervous he was. For this plan to work, they all had to listen to him and do exactly as he said.

Ernst led them to the secluded place where he'd parked the garbage truck earlier that day. "I'm sorry. I know this is unpleasant. But I need you ladies to climb onto this truck and cover yourselves in garbage. Make sure you are well covered. The guard must not see you as we drive out."

"Ewww," Bluma said.

"Be quiet," Shoshana demanded as she helped Bluma onto the bed of the truck.

They did as Ernst told them to do. The smell made Shoshana gag. And she was certain she heard Bluma vomit as they rode toward the front of the camp. But when they arrived at the guard station, all three of them were absolutely silent.

"Dr. Neider. Where is your auto? And may I ask, why are you

driving a garbage truck?" The guard at the gate was not the same one he'd spoken with when he arrived that morning.

Shoshana's heart raced. Her body trembled uncontrollably, and her mouth was as dry as sand.

"Oh, I had to take my car to a mechanic this morning. So, I volunteered to drive this truck filled with medical waste to the dump," Ernst said casually.

"May I look through the contents of the truck?" the guard asked.

Shoshana felt as if she might faint. *If that guard digs in the garbage, he will find us.*

"Of course," Ernst said calmly. "However, I wouldn't suggest it. This garbage is filled with germs and bacteria from contagious diseases. It's mostly waste from patients with typhus. If you touch it, you could easily come down with the disease."

Shoshana held her breath. She was proud of Ernst for being so cool headed. But now it remained to be seen whether the guard would believe him or not.

"Oh . . . well, in that case." The guard shook his head. "I certainly don't want to risk any infection. So, why don't you just go on and drive though. I am sure there's nothing in there I need to see."

"All right, then. You have a good night. Heil Hitler," Ernst said, saluting.

"Heil Hitler." The guard returned the salute.

Ernst let out a long breath. He had to control himself. He almost put his foot down on the gas and sped away from that place. However, he didn't. He continued to drive at a regular pace. Everything was going well. Now, they just had to get to the area where he'd left his car that morning.

It was pitch dark outside when Ernst pulled the truck off the road and parked it next to his automobile. He got out and ran to the back. "All right, you are safe," he said, "Come on out," Ernst said. Then he got the clothes and cigarette ashes out from under the seat of the car where he'd left them. He handed the clothes and ashes to Shoshana.

"I want you and your family to change into these things. But before you put them on, you must rub the cigarette ashes on your body."

"Why?" Bluma asked. "Why cigarette ashes?"

"Don't ask so many questions," Shoshana said, annoyed. "Ernst knows what he is doing."

"It's all right. I'll explain," Ernst reassured Shoshana. Then he turned to Bluma. "In a few hours, once the guards realize that you are gone, they are going to send out dogs to look for you. Dogs have strong noses. They can smell things we cannot. So, the guards will use the blankets and the straw where you slept to familiarize the dogs with your scent. However, we are going to outsmart them. I've brought the cigarette ashes because they will mask your scent, and the dogs will not be able to find you."

"You are really good with children. With all you are doing for us, and all the stress you are under, you are still willing to take the time to explain things to Bluma."

Ernst shook his head. "I think she has a right to know what we are doing and why."

"Well, in my opinion, you are a genius. This sounds like a brilliant plan."

"No, I am not," he said humbly. "Let's just hope this works. Now I am going to walk away to give you girls some privacy while you are changing clothes. I'll be right back. Please hurry. It will be dawn before we know it, and I'd like to put as much distance as we can between us and the search parties before they realize you're missing."

CHAPTER SEVENTY-TWO

♊

Ernst walked several yards away and turned his back to the women. He waited for almost ten minutes and then he returned. When he looked at the three women he was taken aback by how authentic Naomi and Shoshana looked with their blonde wigs and Nazi uniforms. Bluma looked like a little German girl in the dress he'd bought for her. He nodded at them all, satisfied. Then they got in the car: Shoshana in the front seat beside Ernst, Bluma and Naomi together in the back.

"Are you ready?" Ernst asked Shoshana.

She nodded. "Yes."

"Here we go."

"May God be with us," Naomi said.

"May God be with us," Shoshana repeated.

Ernst started the engine, and they were on their way.

"Where are we going?" Naomi asked.

"Switzerland," Ernst answered. "But it's not going to be easy. Unfortunately, we are going to have to climb some mountains to cross the border. I considered crossing at the checkpoint. But I just didn't want to take the risk. I think this is safer."

"Climb mountains on foot?" Shoshana asked. "Do you think we'll be able to do it?"

"I hope so," he said. "I've packed food and supplies. We'll do the best we can."

"I'd rather die a free person than live in that place," Naomi said. "They killed Perle, and they have probably murdered Herschel too. It would only be a matter of time before they killed us."

"They killed Ruth too," Shoshana said.

"I didn't know," Naomi said.

"Yes, they took her away when we first got to the camp."

"I'm so sorry," Naomi said.

Shoshana nodded.

"I am ashamed to say that I am a German. They've killed too many people. And for no reason. In my opinion, one is too many," Ernst said.

"But not all Germans are bad. You're proof of that," Naomi said kindly. "One day when we are safe in our new home, I'll tell you about a German friend I met in the forest. A man who helped me to survive."

Shoshana turned around and looked at her mother. But she didn't say anything.

Ernst maneuvered the automobile down a winding road. He was going so fast that the car almost turned over.

"You're driving too fast," Bluma said.

"I know," Ernst answered. But he continued to speed down the dark road.

CHAPTER SEVENTY-THREE

♊

Ernst hadn't wanted an automobile. He hadn't seen any reason to buy one. But Gisele had convinced him that it would be a convenience, and now as he was driving through Czechoslovakia with Shoshana and her family, he was glad he'd listened to her. *If I didn't have a car, I could never have helped them escape*, he thought. Day was dawning, and the sun was rising to reveal a crystal-blue sky. He stopped to fill the car with gas. By late afternoon he hoped to be crossing into Austria. They were making good time, and so far, he was relieved that they had not been detained at any of the checkpoints. The uniforms were working their magic. It was cold, and they were all tired, but the promise of a life beyond Hitler's murderous grasp pushed them all to keep moving forward.

"Do you think they have started looking for us yet?" Shoshana asked when she saw Ernst check his watch to see what time it was.

"Yes, they would have just realized you were gone, and that means they would have just begun. According to my watch, roll call would have ended about ten minutes ago. They will start their search by combing through the entire camp. This will take them several hours. And that is good for us. Next, they will release the dogs. They will think you three are in the forest, because if we didn't have an auto, it would be very difficult for us to get very far away. Yesterday, before I left, I saw Dr. Mengele, and I told him that I would not be coming into work today.

"You have been taking a lot of time off. Won't Mengele be angry?"

"Of course. He was angry. I am certain he is thinking about firing me, instead of putting the puzzle pieces together when you and your family are missing from roll call. He'll be so fixated on how he will work his evil plan to fire me, that he won't realize that I am with you. At least that's what I am hoping for." Then Ernst turned his head to glance at Shoshana for a moment. He smiled "But that won't matter, will it? Because I am never going to return to Auschwitz, and by the time he realizes that we are together, we'll all be safe in Switzerland."

"That sounds so wonderful." She sighed.

"And it will be."

"But the mountains are perilous, and even though it's early spring, it's not as bad as winter, but it's still cold, and I am sure we will encounter some ice and snow. So, I am a little worried about how we are going to cross them," she said.

"Yes, I know. That's why I hired a guide for us. Someone who I am fairly certain we can trust. He is going to meet us at the foot of the mountains in Austria. He'll lead us from there."

"A guide. Are you sure you can trust him? How did you find him?"

"It's really quite the story. A few months ago, I had just left work and was on my way home when two young men called out to me from behind a building. I was a little on edge, but one of them came out and told me that he knew my name; he knew I was a doctor and that he and his friends desperately needed my help. He said that there were three of them, and one of his friends was dying. I was a little nervous. I mean, after all, I wore a German uniform. That alone was a reason for a Polish man, who I was sure was in the underground, to want to kill me. But I couldn't just let someone die. I had to try to help if I could. So, I followed the man behind the building, and there I found two other men. They were huddled around a young man who had been shot. I saw the wounded man and immediately agreed to help him. He was in bad shape. But the first thing we had to do was to get him out of the alley. One of them suggested that we take him to his home because this would be a private place where I would be able to work on him. I agreed. We helped the wounded man to his feet. Then he leaned on two of us, and we took him to an old, dirty apartment. There I removed the bullet, cleaned his wound, and stitched him up. He'd lost a lot of blood, but he was young and strong.

"Every other day that week I brought food for him and medicine for the pain. By the end of the week, he was recovering. He offered to pay me, but I told him I didn't need his money. I said I was sure he needed it far more than I did. Then he told me that they were indeed members of the Polish underground, and if I ever needed their help that I was to contact him, and he would do whatever he could to help me. He gave me a phone number. I kept it, but I never thought I would use it. Then last week, I realized I needed him. So, I telephoned and left a message for him. Three days later, he came to my apartment late in the night. I explained our situation, and he found us the guide. He refused to take any money from me. But I gave him money to give to the guide; that was so he would be able to get us anything we might need to make the journey."

"Did anyone ever find out what you did when you removed that bullet?"

"No. I knew I was taking a chance by helping him. I figured he was in the underground. And I knew that the Nazis wouldn't be too pleased with what I had done. But I became a doctor to help the sick and the injured, so that was what I did."

"You are so good, Ernst," Shoshana said.

"This man in the underground is a good man too. He went out of his way to arrange a capable guide for us. I believe that under his direction, we will be safe."

CHAPTER SEVENTY-FOUR

♊

They met the guide at the base of the mountains. He was a healthy, strong, and muscular man. And he told them straight away that he was a member of the Polish underground. "I'm Alex," he said. "I have taken people across the border into Switzerland using this route before," he said. "It's not easy, but it's not as bad as some. Stay alert. Do as I say. And you'll get across the border into Switzerland safely."

Ernst took Shoshana's hand. She didn't flinch at the touch of a man. She welcomed his strength.

"I brought food and water. Have you eaten?" Alex asked.

"Yes," Ernst said. "We ate during the ride. I brought food and water too."

"Good. We'll stay at a safe house at the foot of the hills until tomorrow. If we leave now, we'll be in the mountains during the night. It's much safer to travel by day. So, we'll leave early in the morning. I want to cross the border before nightfall."

"A safe house?" Ernst asked.

"Yes, it's the home of Nazi resisters. I've stayed there with parties of escapees before. It will be fine."

Ernst looked at Shoshana. "All right?"

She nodded. "All right with you, Mama?"

"Yes," Naomi said.

"No one asked me," Bluma said. She wrapped her arms around her chest.

"I'm sorry, Bluma. I should have asked you," Ernst said. "Is it all right with you?"

"Yes," Bluma said, satisfied.

"We'll have to hide the car so it can't be seen from the street." Then Alex said to Ernst. "Pull it over there under the mountain ledge. We'll wait for you here."

Ernst did as he was instructed, then he walked back over to the guide.

"All right, let's go. Follow me."

They walked for a little less than a mile when they came to a small house nestled in the mountains. "We're here."

A young woman with blonde braids opened the door. "Alex," she said to the guide. "It's good to see you."

"I brought a group and some money for you and Leon for your trouble. Is Leon here?"

"He's in the house. Come on in."

They walked inside. It was a small, sparsely furnished home, but it was clean.

"I am Jeni," the young woman said. "This is my husband, Leon. I am assuming you will be staying the night with us. I have a pot of hot soup cooking. You'll have a good hot dinner tonight. And I have some coats that we keep for this purpose. They might be a little too big, but you'll welcome them when you are out in the elements."

"Thank you," Naomi said.

"Yes, thank you," Ernst said.

Shoshana nodded.

"Right now, you might want to get some sleep. There are cots on the floor in the living room." Jeni showed them the cots.

"Yes, thank you. We are all tired," Ernst said.

Shoshana and Bluma shared a cot with Naomi. There wasn't much room, but they were all small and very thin. Ernst slept alone.

Shoshana was so tired that she fell asleep almost instantly, and she slept until she felt someone gently shaking her shoulder. "It's time for dinner." It was Ernst. "After dinner you can go back to sleep."

She opened her eyes. "I can't believe we are here. We are free," she said.

"Not yet. But almost." He winked at her.

"Yes, almost."

They all sat down at the table. Jeni poured hearty ladles of potato soup into bowls and served everyone. "Don't eat too much or too fast," Ernst warned. "Your stomach isn't used to it, and you will get sick if you do."

The soup was hot and thick and delicious. It was made with potatoes and a hint of onion. Shoshana had never enjoyed a meal as much. She had to force herself to remember to eat slowly and not to eat too much. Several times, Naomi took the spoon out of Bluma's hand to slow her down.

"I'm hungry, Mama," Bluma complained. "I want to eat."

"I know. But you heard what Ernst said, didn't you? He's a doctor. He knows what to do. We all must listen to him."

Normally Bluma would have said something derogatory about Ernst. But she didn't. It seemed to Shoshana that Bluma was starting to see that Ernst was a good person. He was not like Mengele or Otto.

After dinner, Jeni asked them to follow her into the other room. "Before you go back to sleep, let's take care of this." She pulled a box of old coats out from under the bed. "All right, let's see what we have here," she said as she rifled through the coats.

"This should fit you. And this one looks about your size," she said to Naomi and then Shoshana. "This is the smallest one I have." She pulled a woman's coat out of the pile and placed it in front of Bluma. "We haven't had a lot of children on this escape route. Unfortunately. I wish more children had been able to get away," Jeni said wistfully. Then she added, "Try it on."

Bluma put the coat on. It was huge. But it would have to do; there was nothing smaller, and she was going to need it for warmth.

"Now that you have coats, you're going to need to get as much rest as you can. Mountain climbing isn't easy, I'm afraid. Still, it's the safest way to enter Switzerland. Alex told us that you were coming by car. It would have been easier to just drive across at the checkpoint. However, because Switzerland is neutral, they are very careful at the checkpoint. Too careful. And I am sure that's why Alex decided not to risk it."

Everyone walked back into the other room. Jeni was carrying a large-sized man's coat. "This is for you," she said, handing it to Ernst, who was downing a shot of bourbon. "You're going to need it in the mountains."

Ernst stood up and tried the coat on. It fit. He nodded. "Many thanks," he said. Then he pulled a roll of reichsmarks out of his pocket and took off a few bills. He handed them to Jeni.

"You already paid," she said honestly.

"Yes, I know, but here is a little extra so you can replace these coats. You're going to need them for the next group who comes through here," Ernst said.

"That's very thoughtful, kind, and generous of you."

Ernst blushed. Then he turned to Shoshana and her family. "Let's get some sleep. We have a big day ahead of us tomorrow."

CHAPTER SEVENTY-FIVE

♊

The mountains were beautiful, but also treacherous, because sometimes there were patches of half-melted ice. Bluma's coat was so long, that she caught the toe of her boot on the lining just as she was walking by a thick root that protruded from the ground. If she had been able to free her boot, she would not have fallen. But the toe was so enmeshed within the lining that she could not regain her balance. Falling forward, she hit her arm on the tree root. A cry of pain escaped her lips. Ernst turned quickly and went to her.

"What hurts?" he asked.

Bluma indicated her arm. "It hurts real bad," she said biting her lip to keep from crying.

"Let me have a look," Ernst said.

Alex shook his head. "We'll never make it by nightfall if we stop."

"Take off your coat," Ernst said, then he gently examined Bluma's arm. "It's broken," he said shaking his head.

"Oh no." Shoshana put her arms around Bluma. "What are we going to do?"

"I'm going to set it," Ernst said. "I need two tree branches." Then he unbuttoned his coat. "Do you have a knife?" he asked Alex.

Alex nodded and handed him a small knife. He cut the bottom of his shirt and then tore off a long piece of cloth.

Naomi found two tree branches. Ernst cut them and then broke them into the correct size.

"Put your coat back on," Ernst said. Bluma did as she was told. Then Ernst sliced open the sleeve and carefully set the broken arm by holding it straight with the two branches and then wrapping the whole thing with the fabric from his shirt.

"It still hurts, but not as much," Bluma said.

"I know," Ernst said. He patted her head. "It will be all right. I promise."

They began walking again. "I can't believe how fortunate we are that you are a doctor," Shoshana said.

Ernst smiled. "I'm glad I could help."

"Will you hold my hand, so I don't fall again?" Bluma asked Ernst. This was the first time she'd ever shown that she felt she could trust Ernst. He looked at Shoshana, who smiled, but he could see that she, too, was surprised that Bluma was finally going to accept him.

"Of course, I'll hold your hand," Ernst answered.

Bluma put the hand of her unbroken arm in Ernst's hand, and they began to walk again.

The higher they climbed, the thinner the air became. Naomi got a nosebleed, but she refused to slow down. She leaned her head back and pressed on her nose with the bottom of her coat, and then with handfuls of snow from the ground until the bleeding stopped.

Shoshana was worried about Ernst. The strenuous exercise and the thin air were affecting him. He was having trouble breathing. She hooked her arm in his and walked with him slowly as he struggled to continue. "I can't go on. Take the women across," Ernst said to Alex as he sat down on a rock.

"Don't you dare quit on me," Shoshana said as she sank down

beside him. There were tears forming in her eyes. "You're coming with us. Or I am staying here with you."

Ernst looked into her eyes. "No one has ever cared that much about me," he said sincerely.

"I do. I care about you," Shoshana said. The icy wind whipped across her face. She felt the tears freezing on her eyelashes. "I care a great deal. Much more than I can say."

He touched her face and wiped the tears away with his cold fingers. "I love you, Shoshana," he said.

She began to cry. "Please get up. Please continue." Then in a soft voice, she whispered, "I love you too."

He forced himself to get up. His breath was ragged, his chest ached, and his legs and feet were on fire. But his heart was full of song. *She loves me*, he thought. *She really loves me.*

The night was even colder than the day because there was no sunshine to keep them warm. But they all huddled together, and Alex made a fire.

It took three days until Alex announced, "We made it. You have just crossed the border. You're safe. You're in Switzerland."

"Are you sure we are free?" Shoshana asked.

"I'm sure," Alex said.

They were all exhausted, worn out, and cold, but the joy of knowing that the journey was over gave them new strength and renewed energy. They began to shout for joy, their breath turning white in the frigid winter air. Shoshana and Ernst embraced. Naomi held Bluma close to her.

As they began their decent down the mountain onto Swiss land, Alex stopped them. "You are safe now. I must leave you. I must return to my work with the resistance in Poland. It's been a pleasure. Good luck with your future," he said, then he turned and began heading back the way they had come.

"Thank you," Ernst cried out. Then he added, "Do you want the keys to my car? It's yours if you want it."

"Yes," Alex said.

Ernst tossed him the keys. Alex caught them. He held them up. "Got it. Thank you," he said, and then he walked away.

CHAPTER SEVENTY-SIX

Ernst knew that he wanted to settle with Shoshana and her family in a place where they would not feel the constant sting of Jewish hatred. So, before they left Auschwitz, Ernst had done some research. He discovered that there was a nice-sized Jewish community in Zurich, Switzerland, so he decided that was where they would begin their new lives.

With the money Ernst had saved from his time working with Mengele, he bought a small home. And then he found work at the local hospital. One night after they had settled into the new house, Ernst turned to Shoshana and said in a choked-up voice, "I want to marry you." Then he added, "I was wondering how you feel about that?"

"Are you proposing?" She laughed.

He nodded. "Yes, I am. I realize I am rather clumsy, but I just didn't know how to ask..."

"My answer is yes."

"I love you so much," he said, taking her hand in his and kissing it.

"I love you too. No one has ever been as kind to me and my family," she said.

They were both quiet for a few moments. Then Ernst said, "There's a reformed Jewish rabbi here in town. I met him when he came to the hospital. He needed stitches on his finger. He seems to be a very nice fellow. I'm going to his synagogue and speak to him tomorrow. I am going to see if he will marry us."

"You aren't Jewish. I don't know if he can."

"So, I'll convert."

Oh, Ernst, I can't believe that you are willing to convert for me. You know how hard it is to be a Jew."

"I climbed a mountain for you, didn't I?" he said, smiling. Then he winked. "So, this should be a breeze."

CHAPTER SEVENTY-SEVEN

♊

Shoshana and Ernst were married under a chuppah, a canopy, in the rabbi's study at the reformed Jewish temple in town.

Naomi wore a simple brown dress that she made by hand.

Ernst looked handsome in his black suit, crisp white shirt, and black tie. On his head he wore a kippah, a skull cap. Shoshana was stunning in her beautiful full-length white gown that she purchased at a secondhand store. Bluma looked precious in the dress Naomi made for her.

After the wedding, Shoshana and Ernst took a short honeymoon to a lovely little village called Morcote, where they were finally able to enjoy being in love. They walked through the quaint little city hand in hand, in love and hopeful for the future.

While Ernst and Shoshana were away on their honeymoon, Bluma talked to Naomi about how much she missed Perle. "Sometimes I can still feel her with me," Bluma said. "I miss her so much."

"I know. I know how close twins are. I still think of my twin sister, Miriam, every day. And I miss Perle too. But I tell myself that I must be grateful, because at least I still have you and your sister."

"I miss Papa too."

"Yes, I know."

"Someday, I am going to kill Nazis. I am going to go back to Poland and kill the Nazi guards," Bluma said. There were tears forming in her eyes.

"You are just a child."

"I hate them. I hate them all. And someday, I will get revenge for what they did to my family. Especially for my sister."

Naomi put her arms around her daughter and hugged her. "Try to be happy, little one. Try not to think about what we went through."

CHAPTER SEVENTY-EIGHT

1945

In 1945, the Nazis were defeated, and the Third Reich fell, but the world they left behind was a dark and damaged place. Homeless and displaced persons shuffled through the bombed-out streets desperately searching for a family member, an old friend, or even a neighbor.

Hitler was assumed dead. It was said that he committed suicide in his bunker along with several of his closest friends, including his wife, Eva Braun and Dr. Goebbels, his wife, and their six young children. However, the bodies of Eva, Dr. Goebbels, Marta, Goebbels' wife, and their six children, were found in the bunker, Hitler's body was not. Mengele, like so many other Nazi cowards, ran like a scared rabbit all the way to South America, where he settled under an assumed name in Brazil.

After the war ended, Naomi found that she needed to work, she needed to feel useful. So she took a job with the Red Cross, searching for displaced persons. It gave her life purpose.

Naomi had access to the files, but she was unable to find her twin sister in Lithuania. There was no record of Miriam or her husband anywhere. And although everyone told Naomi that Miriam had probably perished, she continued to search, but she was not successful. However, she did find Herschel's name on a list of people who had been murdered. She wept for him, and she sat shiva for seven days. Even though she'd never been in love with him, she loved him. And she remembered how in the end he had given his life for hers.

Then one afternoon, she was scanning through a list of missing persons for a man who had come to her in search of his father, when she saw a name that sent an electric current through her body. "Eli Silberberg."

For a moment, she couldn't breathe. "I'm sorry," she said to the man waiting for an answer about his father. "I just found the name of someone I know very well. Excuse me, please. I need to go outside. But, wait right here and I'll get someone else to help you."

The man understood what Naomi was going through. There were millions of displaced persons, most of them dead.

Naomi sent another worker to help the man, and then she took the papers outside behind the building where she could read them alone. "Eli Silberberg, alive, living in Britain." Naomi read it over twice. *He is alive. I have his address*, she thought. *I know he is living with his wife. But he is the only man I have ever really loved, and he is still tied to a world I miss every day, a world that has vanished. I know I should leave him alone. He is probably happy. But I am selfish. I must see him. Even if it's only to say hello.* So, that evening when she got home, she asked Shoshana to watch Bluma while she left for a week to go to Britain to seek out an old friend.

When Naomi arrived in London, it was crowded. She was a little overwhelmed by the bombed-out buildings. And she felt a little self-conscious because her clothes were old fashioned compared to the women she saw on the street. But none of this mattered. She had to find her way to Eli's address. When she asked directions, most people walked away without answering her. She was speaking Yiddish, but they didn't realize it; they thought she was speaking German, and the British hated the Germans. The war had left them bitter. Little did they know that she was Jewish, and she hated the Nazis as much as they did. Finally, after wandering the streets for hours asking for directions, she ran into a man who spoke Yiddish. He recognized Naomi as a Jew right away and gave her directions to Eli's home.

Eli's address turned out to be located in a run-down apartment building on the poor side of London. Naomi entered the building. She searched the names on the mailbox. There it was: Eli Silberberg. Her hands trembled as she pressed the bell.

"Who is it?" a male voice with a heavy Yiddish accent asked in English.

It was him. He was older, his voice was deeper, but she would know that voice anywhere. It was Eli.

Her throat felt paralyzed. She wasn't sure she could speak.

"Who is it? Who's there?" he said, sounding annoyed.

Naomi cleared her throat. "It's Naomi Aizenberg," she croaked in a small, broken voice.

For several moments, there was silence. *Why did I come here?* Naomi thought. *I doubt he wants to see me.* She was about to leave, to go running out of the building and into the street where she might be able to find a way to catch her breath. She felt foolish, and she had to get away from this terrible feeling of rejection.

"Come up. Please. I'm in 204," he said in Yiddish, in a trembling voice.

Her knees felt weak as she climbed the stairs. *It's been years since I last saw him. I still have such strong feelings for him. But I must remind myself that we are nothing more than old friends now. He is a married man.*

Naomi knocked on the door. It seemed like hours, but it was mere seconds before Eli opened it. They looked into each other's eyes. He looked older. There were deep wrinkles around his eyes and mouth, and his hair had turned almost white. When he saw her, he dropped the crutch he had been using to walk and took her into his arms. Then he kissed her long and deep. "I'm sorry. I couldn't help myself," Eli said. Naomi could feel him trembling. "I can't believe you're here. I've dreamed of you. Not a day has gone by that I haven't thought of you."

Naomi began to cry.

"I love you," he said. "I've always loved you."

She took his hand. "I love you too. That's why I came."

Eli guided Naomi to the sofa where he sat down beside her. "You found me? I searched for you, but I couldn't find you anywhere," he said.

"I know. That's probably because I escaped from Auschwitz. I have been living in Switzerland. Shoshana and Bluma are with me."

"Perle too?"

Naomi shook her head. "No, Perle passed away."

"I'm sorry," he said sincerely. "Herschel?"

"He died."

Eli shook his head.

Then she looked at his cane. "What happened to your leg?"

"Bombings. The Germans bombed London like mad. They killed my wife and left me maimed," he said.

"I'm sorry."

Eli shrugged. "It was a terrible war. Terrible for everyone."

"Yes. It was," Naomi said.

"But you're here now. And, you are single, and I am too. Let's agree never to be apart again," Eli said boldly.

He has always been direct and open about his feelings, Naomi thought.

"I would love to be together forever. But I can't leave my family and move to London. Would you be willing to move to Switzerland?" she asked.

"I would go anywhere as long as you are there."

"Then we will never be apart again," she said.

He took her into his arms and kissed her long and hard. The painful memories of all they'd endured during the war faded as they held each other close.

CHAPTER SEVENTY-NINE

♊

In early 1948, Shoshana gave birth to a baby boy. She and Ernst named him Pagiel, a Hebrew name, in honor of Perle. Later that same year, Israel was declared a state, giving Jews around the world a reason to rejoice. They had a homeland now. As long as Israel remained a Jewish homeland, the Jews of the world would always have a place to go if another Hitler ever came to power. And although Bluma was only a child, she knew the importance of all of this. "As soon as I am old enough to go, I am moving to Israel," Bluma said proudly.

Her mother and sister thought Bluma would change her mind as the years passed. However, she didn't. In fact, her convictions only grew stronger. As she grew, Bluma became more discontented with her life in Switzerland. The family lived in a Jewish community, where Bluma had plenty of boys who were prospective marriage partners. But she didn't want marriage and children. She wanted to do something she felt was more important, with her life. Bluma wanted to make a mark on the world. When she turned seventeen, she told her family she was going to move to Israel. Naomi was very upset. She tried to persuade Bluma to stay in Switzerland with her family. But Bluma refused. "I will write to you. I will come to visit. But I will live among my own people. Perhaps all of you should consider coming to Israel with me," Bluma told Naomi. "Israel is our home."

"But we have all established our lives here in Switzerland. Eli and Ernst have good jobs. I think it would be very difficult for us to make the voyage with the baby. You know how active he has become. Stay here with us until Pagiel gets older. Then maybe we will all go and visit Israel," Naomi said.

Bluma shook her head. "No, I'm going now. You will always be welcome to come and visit me. But I am leaving Europe forever." Then Bluma walked out of the room. She packed her bags and, the following week, she boarded a ship bound for the promised land.

CHAPTER EIGHTY

Ⅱ

Epilogue 1979 Tel Aviv, Israel

Bluma was now in her forties. She had lived in Israel since she was a teen. When she'd first arrived, she'd found the life-style she had always been searching for on a kibbutz. It was a form of communal living where she spent all of her work and play time with other Jews. It was there that she met many other Holocaust survivors. They understood her, because these people hated the Nazis as much as she did. Everyone on the kibbutz came to know Bluma as the girl who was young, fearless, strong, and sometimes even a little reckless when it came to her desire to punish the Nazis.

The year she turned twenty, she was contacted by a high official in Mossad. He offered her a job. Grateful to have been given an opportunity to defend the land she loved, she accepted. She knew she would miss the kibbutz and her friends. But protecting Israel was the most important thing to her. Bluma picked up and moved to the city of Tel Aviv where she began her work with Mossad. Over time, she proved herself to be loyal and trustworthy, and that was why her superiors had chosen her for a very important, but top-secret, mission.

It had been presented to her only a week earlier when she was called into the office unexpectedly. "You need to be packed and ready by Monday of next week," her superior said. There hadn't been much time to prepare. But she welcomed this job. This was something she dreamed of every day since she was just a child. Bluma had never been certain that she would ever have this opportunity, but when it was presented to her, she jumped at the chance.

Because this was a top-secret mission, she was informed before she accepted it, that if she got into trouble carrying out the operation, Mossad was not going to stand by her. It was essential that no one in the world ever find out that Israel was behind this.

Over the years, Bluma had more boyfriends than she could count. But her relationships had never worked out. That was because she always put her job before love interests. At present, she was living with Ari. A handsome, dark-haired Sabra, the son of a fisherman who had been born and raised in Eilat. Ari had gone to college in Tel Aviv and had liked it so much, he'd never returned home to Eilat. He'd been married and divorced twice when he and Bluma started living together. And for a while, they had gotten along well because he hadn't questioned her work. But lately Ari had voiced his concerns. He said he was falling in love with Bluma, and he didn't like the dangerous chances she was willing to take working for Mossad. As she packed her bags to go, Ari walked into the room. He looked at Bluma and shook his head. "What is this mission you are going on?" he asked.

"You know I can't tell you," Bluma answered.

"I can't do this anymore, Bluma. I never know where you are going or if you are going to return. If you go, I am not going to be here when you get back," Ari said.

"Oh, Ari," she said. "I'm so sorry." Bluma cared for him, but her love for Israel came first.

"How can you do this, if you love me? How can you put me through all of this worry?" he asked.

"I am going, and that is all there is to it."

"Then at least tell me where you're going and what you're doing," he demanded. "Don't you trust me? We've been together for over a year. I think I deserve that much."

"I can't tell you anything. And I won't betray Mossad. I'm sorry, Ari."

Her bag was packed. She threw it over her shoulder and walked out of the apartment.

Bluma doubted Ari would still be there waiting when she returned. *If* she returned. But it didn't matter. This was something she must do, regardless of the cost.

Bluma drove her black sports car out to the farm where she knew that a private plane would be waiting. After a few quick greetings to her fellow coworkers, she and three other Mossad agents boarded the aircraft.

It was bound for South America, for a remote area in Brazil.

Bluma leaned back in her seat and lit a cigarette. She closed her eyes and inhaled the hot smoke. It was going to be a long flight.

After a stopover to refuel, the flight landed in Bertioga, Brazil. It was easy to locate their target, Wolfgang Gerhard. He was an old man who lived a simple life. Each morning he went for swim in the Atlantic Ocean before having his breakfast. The Mossad agents followed the old man for three days. They watched his every move. Because the man had been living under an assumed name, it was essential that the Israelis make sure that they had the right man. Bluma had no doubt. From the moment she saw his face, and the way he walked, she knew it was him. She would recognize that bastard anywhere.

That coward had escaped the Nuremberg trials. He'd never been forced on the witness stand to tell the world what he did. *He thinks he escaped judgment. He thinks he got away with what he did*, she thought as she followed him into town and watched him as he bought mangos at the market. From a safe distance, where she could not be seen, Bluma kept her eyes glued to the man. He was older than she remembered, of course, much older. He walked more slowly, and his straight black hair had turned white and thinned. But nevertheless, she knew it was him. He still had that space between his front teeth, and when he smiled at the vendor who sold him the mangos, he still looked like a jackal.

Bluma watched him each day as he went for his morning swim. She could see that he was a strong swimmer. But Bluma was much younger, and she had been training her body for years, so she knew she was stronger. "That's where I'll take him down," Bluma told the other Mossad agents. "In the water. It will appear as if he drowned. No one will be able to blame his death on Israel."

The following morning, wearing a skimpy bikini bathing suit, like a tourist, Bluma lay on a towel on the sand. And even though no one else was on the beach, Mengele suspected nothing as he walked into the ocean for his daily swim. Bluma paced herself. She waited until he was so far out into the water that he couldn't get away from her easily. Then she swam out to meet him.

"Hello," she said, smiling.

"Hello," he answered, interested.

Bluma had grown into a beautiful woman, and he was taken with the sight of her. He didn't recognize the little girl he'd once tortured. "Have you ever done it in the ocean?" she asked coyly.

"Done it?"

"Yes, you know, had sex?" she said.

"No, actually I haven't."

"Would you like to try?" she asked.

"Sure, why not," he said.

She pulled him to her. Then she put her arms around him. He smiled.

She tightened her grip. Her legs were powerful as she treaded water. He was having trouble staying afloat, and he attempted to push away. She knew by his face that he was feeling a little frightened because she was holding him too tightly.

"By the way," she said, "do you remember a little girl named Perle?"

"No, should I?"

"You should, Dr. Mengele," she said, using his real name. "Perle was my twin sister. She was only eight years old. You murdered her."

Recognition lit up his face, and she saw the terror in his eyes. He was pushing against her grip as hard as he could. He was trying to free himself. But she clamped down even tighter. Then she forced his head under the water. He struggled and kicked, but he was no match for her. Bluma was in excellent shape. She had been lifting weights, running, and engaging in combat training every day for years.

Bluma held Mengele's head under the water until he went limp and stopped struggling. She continued to tread water while she felt his neck for a pulse. Bluma smiled with satisfaction. Mengele was dead.

"Filthy Nazi bastard." She groaned as she shoved his body away from her. His head bobbed up and down for a few minutes as the waves took him out to sea. Bluma observed him for a moment. Then as she looked up at the sky, tears flowed from her eyes. "You always knew I would swim in the ocean. It's just as beautiful as you said it was in your dream. I wish you were here with me right now. But, I know you're watching, Perle . . . I know you saw what just happened. This was for you."

The end.

AUTHORS NOTE

I always enjoy hearing from my readers, and your thoughts about my work are very important to me. If you enjoyed my novel, please consider telling your friends and posting a short review on Amazon. Word of mouth is an author's best friend.

Also, it would be my honor to have you join my mailing list. As my gift to you for joining, you will receive 3 **free** short stories and my USA Today award-winning novella complimentary in your email! To sign up, just go to my website at www.RobertaKagan.com

I send blessings to each and every one of you,

Roberta

Email: roberta@robertakagan.com

THE PACT

PRE ORDER THE FIRST INSALLATION OF THE NEW SERIES TODAY!

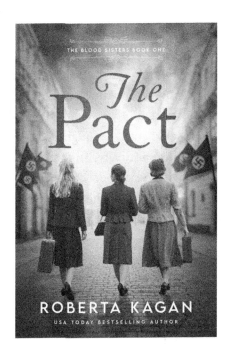

PROLOGUE

Mid-July 1940, The attic

The crash of shattering glass exploded through the silence in the tiny attic where seventeen-year-old Anna Levinstein slept with her family.

Her eyes flew open. Her body bolted upright on her cot. *Could that noise have been another nightmare?* She looked around the room and saw the terror on her parents' faces and the sorrow on her brother's, and she knew...

This was no dream.

"What was that sound?" her mother's lips moved, but she did not speak. Her face cracked with fear. It was the middle of the day, but they had all been asleep. "What was that?" she repeated without a sound.

No one answered.

Then, in a soft voice, Anna's father said to his wife, "Lillian, I think they're looking for us. I think the Nazis are in the house."

"Dear God," her mother said.

Anna's brother Anselm started coughing. He always coughed whenever he was nervous. Frantically, Anna stood up and ran to him. She covered his mouth with her hand. "They must not hear you," she whispered to him. "If they hear you, they'll know where we are."

Anslem nodded. His face was scarlet as he tried to stifle the coughing.

"He's choking," her mother said.

Another crash came from downstairs.

"They're searching the house. They are looking for us," her father said frantically. "You must keep Anselm quiet."

Anna and her mother held a pillow over Anselm's face to dampen the sound of his cough. "Be careful, Anna. We must let him breathe, or we will kill him," her mother said. Anna nodded.

"Jew swine, where are you?" They heard a man's voice coming

from downstairs, and it reaffirmed what they feared: the Nazis were searching for them.

It was horrifying to hear the Nazis tearing the house apart and even more frightening because she could not see what was happening. Her imagination was running wild. Each time she heard glass breaking or heavy things being thrown on the ground, Anna jumped.

Sweat began to drip into her eyes. She wanted to wipe it away, but she couldn't dare to move her hand from the pillow she held over her brother's face.

Then there was a moment of silence. Outside, Anna heard the sound of a siren, a Gestapo siren. It grew loud and then softer and softer until it faded out.

Have they gone? Is it possible they decided we were not here and left? Anna prayed. *Dear God, could it be that they have gone, and we are safe?* A spark of hope filled her with joy, but it was only momentary. Not even a second later, Anna trembled when she heard the heels of Nazi boots as they ascended the stairs toward the tiny hidden attic where the family hid. Each loud step as the boots hit the wooden floor reverberated through her body. Anna's father sighed as he walked over to stand beside the rest of his family. He put his arm around Anna and held her mother's hand. "They're heading right for the attic. It looks like they know there's a hidden attic here. Someone must have turned us in," he said sadly.

"But who? Why?" Anna's mother asked, her voice filled with despair.

Anna's father shrugged his shoulders. "I don't know, Lillian. I don't know. But no matter what happens, at least we are together."

With each deafening step, Anna felt more and more desperation. She wished she could jump out the window and run away, but it was too high. Besides, she would never leave her family to face this alone. They were just waiting now. There was nothing else to do. There was nowhere to go, nowhere to hide. *The Gestapo agent is getting closer. Could it be they don't know about this attic? Is it possible that they are just checking upstairs in the house? Maybe they will go away.* Anna's young, idealistic mind sought comfort.

But the comforting thoughts were obliterated by a ferocious kick to the hidden door. It burst open as it flew off its hinges, revealing the terrified Jewish family.

Anslem coughed harder as Anna released the pillow. There was no point in silencing him now. They'd been discovered, and now they must face whatever the Nazis had in store for them.

"Jews," a giant man in a Gestapo uniform said. "We knew you were here, you sneaky rats."

There were two of them. Two Gestapo agents came to arrest her defenseless family. But only the giant entered the attic. The other one stood behind him. Anna felt herself fill with panic. They were helpless.

Anna glanced up into the giant's eyes. She was hoping she would see some sympathy. But she saw no humanity, none at all. His eyes were dark and hard, devoid of emotion. Anna's heart beat fast, and her chest ached. *What are they going to do with us? Are they going to shoot us right here, right now? I am so scared. Dear God, help me; I am so afraid. What does it feel like to die? Will it hurt? And what about my family? I can't bear to watch them die or, worse, watch them suffer. The Nazis might take us away. But where? Maybe somewhere to work? But will we be together if they take us, or will they separate us? Dear God, please help us. I beg you, please.*

"Don't hurt us. Please, please don't hurt us," Anna's mother pleaded. Anna saw her mother's knuckles turn white as she clung to Anslem's shoulder.

The giant slapped Anna's mother across the face with the back of his hand. "Don't speak to me, Jew. Don't speak unless I tell you to." Then he looked Anna up and down and said to his partner, "Too bad it's illegal to fornicate with Jews. I'd like to have my way with that young one."

Anna felt her breath catch in her throat. *No, please, not that. Please, God, not that.*

The giant was mumbling obscenities. Filthy terrible obscenities. Anna wanted to cover her ears with her hands, but she dared not move. Then the giant's voice grew muffled, and she couldn't hear him. In her mind, she heard her bubbies voice. It was strong and clear, even though her bubbie had been dead for years. "Be brave, Annaleh. Be brave."

But I am not brave like you, bubbie. I'm scared.

"I know, Annaleh. That's when you must look deep into your heart to find courage. Your parents were brave. They escaped pogroms in Russia. You come from strong stock. It's in your blood. Be brave..."

"Let's go. Move, *mach schnell!*" The giant said, nudging Anna's father with the butt of his rifle. "Right now, you lazy pigs. All of you."

Anna held on to the side of the bed and eased herself up, but then the room went dark. She reached up and touched her face. It was wet with tears. She didn't even realize she was crying. Then, silver and black floaters appeared in her eyes, and they were all she could see. Her heart pounded loudly in her ears. She could no longer see or hear the giant, but she knew he was there. Anna lost all strength in her legs and fell to the floor, fainting.

———

Get your copy today! Available to buy on Amazon and free on KindleUnlimited!

ABOUT THE AUTHOR

I wanted to take a moment to introduce myself. My name is Roberta, and I am an author of Historical Fiction, mainly based on World War 2 and the Holocaust. While I never discount the horrors of the Holocaust and the Nazis, my novels are constantly inspired by love, kindness, and the small special moments that make life worth living.

I always knew I wanted to reach people through art when I was younger. I just always thought I would be an actress. That dream died in my late 20's, after many attempts and failures. For the next several years, I tried so many different professions. I worked as a hairstylist and a wedding coordinator, amongst many other jobs. But I was never satisfied. Finally, in my 50's, I worked for a hospital on the PBX board. Every day I would drive to work, I would dread clocking in. I would count the hours until I clocked out. And, the next day, I would do it all over again. I couldn't see a way out, but I prayed, and I prayed, and then I prayed some more. Until one morning at 4 am, I woke up with a voice in my head, and you might know that voice as Detrick. He told me to write his story, and together we sat at the computer; we wrote the novel that is now known as All My Love, Detrick. I now have over 30 books published, and I have had the honor of being a USA Today Best-

Selling Author. I have met such incredible people in this industry, and I am so blessed to be meeting you.

I tell this story a lot. And a lot of people think I am crazy, but it is true. I always found solace in books growing up but didn't start writing until I was in my late 50s. I try to tell this story to as many people as possible to inspire them. No matter where you are in your life, remember there is always a flicker of light no matter how dark it seems.

I send you many blessings, and I hope you enjoy my novels. They are all written with love.

Roberta

MORE BOOKS BY ROBERTA KAGAN
AVAILABLE ON AMAZON

The Blood Sisters Series

The Pact

My Sister's Betrayal

When Forever Ends

The Auschwitz Twins Series

The Children's Dream

Mengele's Apprentice

The Auschwitz Twins

Jews, The Third Reich, and a Web of Secrets

My Son's Secret

The Stolen Child

A Web of Secrets

A Jewish Family Saga

Not In America

They Never Saw It Coming

When The Dust Settled

The Syndrome That Saved Us

A Holocaust Story Series

The Smallest Crack

The Darkest Canyon

Millions Of Pebbles

Sarah and Solomon

All My Love, Detrick Series

All My Love, Detrick

You Are My Sunshine

The Promised Land

To Be An Israeli

Forever My Homeland

Michal's Destiny Series

Michal's Destiny

A Family Shattered

Watch Over My Child

Another Breath, Another Sunrise

Eidel's Story Series

And . . . Who Is The Real Mother?

Secrets Revealed

New Life, New Land

Another Generation

The Wrath of Eden Series

The Wrath Of Eden

The Angels Song

Stand Alone Novels

One Last Hope

A Flicker Of Light

The Heart Of A Gypsy

Printed in Great Britain
by Amazon

47612210R00179